JUDAS FLIGHT

Frank Adams a Charter pilot working around the Indonesian islands is asked to transport the body of a Chinese girl to Semadang. Instead of the girl Frank found the mutilated corpse of a Tong victim. Everyone had more sense than to want to get involved with the Tongs – the oriental equivalent of the Mafia – but by then it was too late. Two rival Tongs were at each other's throats, and Frank was in the middle, with his co-pilot Matt, a fleeing Chinese family, and half a million dollars in gold.

OTHER TASMAN BEATTIE TITLES IN LARGE PRINT

Zambesi Break

Panic Button

Judas Flight

JUDAS FLIGHT

DATE DUE

NOV 19 1987			
OCT. 14 1988			
NOV. 10 1988			
DEC. 7 1988			
JAN. 4 O 1993			
AUG. 21 1995			

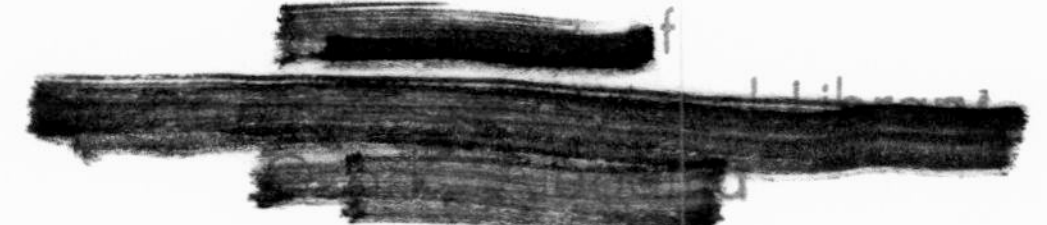

JUDAS FLIGHT

by

TASMAN BEATTIE

MAGNA PRINT BOOKS
Long Preston
North Yorkshire . England

British Library Cataloguing in Publication Data

Beattie, Tasman
Judas flight. – Large print ed.
I. Title
823′.914[F] PR6052

ISBN 0–86009–354–9

First Published in Great Britain by Eyre Methuen Ltd.

Published in Large Print 1981 by arrangement with Eyre Methuen Ltd. London

Printed and bound in Great Britain by
Redwood Burn Limited Trowbridge

For Gidget Anne George

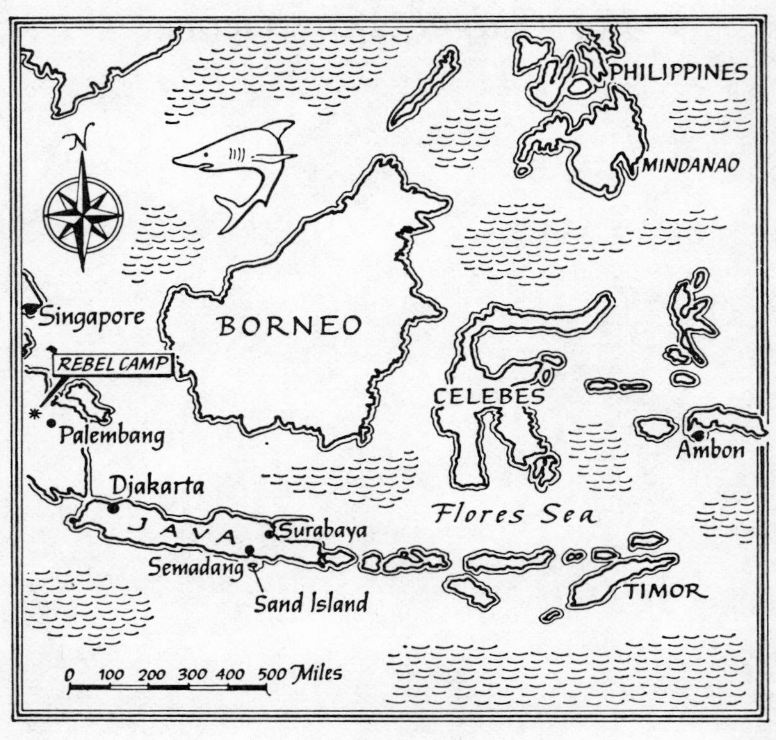
PHILIPPINES
MINDANAO
N
Singapore
BORNEO
REBEL CAMP
Palembang
CELEBES
Ambon
Djakarta
JAVA
Surabaya
Flores Sea
Semadang
Sand Island
TIMOR
0 100 200 300 400 500 Miles

PART ONE

Chapter One

JUGEE HUDYNOTO was a crafty little bastard. No! Let me get this in context. Jugee Hudynoto – Hudy for short – *is* a crafty little bastard. He's still around as far as I know, wheeling and dealing.

At the time this whole thing started I was working for Hudy. We were good for each other. I had a set of principles which let me bend the law sometimes – aviation law that is – and he had a seemingly endless supply of contacts – and money. I'll say that much for Hudy: he always paid – in cash, American and on time.

I was sipping a quiet beer in the Bali Hai – Java Sea variety, nothing to do with South Pacific – when a new shadow fell among the banana fronds. The man himself.

'Ah! There you are Frank.'

Hudy managed to convey a fancy-seeing-you-here expression but I knew he would have been combing Djakarta, checking out all my haunts. I never stuck to a routine – Hudy would find me anyway, so why make it easy for him?

'Sit down, Hudy. I've been expecting you.'

He raised one eyebrow. They were nice eyebrows, more suited to the female of the species but not uncommon among well-bred Indonesians. And Hudy was well-bred, well-heeled and a complete bloody rogue. I liked and admired him – but trust him? Not on your life.

He signalled a waiter and ordered iced tea, the Muslim excuse for drinking in the company of an unbeliever. He didn't offer me a beer – against his principles he once told me. Religious of course. Hudy's religion being the mighty dollar. He wouldn't spend one if there was a way of avoiding it.

Settled comfortably across from me in a cane armchair, he spread his slim fingers into a steeple. His expression was innocent. 'Why do you always accuse me of hounding you on your day off, Frank? This is just a social call.'

'Chamberlain made a social call on

Hitler once. Anyway, who's accusing? I'm sure your being here has nothing to do with the Chong Bee charter tomorrow.'

'So you know!' His finely-chiselled features crinkled. 'I should have guessed. I suppose Santi told you.'

'Santi's your man Hudy, you know that. That bugger would break his watch rather than tell me the time. Just accept that I know and it's not going to be like last time.'

'Last time was different, Frank. We were all caught off-guard.' His white teeth flashed. 'Anyway, I understand you were well taken care of.'

There was no point in disillusioning him; Hudy wouldn't believe it anyway. Chong Bee had laid on a sumptuous dinner when we reached Ambon. Halfway through the meal I figured out the gentle sniggers of my crew – the Chinese maiden at the end of the table was my bonus for being a good co-operative captain. Everyone knew it except me it seemed. I'm no prude but I like to select my own brand of cigarettes, and my women. And I especially don't like deflowering thirteen-year-old Chinese virgins. Not that I ever have, but I did appreciate the gesture. Chong Bee must have been very grateful indeed to offer such a rare prize. I took the girl to my room and ten minutes later sent her on her way – untouched. She smiled her relief and I knew our secret was safe. There would be no loss of face on either side. As far as Chong Bee was concerned he had squared the account. But not as far as I was concerned – not by a long chalk.

I had arrived at Kamayoran Airport to find the Dakota loaded and ready to go. Fifteen passengers occupied bucket seats either side of the aircraft – the centre aisle was piled high with freight, all properly lashed down, loadsheet in order. Only the loadsheet wasn't in order – it was the biggest pack of lies I'd seen in a long time. I started my take-off on a runway long enough for a 707 and was a third of the way along it before the tail would come up. Charlie Delta lumbered into the air with the flying characteristics of a brick shithouse – so overloaded that anything but a DC3 would have baulked at the attempt. Charlie Delta was actually a C47, the freight version of a Dak with a beefed-up floor and wide loading doors. When we landed at Ambon and I checked on what was hidden under those innocent looking tarpaulins, I was very glad of that heavy-duty flooring. Not that it would have saved us if an engine had failed on take-off. No one could have held her – not me and Samson both.

I read Chong Bee the riot act and threatened him with everything from castration to homicide. He took it in good part – by that I mean he adopted a Confucian expression and spread his hands in a helpless attitude. Finally, he summed it up. 'Your superior skill got us here, Captain. I am not ungrateful – you will see.' And see I did. Thirteen-year-old virgins are a rarity anywhere these days.

Hudy took out a packet of cigarettes – the clove-scented Indonesian variety which taste alright with apple pie. I reached for one of my Chesterfields – I'm not that much of a masochist. Hudy used his gold Dunhill on both of us and drew in deeply.

'There will be no overloading this time, Frank – you will be going empty and there is only eighty kilos for the return load.'

I gave him one of *those* looks. Twelve hours flying for the round trip at two hundred dollars an hour, that was thirty bucks a kilo. There aren't too many cargoes worth that kind of money, although I could think of some. I shook my head.

'Forget it, Hudy. I told you, I don't carry guns or drugs.'

'You don't understand – it is Chong Bee's sister you will be collecting.'

'Eighty kilos worth? Jesus! She'll be a big girl when she grows up.'

Hudy looked sad. 'She's dead, Frank. You are to collect her body.' He caught my expression and said, 'No tricks, Frank, if that's what you're thinking. I explained to Chong Bee that you do not exactly trust him and he understands. So the coffin will be sealed after you arrive. When you have inspected everything and are satisfied, it will be put on board. Only then.'

'Okay, Hudy. I've carried stiffs before

– it's no sweat.'

Under the circumstances I could hardly refuse. But what was Hudy himself doing here? He usually didn't waste his remarkable talents of persuasion on anything less than a hard sell. I finished my beer and signalled the waiter for a replacement.

'Why does Chong Bee want her brought to Djakarta, Hudy? There's a big Chinese cemetery in Ambon. I've seen it.'

His eyes had lost their sadness. In its place was a more familiar expression – a combination of hesitant furtiveness and plain skulduggery. I sat quietly, waiting for the con. It came and I couldn't have expected less. I should have known the little bastard by now.

'Well, actually, Frank, the body is not coming to Djakarta. You must deliver it to Semadang.'

'How? By bloody parachute?' So there it was – Hudy *had* a selling job to do. Well, I had my pride. Unfortunately, I also had my price and he knew it. I said angrily, 'Listen, Hudy, if you ever get off your arse and learn something about flying instead of acting like Lord Brabazon, you'd save yourself a lot of grief. Semadang airstrip is not quite big enough for Tiger Moths and you know it.' I got another thought suddenly, pregnant with intuition, or clairvoyance or something. 'What am I supposed to do, Hudy? Prang the bloody thing because you've changed your mind about insurance? Is that it?'

At forty, having missed out on the jet age, I had satisfied my professional pride in other directions and there wasn't much I couldn't do with a Dak. But Semadang was something else – fifteen hundred feet of lumpy gravel and only about half the minimum length I like to work with.

I did some quick mental arithmetic. There would be no load to uplift. If I wangled my fuel to leave just enough for the run home to Djakarta . . . it might just be possible. It would mean pulling Charlie Delta into the air before she was ready to fly, but if I could mush her over the beach for say, ten seconds, I might make it. Now I had something to work with. Those ten seconds were going to be worth fifty bucks apiece. I would take forty.

I picked up my beer, sipped slowly and gave Hudy my fish-eyed look over the bubbles. It was bargaining time. I started off by flatly refusing, mellowed to a remote 'perhaps' when Hudy mentioned money, and finally agreed on four hundred and twenty-five dollars bonus for the job.

He finished his iced tea and stood up. 'You strike a hard bargain, Frank.' I caught the satisfied gleam lurking in the back of his eyes and realized I had sold out too cheap. Chong Bee must have already settled bonus arrangements with Hudy. Judging by his expression, some of it was left over.

'Goodbye, Hudy. Don't call me, I'll call you.'

'That's what I like about you Frank – so respectful. One day I'm going to have to fire you. You know that, don't you?'

Yeah. I knew it. And one day pigs might fly. Hudy was stuck with me. The Indonesians had made licensing difficult for foreign pilots, and there weren't enough Indonesian pilots to go round. I had the magic piece of paper – and a job with Hudy as long as I wanted it. I flicked my fingers at him. He feigned a sad smile but a man like Hudy could never be sad. Not with such a happy wallet.

'I'll send Santi over with the envelope, Captain.' He pushed through the bead curtain and was gone.

Hudy always dropped the old pal's act once the price was settled. The parting 'Captain' was his way of re-establishing the master-servant relationship. Even sending Santi with the four hundred and twenty-five bills was part of the scene. Hudy felt naked without at least a thousand bucks nestling in his pocket, but procedure was everything, and protocol all the rest. I ordered another beer, looked across to where I knew the sun would be setting and dreamed pleasant dreams – like how it would be to be rich one day, like Hudy. The beer was my sixth, a strong chemical brew with a bite guaranteed to turn any man into a philosopher. I consoled myself. 'Hudy's only dollar rich, while you, Frank – why – you're superman! You're the intrepid ace who's going to get Charlie Delta in and out of Semadang tomorrow afternoon. Stupid, over-confident bastard.' I emptied the glass, beckoned the waiter and ordered my seventh.

The coffin was a big, ornate, Chinese kind with a domed roof which looks as if it should weigh a ton, but doesn't. It was resting across two coffee tables in the small passenger lounge. Chong Bee was there too, looking suitably sad if you could ever describe his bland face as looking suitably anything. He had precious little hair, with eyebrows to match, and I would hate to be staring into that blank expression over a poker hand – with my life's savings lying on the table.

'Good morning, Captain Adams.' His head was inclined forward just the right couple of degrees to show the depth of his grief. I took the podgy hand and muttered my condolences. 'I have arranged lunch for you and your crew, Captain. Then perhaps we could leave.'

'We?'

I gave him a searching look and he said, 'I have decided to come with you. The funeral is not for two more days but I will feel better if I accompany my dear sister on her last journey.' His chin was almost resting on his knees by now.

'OK. Chong Bee. Let's dispose of the formalities first.'

The coffin lid was hinged. It raised easily at Chong Bee's touch and I looked down at the departed sister. She could not have been more than twelve – just a kid. Her young face had been painted in bright make-up; her long black hair was brushed symmetrically onto the shoulders and someone had painstakingly extended each closed eyelash onto the cheeks with wisps of mascara. The effect was grotesque. Underneath all that goo was probably a very pretty child. She was dressed in a full length cheong-sam with dainty slippers just visible on her feet. Despite the macabre way in which she had been prepared to meet Buddha, she looked at peace.

I nodded slowly. 'Alright, Chong Bee.'

Closing the lid, he motioned to the two

Zamrud Airways porters hanging around the doorway. I followed the hand trolley out to the aircraft and helped drag the coffin aboard. We lashed it down about halfway along the fuselage. I tested the knots and was satisfied. I jumped down to where Chong Bee was waiting on the tarmac. Matt Duncan, my co-pilot, was coming from the control tower and we walked towards him.

'Any flak, Matt?'

He shook his head. 'No sweat.' He waved the sheet of paper in his hand – our copy of the flight plan. 'We're legal.' That was one problem out of the way.

The airport restaurant would not measure up to transport café standards in some parts of the world. Its bare wooden walls had never seen paint and the furniture was modern basic. But in the Far East you don't judge an eating house by its appearance. Chong Bee had ordered crab claws cooked in soy, bean cake and rice. The three of us tucked napkins into our necks and got our fingers greasy.

'What did your sister die of, Chong

Bee?'

Matt had finished eating and had managed to wipe his mouth nearly clean. A trickle of grease ran down one corner onto his five o'clock shadow. He was one of those black-haired Englishmen who could shave six times a day and it wouldn't make any difference.

Chong Bee looked blankly over the large crab claw he held in both hands. 'Ling Ma was shot.'

I saw Matt's eyes widen and my own must have done the same. I temporarily stopped chewing as I waited for the Chinaman to continue.

'There was a gunfight in town. My sister was coming from school and she got in the way.'

'A Tong fight?'

'Perhaps.'

I had lost interest in the food, suddenly very sorry for Ling Ma. I had almost gone the same way myself two months earlier. Stuck in Ambon for the night I had wandered into a bar for a couple of quiet drinks. The shooting started suddenly, and there were five bodies on the floor when it finished. I was also on the floor, under the table. The police arrived promptly but there was nothing they could do. The gunmen had fled. I learned later that three of the dead were members of the same Tong, the other two just innocent drinkers. These secret societies – Mafia, Chinese style – were the curse of the Far East.

I threw Matt a 'don't press it' look and said quietly, 'Let's go. We stood up. 'Five minutes, Chong Bee.' He nodded and I followed Matt out into the hot sun.

Matt said, 'Talkative bugger, isn't he?'

In the strong sunlight, Matt's face looked almost as blue as the cap perched jauntily on the back of his head. Hands stuffed in his pockets and circles of perspiration staining his armpits, he looked a scruffy bastard. I gave myself a quick once-over. We were a pair of scruffy bastards.

'You drain the fuel, Matt. I'll do the walk-around.'

Four hours out of Ambon, the island of Bali appeared on our left. We should have made it in a little over three but the westerly on our nose was blowing close to forty knots. Semadang lay on the south Java coast, ninety miles away. We wouldn't make it to Djakarta in daylight. The afternoon thunderstorms were already active along the mountain chain which spines Java and rises to eleven thousand feet in places. For once I was ready to take on those storms. It would be a small price to pay in return for forty knots of wind down that short runway. But we had a fuel problem. We would have to double back and refuel at Surabaja.

Chong Bee wandered into the cockpit a couple of times, concerned at our slow progress. All I could do was point at the white horses dancing on the sea eight thousand feet below, and shrug. We were going as fast as we could and in any case, what was his hurry? It wasn't going to make any difference to Ling Ma.

The airstrip ran roughly parallel to the beach, half a mile inland and north east of the straggle of atap dwellings which was Semadang. Two larger roofs stood out from the rest as I turned Charlie Delta into the approach. One would be the District Administrator's residence, the other the Police Post. The town had no hotel.

I eased the Dak onto a long, dragging final approach. There were no forty knots blowing but the windstock stood at right angles, indicating at least twenty miles an hour. I wasn't too worried about the landing – getting airborne again was my real concern. Just the same, I nursed Charlie Delta through those last few seconds – holding her main wheels off the six foot lalang grass and letting them grab at the gravel three feet into the runway. It was a neat, satisfying piece of flying – nothing spectacular but no problems either.

An ancient, square-bodied lorry was parked at the side of the strip and as I taxied alongside two men jumped from the vehicle and waved. They were Chinese, dressed in what is almost a uniform in the Far East – white shirt, khaki trousers, brown shoes.

As Matt pulled the mixture controls the engine died and I left my seat, heading aft. Chong Bee was already at the rear door, pushing it open. I slotted the metal steps into place and stood back. Chong Bee was immediately on the ground and in earnest conversation with the two men.

I don't know what first caused the hackles of suspicion to rise, but suddenly my back hairs were prickling with an urgency of something wrong. There should have been some sort of ceremony taking place – gong beaters, wailing women, banners. The Chinese make a special fuss of their dead, even hire professional mourners. This scene was all wrong.

Matt was making his own way down the fuselage towards the door. I motioned him to stay where he was and walked towards the coffin. 'Something smells Matt – help me untie these ropes. I want another look inside.'

He raised one black eyebrow, seemed on the point of saying something and changed his mind. I grabbed at the knots with an urgency I couldn't understand. Caught up in the fever, Matt did the same. Thirty seconds later the lashing ropes lay in a tangle at our feet. I took a deep breath and raised the coffin lid.

'Christ!'

Matt stepped back, his face the nearest to white I had ever seen it. Two dark brown eyes looked up from inside the coffin, wearing an expression of terror – and pain. A piece of broad tape covered the man's mouth, but it was his hands that riveted attention. They were tied together across his chest in the usual burial position, but each fingertip was a swollen, pulpy mess – all his fingernails had been torn out.

'How very unfortunate.' The voice came from behind.

I turned, startled, letting the lid fall back in place. One of the Chinese was on the steps, climbing aboard. His lips were parted, eyes unsmiling. The man outside the aircraft was pointing a gun straight at me and Matt. The first man walked quietly towards the coffin keeping out of the line of fire. He raised the lid and peered inside briefly, a thin smile on his lips. Then, letting the lid fall shut, his voice barely above a whisper, he said, 'Have you never heard about curiosity, Captain, and what it did to the cat?'

Chapter Two

I STOOD in the doorway for a second, staring at the gun three feet away. The man with the gun was younger than his companion. A thick hank of black hair hung over his forehead and his eyes flickered from side to side. His moist lips showed signs of nervousness, but not the hand holding the gun – that never moved. Chong Bee was standing on the tarmac about ten feet away, his brow wrinkled, concerned. I felt a gentle prod in the back.

'Climb down, Captain. Slowly.'

I glanced behind me. Matt's face was expressionless. I tried to give him a reassuring wink, but it didn't quite come off. I turned away quickly and stepped to the ground, the gun motioning me to stand clear. I moved towards Chong Bee, sideways, not taking my eyes off the revolver. The barrel was pointing slightly away from me now, covering Matt as he stood in the doorway, but it was no time for heroics. Or so I thought. But I hadn't counted on my co-pilot. I caught a movement in the corner of my eye as

Matt's leg lashed out, then everything was confusion. I think I heard the sound of a shot, I'll never be sure. But I do remember the gravel rushing up to meet my face as I thudded into it, small stones tearing at my nose and lips as I blacked out.

The noise was deafening. I tried to open my eyes as pain lanced viciously, coming from somewhere behind my right ear and spreading outwards in waves which seemed to extend beyond my body. I was conscious of a pale light as I attempted to sit up. The floor was moving beneath me. Things came briefly into focus and I was seized by a sudden panic. I was in the aircraft – moving. Matt was attempting a take-off and we'd never make it. He wasn't good enough. Somehow I got to my feet, standing, yet not standing, spread-eagled across something which gouged into my face. I started at the strange object resting against my nose, a row of twisted, yellow warts stretching to infinity. A beam of bright light stung my eyes and caused the nodules to shimmer like liquid gold.

It reminded me of the way sunlight can move through a turning aircraft, splashing along the windows. Consciousness was winning. I *was* in an aircraft and that was what I had to do – stop Matt from making this take-off before he killed us both.

I heaved myself erect, fighting off a new wave of nausea. The warts took shape – the long, spindling curls of a dragon embossed on the coffin, hand-carved and gold-painted. I pushed away from the domed lid, memory returning – right up to when Matt had been standing in the aircraft door. What the hell had happened after that? Whatever it was, Matt was a winner so far – but not for much longer. I staggered towards the flight deck.

The cabin door was ajar, swinging gently. I grabbed the bulkhead and rested my head against it, holding back the dizziness. The pain settled to a steady throb but the spot behind my right ear was on fire. My exploring fingers came away sticky with blood. I pushed the door wide and stumbled through.

The right seat was empty. Matt sat on the left, my side of the aeroplane, and it took several seconds to sink in that we were flying. God knows how he'd done it, but he'd actually got us airborne. He was better than I'd thought.

Other things registered during those brief seconds and somehow my confused mind had taken them in. The instruments indicated a climbing turn which was already through seven thousand feet. So we had been in the air for some time. I glanced instinctively at my watch but the hands told me only that it was six thirty-four. My brain refused to make the comparison I needed. I didn't know whether I had been unconscious for ten minutes or sixty.

But what the hell was Matt doing? This climbing turn would gain us nothing but altitude. Was Matt planning to try for a direct run over the mountains to Djakarta? Something was forcing its way to the surface of my memory, desperately trying to tell me that Djakarta was wrong. Then it came all the way through – fuel. We didn't have enough fuel to reach Djakarta.

I must tell Matt – Surabaja had fuel, go to Surabaja; and you don't need all this height, Matt; we can go low level, follow the river; it will be dark soon, get her down Matt, take her *down*. I stumbled the last few feet into the cock-it, my mind screaming silent orders – Get her down, follow the river Matt; you're doing it all wrong – do what I tell you. *I'm* the captain of this fucking aeroplane.

A red glow crept over the nose, splashing Matt with slivers of fire and gold as I reached his side. My mind unconsciously registered a westerly heading, facing the setting sun. Something told me that was wrong. It didn't tell me why.

Matt was slumped in his seat, held there by the harness. A patch of wetness glistened on his right shoulder, black and shiny in the glow of the distant fireball. It darkened to red as the nose of the aircraft deserted the sun and shadows began to fill the cockpit. I touched Matt on the cheek. His head moved sideways and the eyelids flickered but did not open. At least he was alive. I moved clumsily into the right-hand seat.

The feel of the yoke in my hands was comfortably familiar, but it refused to obey my correcting pressure. Instincts were taking over – first thing to do, disengage the auto-pilot. Matt had managed to switch it in before losing consciousness but it must have been a close thing. He had not had time to align the indices. My head felt as if it would fall off as I bent to the lower pedestal for the lever. Then I had an aeroplane in my hands again – obedient, responsive.

Surabaja was to the north-east of Semadang. I turned Charlie Delta in that direction, levelled the wings and reduced power. We didn't need all this altitude and the eastern sky was darkening so rapidly it was difficult to see what was below. Yet I could swear that beneath us was nothing but water. That couldn't be right; we *couldn't* have moved far out to sea. There hadn't been time. But how did I know there wasn't? Logic said I had been unconscious for not more than forty minutes, but a Dak can travel a long way in that time. And how *compos mentis* had Matt been before he finally passed out? Had he steered some weird course with his mind tottering on the brink of reason? It was possible. Christ! Anything was possible – we could be any-bloody-where.

Now down at five thousand feet and still descending, the illusion was gone. That *was* water down below – dark grey sea water and lots of it. 'Forget about Surabaja, Frank. Start thinking about staying alive. Land is to the north.' I didn't want to look at the fuel gauges but I flicked them anyway, trying to reassure myself that fuel gauges are notoriously inaccurate and that the tanks needn't necessarily be empty just because the gauges said so. The carburettors could be slurping at the last drops right now and there wasn't a damn thing I could do about it. No! There was *one* thing I could do. Start thinking about being dead. If the coastline was only five miles away it would be dark before we got there. I would have to rely on a line of breakers between sea and shore to show me where the ground was. Even if I *was* that lucky – what the hell did I do for an encore?

I knew it was hopeless and because my head was not quite my own, I didn't care a hell of a lot. It had to end sometime – somehow it was fitting this way. Noble almost. Despite the feeling of resignation, I turned the aircraft due north. There was a faint light in the sky to my left as the sun did its swan song over the horizon. I involuntarily glanced that way.

My heart skipped a beat. It was little more than a strip of coral with palm trees, maybe a mile long and half as wide. But it was land – one of the three thousand dots in the ocean which make up Nusantara Indonesia. It was less than half a mile away, the scraggy beach lined up conveniently into the wind. And we could make it.

Charlie Delta was so light she just wanted to fly right on past the island into the darkness. There was no time for circling to lose height. I pulled off power, banged down gear and flaps and drove her towards the beach. I had intended raising the gear at the last minute and doing a belly landing but fifty feet from the ground I could see it wasn't necessary. The dark blotches in the sand were not rocks, just rotting coconut husks. I slammed Charlie Delta onto the beach, stood on the brakes and pulled up in less than two hundred yards.

Matt had been thrown forward against his harness at the rapid deceleration. As the engines died I could hear faint whimpering sounds as he tried to lift his head. Then he was staring at me, glassy-eyed, bubbles of saliva staining his lips. I climbed out of my seat, slowly, pain throbbing madly behind my right ear with the potency of a toothache. I switched on the cockpit dome light and carefully unfastened Matt's harness. Then I propped him gently back in the seat, pulled his shirt to one side and bent to examine the wound. A gaping hole below his right shoulder oozed a thin liquid, forming a trickle down the thicker blood, already sticky in congealment. I gingerly pulled Matt forward looking for the exit wound in his back. There wasn't one. I felt my own blood run cold.

His voice was croaking at me, trying to say something. Then I got it – knife. Matt was telling me he had been attacked with a knife. All I could think was, 'Thank God'. No bullet to be dug out, nothing festering inside ready to swamp him with poison as fatal as snakebite. There was a first-aid kit on board somewhere. Now I could think about using it with some hope of success. Dress the wound, keep it clean, stop any further loss of blood and Matt had a chance – a good chance. Better than good in fact; his mind must be working properly or he wouldn't have told me about the knife. He must have known what was bothering me which meant he was thinking straight – not trapped in the delirium of fever. I made him comfortable and remembered where the first-aid kit was stowed – aft, in the toilet.

The two cabin dome lights showed an eerie picture as I flicked the switch and stepped through the connecting door. The coffin had slid forward during the landing and was lying askew, jammed against the forward bulkhead. Beyond it, the lashing ropes lay in a tangle like strands of the Gorgon's hair. Meccano-like bracing-struts along the unlined fuselage threw odd shadows, adding to the macabre scene as I sidled around the coffin. I was tempted to lift the lid and reassure the occupant but if he needed more than reassurance that could delay me. First, Matt, then I could look after the Indonesian.

The toilet door resisted my efforts to open it. I thought the inside lock might have jolted into place, then I saw the rubber wedge jammed into the door from the outside. My brain must have been a bit switched off because I didn't even stop to wonder what it was doing there. I used my pocket knife to pry the wedge loose, opened the door, and suddenly understood.

Huddled in the corner, eyes wide with fear, was Chong Bee.

Chapter Three

I TOOK a step towards him, fists clenched, gripped by an anger I didn't know I was capable of. Chong Bee shrank further into the corner and his hands came up to cover his face.

'No, Captain. No.' His voice was shrill, seeming to take on the texture of the surrounding metal. Thunder boomed somewhere, quite close – the night-equatorial storms were starting early tonight. Chong Bee was babbling, still in that high-pitched voice. 'I helped, Captain, I helped. Ask your co-pilot – I helped him. Please . . .'

I hesitated for a moment, and the moment was lost. The blinding pain in my head was suddenly just pain, no longer agonizing white-hot anger. My hands fell to my sides and I just stared at the crumpled Chinaman. He looked pathetic. He might have helped Matt – after it was obvious which side was winning, but Chong Bee had gotten us into this mess in the first place. Questions could come later. The green canvas first-aid kit stared at me from the rear bulkhead. I pulled it from its bungee stowage, glared at Chong Bee and closed the door. Whatever assistance had come Matt's way, he had still felt it necessary to lock Chong Bee in the dunny. I picked up the rubber wedge and rammed it home with the heel of my palm.

Heavy drops of rain were rattling on the aircraft as I made my way forward. Matt seemed a little brighter; his eyes were wide open and looked alert. The remains of coffee in the thermos behind my seat would probably be cold by now but I poured a small quantity into the plastic cup and held it to Matt's lips. He took a couple of sips and pulled his head away.

'Thanks, Pappy.'

'You're welcome, Sunshine.'

I snapped open the first-aid kit and rummaged around for what I wanted – gauze, plaster and penicillin powder. I didn't want to disturb the wound with too much probing so I didn't bother to clean the blood away. I just poured in the penicillin, slapped on a dressing and taped it in place. A packet of six morphine ampoules lay in a side packet. I picked it up.

'Want one of these?'

He shook his head. 'No . . . just a cigarette.'

I lit two Chesterfields and put one in

his mouth. 'Will you be okay for a minute, Matt? I want to open up Pandora's box again. I hope the poor bastard's still alive.'

'Before you go Frank . . . Chong Bee is in the loo. I locked him in there.'

'I found him. He's still locked up. Don't worry. I'll be as quick as I can. Maybe you'll feel like talking when I get back.'

Matt used his good arm to get comfortable in the seat. He winced at the effort, but there was definitely more colour in his face, not just five o'clock blueness either. His voice was strained at first, then got better. 'I think we'd better talk first. Frank. I know who it is in the box.' His mouth twisted in an imitation of a smile that couldn't quite make it. 'I recognized him. That's why I started that ruckus back there.'

I was staring at Matt, my head suddenly full of questions. There had been questions there before, but not like this. *Now* they were important. And whatever the answers turned out to be, they could only lead to more questions.

I hadn't really worried about Matt's

motives for behaving like a one-man army back at Semadang. I had just put it down to his background, together with an in-built streak of cussedness that doesn't like being pushed around. Now the whole thing was important – including his background. Matt had come into flying late in life which was why he was still a co-pilot. When he had arrived in Indonesia eight months previously with three years flying experience and nothing bigger than a Cessna in his licence I thought he was pretty damn lucky to land a job with Hudy. But I didn't knock it. We needed another co-pilot and if Matt had connections to swing him an Indonesian licence, that was his good fortune. I taught him to fly Charlie Delta and as a cheeky form of respect for my doyen status, he had labelled me Pappy despite being only three years my junior. I had come to like the guy and his nose-thumbing attitude to authority. As an Australian, I found it something dear to my own heart.

But something hadn't quite added up right. As I got to know Matt and found out more about him I realized he couldn't always have felt as he did now. At one time, Matt had wielded quite a bit of authority in his own right. Eighteen years in the Malayan Police Force – the last six years as chief superintendent, Special Branch. Now I was starting to wonder. Matt being Matt, hellraiser, was one thing. Matt with a reason was something else. Maybe reaction to the last few hours had slowed me down, but it suddenly struck me that Matt had taken a hell of a chance – unarmed and against odds of three to one. If he had not acted on impulse, had done it for a *reason*, then maybe the reason had roots going a long way back. I had run across other airframe jockies in various parts of the world, including Indonesia, who were fellow shitkickers on the surface, and CIA underneath. Maybe approaching middle age made me cynical, but suddenly I was taking a fresh look at Matt. Was *he* some sort of agent, working for foreign interests and hiding behind a pair of pilot's wings? It was a common cover in this kind of country. Pilots had a mobility not enjoyed by lesser mortals. If Matt was one of *them* I didn't want to know. Yet I *had* to know.

'Alright, Matt, maybe we'd better talk first.' I tried to keep my voice normal as I figured out which question I should ask first. The one burning a hole in my head forced its way out anyway. 'How come you know him Matt? And why was it important enough to risk all this?'

His eyebrows raised a fraction, almost imperceptibly, but I caught their meaning. He stared at me for a second, then said slowly, his voice barely above a whisper, 'You're alive Pappy. Isn't that important enough?'

I returned his stare, wanting to say a hundred things and saying none of them.

Matt continued in the same low voice, now more intense. 'I know that man's face as well as I know my own, Frank, and you can thank God I do. It was my job to know him, and others, although I never thought we would meet, certainly not now that I am out of the business. His name won't mean much to you, but fifteen years ago, back in the days of Sukarno's "Confrontasi" – the confrontation between Indonesia and

Malaysia – he was number one on the totem pole. The man most unlikely to succeed if he ever set foot inside Malaysia. His name is Sartono. Twenty years back, when he was an up and coming major, he made *Time* magazine as the "butcher of Mandakan". He organized the massacre of a group of islanders who were disenchanted with the regime.

'Under Sukarno, that got him promotion. Officially, he is now Major General Sartono – retired. Unofficially he is a wheel in the Secret Police and I don't want you getting any funny ideas. I didn't pull that caper back in Semadang to save anyone's life but ours. Once you stuck your nose inside the coffin there was no choice. Those Chinese would have killed us – no ifs or buts, just finito.'

'Why? What were they doing with him?'

Matt had a far-away look in his eyes. 'I don't know Pappy and I don't think I want to know. Have you got another smoke?' I pulled two cigarettes from my pocket, automatically, and passed him one. He drew deeply. 'Right now, Frank, we are facing the same choice the Chinese had.'

'What do you mean?' I asked the question but the sudden churning in my guts told me I already knew the answer. Matt kept his voice calm. 'We should kill Sartono and Chong Bee and bury them somewhere. Then walk away and pretend none of this happened. If we don't, then I hate to think what we've got ourselves involved in. The man in the coffin is a wild beast. I know his file backwards and I'm not exaggerating, believe me.' He blew smoke from his mouth and watched it curl upwards. Then he said quietly, 'I've told you what we *should* do Pappy, but I don't think you've the stomach for it. Trouble is, neither have I. So I guess you'd better go out there and do your Christian duty. But don't be surprised at anything that happens. That really is Pandora's box.'

I drew hard on my cigarette. It didn't help the dryness in my throat or the raspy sound that had crept into my voice. 'There's something you ought to know, Matt. We're down on a coral island. I'm not sure where, but it's not very big and I doubt if it's inhabited. I can't be sure about that because it all happened pretty quickly, but I don't remember any huts. So we're not exactly out of the woods. If there's enough gas to run one of the engines we might be able to take a couple of DF bearings and pinpoint ourselves – and we *might* be able to raise someone on the radio. In the meantime we're marooned on an area slightly smaller than a country racetrack with no food and not much better prospects. I just thought you'd like to know that. You're the expert on these things – see if you can come up with an idea or two while I go talk to your general.'

'In that case Pappy, I'm glad I brought this along. Better take it with you.'

Matt reached down with his left hand into the map pocket and came up with the revolver I had last seen in the Chinaman's hand. I took the gun and let the gnarled butt nestle in my fist. It had been a long time but there is something oddly familiar about the feel of a thirty-eight. If you've had an acquaintance with one before, that is. I had. A long-standing acquaintance which went back ten years and was the reason why I shunned so-called agents like the plague. I was a pilot now – *only* a pilot. I wanted nothing more. If Matt *was* a member of that other brotherhood I was going to end up hating him for it, and for getting me involved. I was finished with all that. It had ended one night in Hong Kong a long time ago.

I slipped the gun into my trouser pocket, leaving my hand there, reluctant to relax my grip. I hadn't been near a gun since that night, had sworn never to hold one again. Now it was like saying hello to an old love that had gone sour, but had only left the pleasant memories behind. I had been good once. A thirty-eight is not supposed to be a marksman's weapon but I had proved the experts wrong. I forced my fingers to let go, and my mind to do the same. It was over – finished. I slowly walked towards the cabin door.

I paused over the coffin, my fingers on

the lid, reluctant to make the final move and open it. Matt had given me a lot to think about and no time to do it. I hesitated. Once I opened the lid I was committed – I couldn't just say hello and close it again. I would have to free the man inside and at some stage I was going to have to free Chong Bee. What came next? Matt and I had to get some sleep tonight. How possible would that be with the other two characters on the loose? Maybe Matt was right; maybe we should kill the pair of them and bury the evidence.

That thought brought a wry smile to my lips, but it was sick humour. Matt had quite genuinely believed that I wouldn't have the stomach for a killing and somehow that gave me childish pleasure. If Matt thought of me that way then I had been more successful at living down the past than I had imagined. I wondered how many men Matt had killed in eighteen years of police work. Probably quite a few when he had started out – as a junior officer he would have done his share of jungle bashing on anti-terrorist patrol. But that was heat of battle stuff.

How would he be on the cold, calculated scene? Could he, even in the line of so-called duty, gun down a man in cold blood? I doubted it. But I had killed four men in just that way – and one woman. Yes! There had been the woman. There would always be the woman.

Thinking of her brought me back to the present – and to the general. The image of him lying in that box was fresh in my mind. I could almost see him through the fancy woodwork, those dreadfully multilated fingers and the frightened brown eyes. But the face was a woman's – *the* woman's. Her eyes had been brown too.

This time I didn't hesitate. I put both hands to the lid of the coffin and opened it wide. The smell hit me at once and I turned my head away, fighting back the bile in my throat. The man had vomited. A small amount of it was on one side of his mouth and there was more on the fancy silk pillow under his head. But that was not the source of the smell. At some time during the last few hours he had defecated – whether from fright or natural causes I would never know. The man was dead. I could see it from the waxy pallor of his skin even before I forced my fingers to touch the cold, clammy forehead.

I stared for some time at the anguished face, then glanced at my watch. It was some forty minutes since I had regained consciousness, but he must have been dead at least twice as long. What I didn't understand was what had killed him. He couldn't have suffocated; there was raised wooden studs between the lid joints which would have let sufficient air into the box. Now that I looked at it more closely, I could see the coffin had been purposely designed that way. So what the hell had happened?

I glanced involuntarily at the toilet door, but even from thirty feet away I could see the wedge was still in place. I looked back at the general, trying to rationalize. The plaster covering his mouth was still there except for one corner which somehow he had managed to work loose. I took out my handkerchief and wiped the corner of his mouth so that I could distinguish the curled edge of the sticky plaster. Then I understood. He had drowned in his own vomit.

Whether the odour of his defecation in that confined space had made him vomit, or whether fear had initiated the sickness and the bowel movement had been the final, protesting function of his tortured body was academic. The man was dead. I tried not to think of his last, frantic moments as I closed the lid. Then I was running for the rear door. I jumped onto the wet sand and fell on my hands and knees, retching uncontrollably.

When I was finally able to stand up, there was nothing left. Physically and mentally I was completely drained – exhausted. I rested my face against the cool aircraft skin and stayed like that for several minutes, like a man with a hangover and no place to go. The lapping of the waves ten feet away brought me back to reality. I went on my knees again at the water's edge and washed my face in the salt water.

I kicked sand over the evidence of my discomfort and hoisted myself aboard the aircraft, heading straight for the toilet. The wedge came away easily and the door opened.

Chong Bee was hunched on the closed toilet box, his eyes still wide with fear.

'What are you going to do?' he whispered.

'That depends. On how you answer my questions.' His eyes fell on the coffin at the far end of the aircraft and I thought he was going to have a fit. He started shaking. I said, 'Sit down Chong Bee for God's sake, before you fall down.'

Outside the daily tropical storm had begun. Lightning splashed the windows and I heard rain swishing heavily on metal skin. I was glad of the soothing sound in the midst of my turmoil. First the doubts raised by Matt, and then the discovery of the general. The sound of the rain would mask our voices in the cockpit, and I wanted a serious chat with Chong Bee. He may have helped Matt, but he was mixed up in this mess, and I was beginning to want some answers.

Chong Bee slumped into a corner on the plywood floor. I lowered a canvas bench on the port side and sat on one end, the gun resting on my knees. My head was throbbing with little stabs of pain like shooting needles of fire, and I could still taste the nausea in my mouth. It was not improving my temper.

'Firstly you little shit, I think you should know we have crash-landed on an uninhabited island so don't expect your friends to rescue you. Now we have established that, your survival will depend on your complete co-operation. Do you understand?'

He nodded slowly, tongue licking at his lips. I had exaggerated our position. There had been nothing crash about our landing; in fact, with fuel, I could probably fly Charlie Delta right out of here. But that was my secret for the time being, along with the general's death.

'I've already figured out that the bodies were switched while we were having lunch. Just one thing whilst we're on that subject. That little girl, Ling Ma. What happened to her? I hope you had her sent back to the funeral parlour you obviously stole her from. Her family would be entitled to that much. Was

Ling Ma her real name?'

It was a totally irrelevant question yet somehow it was important to me. The poor kid had been too young to die. If she was to be denied a proper ceremony as well, it was too much. I wished I had never seen her – now, for some reason which made no sense, I was worried about her. I needed to know that she had been accorded the final privileges, that she had a chance in the other world denied her in this. It was sentimental nonsense yet I waited for Chong Bee's answer, ready to hang on every word.

His face had a grey pallor but there was a change of expression in the eyes – a suggestion of something deep. He spoke slowly, 'Ling Ma was her name, Captain, and I didn't steal her. Chong Ling Ma was my mother's last child. She came very late and my mother died having her. I have a daughter the same age as Ling Ma. She too would be dead if I had not co-operated.'

I studied Chong Bee's face, looking for something . . . anything. I didn't see it. He was telling the truth. I felt my blood run cold. What sort of people were we involved with? What sort of people kill a twelve-year-old girl just to convince someone that they are quite capable of killing another twelve-year-old girl?

I pulled the packet of Chesterfields from my pocket. There were only two left, but there was no danger of running out of smokes in the next few hours. I had half a carton in my flight bag. I put both cigarettes in my mouth, lit them and passed one to Chong Bee. Surprise flashed briefly on his face, then his features relaxed. He took the cigarette gratefully. 'Thank you, Captain. Then you understand?'

I nodded. I understood alright – a lot of things. I understood that if the people who had killed Ling Ma were within range I would have gunned them down there and then and to hell with the New Year resolution I had made ten years ago. And then I knew I hadn't lost it – buried it maybe, kept it hidden, but it was still there. Not a killer instinct, something deeper, something that becomes part of your character when you're still a foetus: the ability to kill for money. Whatever this thing is, you're born with it. *I* was born with it and sixteen years ago, Fleming had recognized it. And for six years he had made use of it. They were six years of good living, not marred by the inconveniences of a conscience. Six years of cold, uninvolved, occasional killings, but then there had been Hong Kong, and the woman, and I had called a halt.

It hadn't been easy to quit. Fleming was not an easy man. But I had been a pilot when he found me and I could go back to being a pilot. I told him so and he had smiled.

'Alright Frank. Go play at being Douglas Bader for a while if that's what you want. But don't try and make a career of it. You'll be back.'

I hadn't gone back. But I hadn't made much of my career either. Even when the big airlines were recruiting, Frank Adams couldn't make it onto their seniority lists. After half a dozen interviews that led nowhere I finally got the message. The whisper had gone round – Frank Adams was a dirty word. Fleming was playing the game his way.

So there had been ten years on the

shitty side of the sky. While guys I had trained with were donning white gloves and tooling pretty jets around the heavens, I had gone cap in hand from one stringbean outfit to another. It hadn't been much, but it was flying, Daks mostly. Frank Adams, DC3 specialist. Now my other hat was back on my head – Frank Adams, killer. A woman in Hong Kong had buried it; a twelve-year-old Chinese girl with the name of Ling Ma had resurrected it. And I had better learn to live with it.

I drew slowly on the cigarette and was surprised at how soft my voice had become. 'Tell me the rest of it Chong Bee. Take your time and tell me everything you know.'

Chapter Four

THE flight deck appeared to be in darkness as I walked through the door, but a red glow from the instrument panel said Matt had the rheostats turned down.

'I was saving juice, Pappy. If you want to start one of these donks then we need some battery.'

'Good idea.' I rummaged in my flight bag and came up with two packets of Chesterfields. I tossed one on Matt's lap. 'Those'll keep you going for a while.'

'Thanks. What's happening back there? How did you find the general?'

I nerved myself. 'Sartono's dead, Matt. He choked on his own vomit.'

Matt let out a low whistle. 'What are you going to do, Pappy?'

'I don't know yet,' I said. 'I want to cover all the angles before I decide anything. Chong Bee and I have just had a long chat. He was blackmailed into this – they killed his sister and threatened to do the same to his daughter unless he set this deal up.'

'And you believed him?'

'Yes, I believe him.' I didn't like the note of incredulity in Matt's voice. It had sucker-of-the-year undertones.

'Sorry, Frank. Didn't mean to sound like the public prosecutor – too long in a business where the customer is always wrong. Did he tell you what it's all about?'

'As much as he could, I guess, though I didn't get round to telling him about the general yet. I thought I'd save that little item for later on.' The acid had left my voice. I was thinking about how what Chong Bee *had* told me had side-tracked me. Despite Matt's battery-saving measures, I reached across and flicked on the dome light. I wanted to see his face while we talked. There was a thin line of moisture along his top lip and his eyes had a sunken look. He had tucked his right arm inside his unbuttoned shirt in place of a sling. There was one in the first-aid kit. I made a mental note to fix it for him some time.

'How you feeling Matt? Is it bad?'

'Bearable.' He was an incorrigible bastard – there was humour in his voice. 'But I'm not quite walking wounded. I tried to come and join you back there – you don't have a monopoly on curiosity. You *were* a long time.'

I perched on a corner of the spare seat and lit a cigarette, my eyes flitting around the cockpit, looking for something out of place. I didn't see anything but that didn't quell my uneasiness. Now that I had this feeling about Matt it was uncomfortable. I tried to tell myself it was also unnecessary, but that didn't work either. Matt could be exactly what he purported to be, just another copper turned pilot – there was nothing to say different. Nothing except this feeling in my guts. Christ! This bloody business was complicated enough already without adding fuel to the fire. I wanted to trust Matt, needed to trust him in fact, for many reasons. I just wished I could do it without looking over my shoulder.

'What do you know about a crowd calling themselves the League of the Lotus, Matt?'

'Are *they* involved?' Matt had risen in his seat; grown several inches. The bantering tone was missing.

'According to Chong Bee they are.'

Matt was nodding his head, slowly. The silence went on for several seconds and I wanted to break it. I didn't. Matt had the ball. Finally he spoke. 'How much do you know about the Chinese secret societies, Frank? I know you know *of* them. What I'm asking is how much do you know *about* them?'

'Not a hell of a lot if you put it that way. I was nearly killed in a Tong fight once, but that was just because I was drinking in the wrong bar at the time. Until then I always thought of them as some kind of slant-eyed Freemasons.'

'Then I'd better educate you, Captain. By the way, where *is* Chong Bee at the moment?'

'Back in the loo.' Matt's eyebrows raised, a faint smile on his lips. I blurted out angrily, 'Look! I said I believed him; I didn't say I trusted him.'

'OK, Pappy. Just asking.' He fumbled a cigarette from the packet with his good hand and I lit it for him. He was wasting time and he knew it, but I wasn't going to give him the satisfaction of seeing my bated breath. I waited patiently. He could be a cussed bastard at times.

'The Tongs go back a long way, Frank. Some of them *were* just Freemasons, others became the secret service of the local Mandarin. There were Tongs of a pseudo-religious nature, others which ran protection rackets —

you name it, the Chinese had a Tong for it. Jealousies inevitably sprang up so there was fighting, and killing. Kangaroo courts, summary executions, terrorizing. An earlier version of the Mafia if you like, served up with rice instead of spaghetti.

'The colonizing British, in their wisdom, banned these secret societies in an effort to stamp out the Tongs. Britain never actually colonized China of course, so there wasn't much to be done on home ground, but in other places – Hong Kong, Singapore, Malaya – the Tongs were outlawed. This only drove them underground, then gradually, between the wars, they started to emerge quietly into the open again and now a more enlightened colonial government recognized that certain benefits were to be derived by leaving the Tongs alone. Some of the societies were very innocuous, businessmen's associations, trade associations, that sort of thing, who seemed to be able to settle civil disputes without overburdening the already crowded law courts. There was still the criminal element, the Tong

Gangs as they came to be called, but there always had been those, and the police still cracked down on them when they got the chance.'

'However, the more respectable Tongs were left alone and when the British moved back into their old possessions after the Japanese occupation they had more important things to worry about than a few secret societies.' Matt lit another cigarette from the butt in his hand. 'The reason I am telling you all this, Frank is to let you know that there are Tongs and Tongs, some quite harmless, and others ... Well, I think you've got the idea.'

'The League of the Lotus is a relative newcomer. Nobody is quite sure when it was formed but it first came under notice in 1949 after the British Governor, Sir Henry Gurney, was killed in ambush by communist terrorists. The League name cropped up during interrogations – several times as a matter of fact.'

'By the time I got into the act in the mid-fifties, as a young assistant superintendent of police, the League of the Lotus was well established as a powerful new element in the secret society business – the political Tong. It operated along political lines for quite a while – 'change-by-force' was its chief maxim. Members who were captured and who talked were mysteriously executed, some of them in maximum security prisons. League members were soon caught in a cleft stick. If they talked, their own people got rid of them. If they didn't, we hanged them. Not surprisingly, the League was driven even further underground until finally it was thought to have disbanded.'

I sat listening in quiet fascination. Matt knew his stuff and as far as I could see he was not trying to be evasive or hold anything back. Maybe I had misjudged him. It was a comfortable thought, but comfortable thoughts were a luxury I couldn't afford right then. I lit another Chesterfield, my third in less than half an hour, and let him continue.

'Eventually Malaya and Singapore got their independence and, apart from a few communists deep in the jungle, the terrorist war was over. The emergency laws were rescinded and things got back to normal. Normal if you forget the squabbling between Malaya and Chinese-dominated Singapore, and Sukarno's ridiculous Confrontasi, that is.'

'Then, one day in October 1969, a deputy governor of the Reserve Bank was kidnapped. We must have arrested one in three of the Chinese population of Malaya on that caper. We didn't catch the criminals and eventually the ransom of two million straits dollars was handed over and kissed goodbye. But during the hundreds of interrogations which went on, a whisper started which soon became a shout. The League of the Lotus was back, apparently out of the political business and in the kidnapping business. I say apparently because some later kidnappings had political motives, plus money of course. They never failed to demand money, and get it.'

'I became personally involved because one kidnapping – I can't tell you the details – threatened state security, and that made it Special Branch business. The League was making a good thing out of kidnapping and extortion. I spent just about my last four years on the force trying to find a chink in their security. I never found it.' He stubbed out his cigarette, not reaching for a fresh one. 'It's odd to run up against them again – here. I hadn't known they had spread to Indonesia but it was to be expected. They're probably everywhere between here and Hong Kong by now.'

'Thanks for filling me in Matt. I find Chong Bee's story even more believable now.'

Matt gave me a funny look. 'I saved the best bit for last, Pappy. I suppose I should have recognized this as League work when I saw the General's fingers. That's their trademark.'

'You mean they tear the fingernails out of all their victims?'

'No. Not exactly. But they never send them back in one piece either. The ransom demand is always accompanied by a little item to show they mean business. A toe, a finger, an ear. The State Security wallah I was telling you about has no top lip anymore. That is why the League is so successful. Nobody doubts their intentions so people pay up.

Quickly.' He looked thoughtful for a moment. 'But every fingernail? They haven't gone quite that far before to my knowledge. They must have wanted to torture the general. I wonder why?'

The rain had stopped. Lightning flashed in the distance and occasionally thunder rolled quite close by. There would be more storms before the night was over but for the moment it was peaceful. I slid open the storm window and could hear waves lapping the beach. The air tasted fresh – too fresh. It set my head aching again. I reached for another cigarette. I was smoking too damned much.

Matt said, 'What happens next, Pappy?'

I shrugged, I had to do something soon but my mind was too confused for any clear picture to emerge. I decided to go and play my trump card with Chong Bee.

The Chinaman looked up at me, expectantly, as I opened the door. The barely discernible eyebrows on his round face gave him a faintly comical look at the best of times. When the eyes were open wide, staring, as they were now, he looked like a clown.

'One thing I forgot to tell you, Chong Bee. The general is dead.'

'General?'

I was getting my sources of information mixed up. Chong Bee hadn't mentioned the general; that was Matt. I was pretty sure that Chong Bee had levelled with me – not certain, but pretty sure. His story had been simple – maybe the simple lies of an uncomplicated man – or the simple truth. I had to believe the latter because Chong Bee was not uncomplicated. In Ambon, he was a very successful businessman and you don't get to be that in three easy lessons. Not if you're Chinese you don't. Chong Bee had come up in a hard school and had risen to the top. Which was why, according to him, the League of the Lotus had approached him in the first place. I had wondered why, if that were true, the League hadn't bought his co-operation with money. Since my talk with Matt however, that question no longer bothered me.

The League had needed an aeroplane and an unsuspecting crew – so they had needed someone who used charter aircraft in the normal course of business, like Chong Bee. What they hadn't bargained on was a captain with a nose as long as mine. Nobody had, me included.

'Yes, Chong Bee. Our special passenger has been identified as General Sartono of the Secret Police.'

'General Sartono . . . here . . . dead?' He was babbling again and the ash colour was back on his face. He buried it in his hands in a gesture of despair and started to shake. Chong Bee was not a young man. I guessed he was closer to fifty than forty; at the moment he looked eighty. When he straightened up there were tears glistening in his eyes, real tears.

'My family, what will they do to my family?'

I couldn't share his distress; I didn't really know what he was so upset about. We were in trouble – sure. Probably more trouble than we could explain away, but Chong Bee was behaving like a man in ruins. I didn't know whether to sympathize or tell him angrily to pull himself together. I did neither. With a hand on his shoulder I steered him gently towards the cockpit. I prodded him towards the co-pilot's seat and he fell into it.

'So now we're all one happy family,' I began, 'perhaps we'd better start thinking about what we do now.'

'We?'

'Yes, we Matt. The *three* of us. If you don't like it you can stick it up your arse.'

'Easy, Frank. Easy.' His eyes narrowed. 'I'm on your side, remember?'

'Are you, Matt? That's nice.'

'What's the matter with you, Pappy? To use one of your own expressions, you're behaving like a two bob watch. OK, so the general's dead. I'd say that's something to be thankful for – it saves a lot of complications.'

'Oh! You've got it all worked out have you?' I glanced at Chong Bee. He was taking his time coming out of whatever was eating him. 'Well I think we should listen to what Chong Bee has to say before we start digging holes in the sand. You can see the poor bastard's scared half out of his wits. I want to know why. Maybe it's something we should be worried about too.'

Matt was looking at Chong Bee, his expression speculative. Suddenly he spoke, sharply, and the Chinaman lifted his head. Matt said something else, ignoring the fact that I was now staring at *him*. He was speaking in a Chinese dialect, Hokkien I thought although I wasn't sure, and he wasn't groping for words. I got the impression he wasn't mincing words either. Chong Bee was sitting straight up in his seat, surprise written across his face. But he was also paying attention. Matt turned to me. 'Alright Frank. Let's talk. Chong Bee is ready to answer your questions.'

'You're a man of many surprises, Matt.' My voice was neither friendly nor hostile.

There was a slight edge to Matt's as he answered. 'Yes, aren't I though. I also play the banjo and collect stamps.' He fumbled in his lap for a cigarette. 'Give me a light, Pappy.'

Chapter Five

IT was an odd story Chong Bee had to tell. To understand the ramifications, one had to go back several years and appreciate the hold the Chinese had on commerce in South East Asia. The European colonizers came for power and possession. More jewels in the crown of empire. The Chinese came too, but not in pretty uniforms to the sound of brass bands. They were interested in the commercial prospects of the new colonies. The people of Cathay moved into the Dutch and British possessions in the Far East in their thousands – some were coolies, but others were some of the best businessmen in the world.

The colonial powers got what they came for; rubber and tin from Malaya, spices from the Indies, but the Chinese were there too – ready to cream off a fat middleman profit.

When independence finally came to these countries, the Chinese owned most of the commercial wealth. They were welcome in Singapore where the Chinese constitute seventy per cent of the population. Many tolerated them but Indonesia did not. Many Chinese, even those born in the country, were forced to leave. Not deported as such – just hit with a wave of restrictions and petty persecutions which made life unbearable. Some managed to get their wealth out of the country, many more didn't. A new law was passed requiring fifty-one per cent of any business to be Indonesian owned. A lot of fifty-one per cents were obtained on the cheap and a lot of hitherto profitable small businesses were left in ruins.

Chong Bee moved his headquarters to Ambon. He wasn't ready to leave Indonesia just yet and Ambon was far enough away from Djakarta to give him breathing space. Or so he had thought. He only needed five years – five more years and he could retire to some other part of the world. His target was two thousand ounces of gold and he already had half that amount, salted away in ten ounce bars. Even Matt had raised his eyebrows at that.

In Ambon, Chong Bee had continued to make regular protection payments to the Society of Jade. Then one day an Indonesian had walked into his office with an offer for fifty-one per cent of the business. The Chinaman had known it would happen one day. When it did he was ready to cut and run. He had long accepted the inevitability of it and had prayed for time. Now time had run out.

But the Indonesian's offer was not all bad. True, he was not offering to pay for his fifty-one per cent, but there were other advantages. To begin with, he was quite prepared to leave the running of the business to Chong Bee, and just take twenty per cent of the net profit. The fifty-one per cent on paper would legalize the company and protect it. And the stranger offered another kind of protection. Chong Bee would not suffer any government interference, and from now on, his cargoes would not be too closely inspected by customs. In return for the privilege, he would be required to arrange shipment of a special cargo from time to time.

Chong Bee had weighed the matter quickly in his mind. With a twenty per cent drop in profits the gold bars would take a little longer to acquire, but he could now buy the time he so desperately wanted. Chong Bee ordered the necessary papers drawn up and went into business with his new partner – General Sartono.

And the general kept his word. The business ran smoother than it had ever done. Shipments were allowed to come and go as if on greased rails. Labour unrest, hold-ups at the docks never affected Chong Bee's cargoes, except perhaps in a profitable way. Chong Bee would frequently find himself the only supplier of a certain commodity in Ambon, and his competitors' goods delayed on the docks. Naturally, in these circumstances there was a price rise.

The partnership was only three months old when Chong Bee sat down at his ledgers one day and started working things out. Despite the General's twenty per cent, the business was now doing so well that Chong Bee could be in the same financial state as he was before taking on his partner. If it were not for one thing. The monthly payment to the Society of Jade.

So Chong Bee made his first mistake. He told the Society of Jade to go jump in the lake. By now he knew that the general was head of the Secret Police in Ambon. With someone like that on the board, what did Chong Bee need with the feeble protection of the Society?

The Society of Jade did not see things quite that way. They came to Chong Bee's office above his main warehouses and threatened him. Chong Bee made his second mistake. He told the general.

General Sartono was no businessman, but whatever else he was, he was no fool either. If he started a purge on the Tongs, the Society of Jade in particular, his profitable twenty per cent of Chong Bee's labours would be gone. The Society would take revenge on Chong Bee, a revenge which would include his life. And a dead Chong Bee was no good to the general. The Chinaman's personal contacts throughout the east were the soul of his business. Put someone else in to run Chong Bee Enterprises, even another Chinese, and the business would run down. So the general needed Chong Bee alive, and to ensure the Chinaman's continued good health, he made a deal with the Tong. They would be left alone, free from police interference, if they in turn would leave Chong Bee alone.

It was a neat stand-off, guaranteed as long as the general stayed alive. The Society made one more call on Chong Bee to inform him just that. He was alive as long as the general lived. Chong Bee through greed and lack of foresight, had ended a long-standing business arrangement with the Society in a way that the Society found insulting. Chong Bee was aware of what happened to people who insulted the Society. They were patient people. The general was not a young man – he could not live forever. One day the insult would be expiated. The Society wanted Chong Bee to know this, and that, unlike their delinquent client, the Society always paid its debts.

Chong Bee decided to run. The gold bars now totalled eleven hundred ounces, not enough to retire on, but more than enough to start a business elsewhere. It was not what he had planned, but the situation had changed. However, the Tong had anticipated Chong Bee, and acted accordingly. *He* was still free to come and go as he pleased – his business demanded it. But his family was under surveillance night and day.

There was nothing Chong Bee could do about this. The Society was not pestering him – just watching and waiting. It was no good going to the general again. He had made a deal with the Tong and as long as they didn't break it, he would do nothing. Chong Bee considered redeeming the insult with money – offers to make good, backpayments to the Society. But he knew it would be useless. His debt to the Society could only be paid in blood – it was the way of things.

As Chong Bee unfolded his story I couldn't help thinking he had asked for it in a way. He was a grown man and should have known what he was doing when he decided to be greedy. Then Matt had asked a question. How long ago had this happened?

I knew what was in Matt's mind. I had been wondering too; the timing didn't make sense. Until Chong Bee answered the question. Even then it wouldn't make sense to an occidental mind which thought of Chinese patience as a game of cards. But I had grown accustomed to the strange ways of the orient. I believed it, and I could see Matt did too. The Society of Jade had kept up their surveillance for six years, never relaxing it for an hour in all that time.

I could now understand why Ling Ma had been killed. Chong Bee was unreliable – he would have to be convinced beyond any shadow of doubt that his only choice was co-operation. The League of the Lotus was not going to give Chong Bee the opportunity to betray them too.

I looked at Chong Bee long and hard. He had told his story almost in a monotone, his face expressionless, but I could sense the turmoil taking place inside. He could break at any time. Matt and I prodded him with questions which he answered in the same dead voice. He did not know why the League had kidnapped the general – or why they had wanted him taken to Semadang. I could guess the reason for that. They had wanted him on the island of Java and

Semadang was an obvious choice. It was one of the most deserted airstrips on the island, rarely used and unstaffed. Ideal for the League's purpose, whatever that purpose might be. One could only guess at that.

Chong Bee sat in the co-pilot's seat and I had parked myself in the gangway, sitting on my flight bag. I stood up and stretched my legs. The effort set my head aching again. The Chinaman's tale of woe had been interesting but it hadn't told us a hell of a lot. Just that he was in the shit up to his ears. I wondered how Matt and I would stand with the League when they discovered our part in robbing them of the general. They had obviously wanted him alive and we had spoiled that for them. One thing I was sure of – they were not the kind who forgive and forget. I suddenly felt naked and very vulnerable. We were no better off than Chong Bee. The Society would take care of him now that his insurance had expired – and the League would sure as hell take care of us. If sharks or starvation didn't get us in the meantime. It would help if we knew where we were.

Maybe now was as good a time as any to find out.

A startled expression appeared on Chong Bee's face as I started the starboard engine. He had sunk down in his seat, round and fat, a picture of doom and despair. Now his eyes were alert, interested. I reached into my flight bag for the appropriate chart and fiddled with the automatic direction finder. I got a good bearing from Surabaja and a shaky one from Djakarta. I drew the position lines in on the chart, a satisfied smile on my face.

Even allowing for night-effect and coastal refraction, the crossed lines put us south east of Semadang, not more than eight miles from the coast, and possibly as little as four. I felt elated. There were sure to be fishing boats this close to shore, and if there weren't, we had the rubber dinghy to fall back on. But the dinghy would be second choice. It was an ex-RAF Q-type which hadn't been inspected for years. It lay inside a grey canister at the rear of the aircraft and I wasn't kidding myself. The rubber could have rotted away by now, and the

CO2 bottle might be green with corrosion.

I shut down the engine. Chong Bee was staring at me, his features agitated. When he spoke there were signs of life back in his voice. 'Will this aeroplane . . . fly, Captain?' His eagerness brought a smile to my face. We were supposed to have crash-landed.

I nodded. 'There's fair chance – if we had some fuel.'

'Then we didn't crash?' He seemed to be taking his time digesting this. His expression had gone blank again, more as I was accustomed to seeing it. But I didn't immediately recognize it as his business face. Not until he spoke. 'Captain, I want to make you a proposition – for which you will be very well paid. I must get my family out of Ambon. If you will help I will make you both very rich men.'

Matt and I exchanged glances, then I was shaking my head. 'There's not enough money in the world to make me go back to Ambon right now. Not after what has happened. In any case, I told you we don't have any fuel. Without it, this is just a hunk of useless hardware. You'd better stop thinking of it as an aeroplane.'

The flush of excitement was on Chong Bee's face. He was gesticulating with his hands again and the words were literally tumbling from his mouth. 'But it *is* an aeroplane, Captain, and we can *get* fuel. And you wouldn't have to fly to Ambon. There is an island close to Ambon. It is only used by fishermen and there is a long, straight beach.'

The guy was crazy, clutching at straws. He had seen a chance for life and was seizing it with both hands – but it was impossible. Taking off for Semadang had been bad enough. I had known it was a small airstrip but it *was* an airstrip. To fly six hundred miles with only a beach at the other end was not on. However, I was interested in the Chinaman's statement that we could get fuel. He seemed very positive about that. I was entertaining other thoughts – of flying Charlie Delta out of here, right out of the country, to Australia perhaps.

I heard Matt say quietly, 'How rich is rich, Chong Bee?'

It didn't matter how rich was rich. You can't spend it in a pine box. Yet there is a touch of greed in every man – I was no exception. Despite the impossibility of it all, I found myself waiting on Chong Bee's answer. My mouth had gone dry.

Chong Bee had calmed down. Once again he was the successful Chinese businessman and I thought I caught a hint of reverence in his voice. I may have been wrong about that but I don't think so. He was talking about money. His eyes blinked once or twice and he licked his lips. There was a shiny glow on his round face.

'I bought my two thousandth ounce of gold five years ago but I couldn't use it. And I was still making money with nothing to spend it on, you understand. So I bought more gold.' He was looking at Matt intently. 'I now have three thousand one hundred ounces. If you help me, I will keep only my two thousand ounces. The rest is yours.' Matt didn't speak, but his expression said, 'Jesus'. Chong Bee allowed himself a faint smile. 'It is indeed a great deal of money. When I started buying gold it cost me less than twenty dollars an ounce. It is worth six times that now – more than six in fact. You would each have a half share in at least one hundred and thirty thousand dollars.'

Matt was looking at me oddly. I couldn't blame him for the taste of riches he had in his mouth. In the last few seconds my good intentions had gone out the window – along with my common sense. I heard myself saying, from a long way off, 'Assuming we could get some fuel and fly out of here, Chong Bee, what exactly did you have in mind?'

Chapter Six

WHOEVER said talk is cheap never sat up half the night in the cockpit of a DC3 using the kind of ten thousand dollar words we were throwing around. Sure, we talked a lot of crap too, but even that had an expensive sound to it. At 2 am I left the others to settle down in the pilots' seats and try to get some sleep. I went back and lay on the canvas bench, my flight bag for a pillow and a cigarette for company. I wasn't ready for sleep – I had some thinking to do.

Chong Bee's plan was crazy, impossible, far-fetched and didn't have a hope in hell of succeeding. And ten minutes ago I had agreed to go along with it. I had convinced myself that I had no choice. Now, lying on the uncomfortable bench in the darkness, watching the glow of my cigarette, I realized there *was* an alternative. I could go back to being poor.

I couldn't stay in Indonesia and neither could Matt. We must leave the Far East by the quickest possible means and hope to hell the League of the Lotus wouldn't be inconsiderate enough to come after us. Not that I had to spend the rest of my life looking over my shoulder, I only had to say the word and I could have all the protection I needed. I would be welcomed with open arms if I went back to Fleming. He would give me the long-lost brother routine, ask how I was, send me down to accounts just to get me reaccustomed to the high life, and he would smile that knowing, smug, Fleming smile. Then he would shove a gun in my hand, tell me to get in some practice and go lie on a beach until he sent for me.

I could take it all, even the gun. That didn't bother me any more. But I couldn't take the Fleming smile. There had been too many years, too many jobs for the wrong companies in the wrong aeroplanes for the wrong reasons. Fleming's reasons. Seven thousand hours had gone into my log book in the past ten years, and I owed Fleming back for every one of them. Seven thousand pinpricks add up to a lot of resentment. I wouldn't work for Fleming, and I couldn't stay in Indonesia and continue to work for Hudy.

So Chong Bee's money could make the difference. Maybe I could buy a share in a flying outfit somewhere – Australia, South America, Africa. Get into a freight company – there's money in air freight. Christ! If Matt and I pooled our resources we could start our own freightline. Adams and Duncan

Airfreighters Limited. No, maybe Duncan and Adams had a better sound to it. What the hell! If we were partners, fifty-fifty straight down the line, it didn't matter whose name came first on the letterhead.

My cigarette left a trail of sparks as I flicked it through the open doorway onto the beach. I deliberately steered my mind away from unpleasant thoughts. With faint starlight invading the aircraft and waves gently lapping the beach, it was nice to dream a little. I fell asleep contentedly counting my chickens.

There is no such thing as the cold light of day in these latitudes. At six ten by my watch I opened my eyes to an already bright morning. The sun burned hotly in a white sky as I dropped to the beach, walked to the seaward side of the aircraft and tasted disappointment. I could just make out the dark lines of trees, low in the water and closer to fifteen miles away than five. That Djakarta bearing I had obtained was really up the creek. So were we if the rubber dinghy was perished; there wouldn't be too many fishing prahus this far off the coast.

I was suddenly anxious about the dinghy. I also wanted to explore the island, but there was nothing to explore. I could see right across it from where I was. The only vegetation was a straggly green weed and the coconut palms, heavy with fruit. I climbed aboard the aircraft, untied the lashing on the dinghy canister and kick-rolled it through the doorway. It fell onto the beach with a soft thud and I followed.

This time I was half ready to be disappointed, but that didn't take the sting out of it. Some years back – around 1944 I would guess – the dinghy had been neatly rolled up, the folds liberally sprinkled with French chalk to prevent the rubber sticking to itself. The precaution had been a success, even after all this time. The rubber wasn't sticking to itself; it was adhering to the French chalk which the years and humidity had caked into a thin film of cement. We weren't going anywhere in this boat.

I scanned each horizon for signs of a sail – an oar even. Nothing! Not a damned thing. It crossed my mind to float Charlie Delta across to the mainland. She was light enough with no fuel in the tanks. It was a ridiculous thought, though – as ridiculous as the other idea which jumped into my head: turf the general out of his coffin and use it as a canoe. But at least I was thinking, and the useful thing about that exercise is that is leads from one idea to another. It led me right back to where I started – Charlie Delta. The tanks might be stone motherless empty – and they might not. Fifteen miles was about six minutes flying – less than four gallons an engine. Allow another six gallons for the take-off and, provided there was a minimum of fourteen gallons on board, we were in business. But there was no way of knowing. The gauges couldn't read down that far, and in any case they were indicating empty. There was a dipstick somewhere in the aircraft but even that wouldn't give us a true picture. With the aircraft sloping on its tailwheel, any small amount of fuel in the tanks would have slopped to the back and would be undetectable. So it was a pure lottery.

Both engines were delivering power when I had landed last night, and we had managed to run number two long enough to raise our DF bearings. So there was *some* fuel in the tanks.

If I had it figured wrong we were going to get our feet wet. I would fly Charlie Delta out of here on a wing and a prayer, and just so the others wouldn't try and talk me out of it, I would lie a little.

Ten minutes later, when Chong Bee jumped onto the beach, the stage was set and I had my story right. The aircraft step ladder was propped under the wing; the dipstick lay carelessly in the sand. I was sitting nearby, fire axe in hand, beating hell out of a young coconut which refused to open. The Chinaman had a broad smile on his face.

'Can I help you with that, Captain Adams? You seem to be out of practice.'

Matt was back in his seat, right arm now resting comfortably in a black sling, his left hand dangling above the gear and flap levers ready for when I needed them. The two days growth on his face was better than I could manage in a week. Put a black patch over one eye to match the sling and he'd be a dead ringer for Captain Kidd. I swung Charlie Delta round at the eastern end of the beach, facing into the very light breeze which had replaced yesterday's strong westerly.

'Ready, Sunshine?'

'All yours, Pappy. Give her the gun.'

I glanced at the light surf lapping the shore in an unbroken line. Even fifty yards away there was no break in the steady rhythm. I smiled with graveyard humour as I told myself the general was not making waves. He was out there, ten yards off the beach in five feet of water. There was something too final about burying him – quite apart from the fact that trying to dig a deep enough hole in the shifting sand would be a losing battle. So we had settled for Davy Jones's locker.

Somehow, Chong Bee and I had managed to drag the coffin across the beach and into the water, although it was incredibly heavy. It was now heavier still, weighted down with sand which we had scooped into the bow to keep it submerged. If we had to produce the general's body sometime, then it was likely to keep for a few days in salt water. The incriminating stretch of coastline was easy to identify opposite a bent coconut palm. I dragged my eyes away and pushed the throttles wide open.

Charlie Delta started to move, slowly at first and then the paddle blades got a grip on the early morning air and we were accelerating along the firm sand. At seventy knots I pulled her off and she was so light there was no protest, even though we were eleven knots slower than normal lift-off speed. Matt raised the gear and I set up a skidding turn to the right, levelling out fifty feet above the water and reducing power from the fuel consuming take-off setting. Six minutes, that's all we needed. Six minutes, and a friendly stretch of mainland beach. As we peered, the coastline didn't look all that far away, but there was a new surprise in store. I could see buildings on a stretch of coast that should have held nothing but jungle. Two minutes later I recognized it. So did Matt. He looked at me oddly.

'Semadang!'

It suddenly made sense. The erratic Djakarta bearing which had put us further off the coast would also have swung us further south of east. Standing between the two pilot seats, Chong Bee had also recognized the town and there was a hint of fear in his eyes. I didn't blame him. He knew what I knew – that the only area within miles of Semadang suitable as a landing area was the airstrip. The coastline was mostly straggling mangroves, the beaches short and rockstrewn.

I drove Charlie Delta towards the town with mixed feelings. At least the airstrip offered immediate survival and the prospect of an undamaged aeroplane – something which even the most innocuous beach could not guarantee. But Semadang was also the lion's den.

The day before Matt had left the young gunman lying unconscious and the older man, the one with the knife, writhing on the ground with a bullet in the groin. I wondered if the two men had made their escape without attracting official attention. The airstrip was just far enough away from the town, but we could not entirely rule out the possibility of police interest when we landed.

The right engine burbled and lost power, bringing me back to the present with a jolt. I pushed a lever and both engines were feeding from whatever fuel remained in our port tank. The starboard revs recovered as I turned Charlie Delta towards the airstrip three miles away. The runway grew larger under the nose and Matt lowered the wheels at the last minute. Then we were down and rolling and I stopped holding my breath.

Matt was grinning at me as I wiped my wet palms on my trousers. 'Were you worried about something, Pappy?' He offered the cigarettes and I took one gratefully and slid open my side window to let in some fresh air. The cockpit had suddenly become very warm. The soft, metallic pinging of cooling engines broke into the silence, then the birds joined in and the chattering of monkeys started up again in the nearby trees. After the rude interruption of our arrival, the morning was getting back to normal.

A film of sweat formed a moustache on Chong Bee's top lip. 'We must not stay here, Captain. It is dangerous.' He was peering anxiously out of the window, glancing towards the trees as if expecting the danger to appear at any second. But for the moment we had the place to ourselves. The lorry was gone, along with the two Chinese, and there was nothing to say that the previous day's fracas had ever happened. Just the same, the Chinaman was right; we couldn't stay where we were. It was time to ask him about the fuel he had promised.

Having lived and worked around the Far East for a few years, I had catalogued the different races into little compartments. Malays were some of the most friendly people in the world – and probably the laziest; Tamils were tall and very black with perpetually red mouths from chewing betel nuts; Indonesians practised corruption as a way of life; Thai women, pound for pound, were the most beautiful female creatures in the universe. And so on and so forth. Racial and national characteristics were filed away in my tiny brain so that the unusual become the norm, and the norm was often unexpected.

My Chinese file contained a cultured, astute people, basically honest but ruthless in business and some of the world's best manipulators. I never met a Chinaman who said he could 'get it for you wholesale' – that would be completely out of character – but if a Chinese promised something, delivery was guaranteed. That was why I had never questioned Chong Bee's statement that he could organize fuel. Chong Bee was Chinese and therefore if he had a chain of fuel dumps festooning the entire archipelago, it wouldn't have struck me as unusual.

But there were no fuel dumps – and there was no fuel. Not the kind Charlie Delta needed anyway. Chong Bee matter-of-factly stated that a contact here in Semadang could provide as many forty-four gallon drums as we were willing to pay for – standard or premium grade. Matt and I exchanged glances and I gave forth with a vehement 'Shit'. It wasn't Chong Bee's fault. It was mine. I shouldn't have taken it for granted that he would know the difference between vehicle petrol and avgas. If we put ordinary gasoline into Charlie Delta, both her engines would blow up within a few minutes of getting into the air. Our nearest source of aviation fuel was Surabaja. It might as well have been the moon.

Matt shifted restlessly in his seat. He said suddenly, 'We'll have to hire a boat.'

I looked at him sharply. 'What do you think we are – fucking tourists? If we start wandering around the wharves they'll have us inside within five minutes.'

He was shaking his head. 'No, Pappy. If the police were interested in us they would be here by now. This place would be under surveillance if they knew what happened here yesterday, so they don't know. And I've been thinking. Semadang can hardly be a stronghold of the League – it's just a bloody backwater. I'll guarantee the only League members within miles of here are those two we ran into yesterday, and one of them is out of action. In any case, they'll be lying low. When we flew in I noticed two or three boats big enough to make Surabaja and back. Chong Bee could hire one and pick you and me up off the beach; to be on the safe side, it would be better if we are not seen in town. We could be back here in two days with enough gas to get us to Surabaja; we could top the tanks up there and start earning our money.'

Chong Bee's face was not exactly alive with enthusiasm; he didn't like the idea of going to town on his own one bit. But Matt was right. The police *would* have been here by now if they were going to be – and if Chong Bee went about his business quickly he shouldn't attract undue attention. A European in pilot's uniform would, so there was no choice, it had to be the Chinaman. It took less than five minutes to talk him into it, mainly because he realized it was his only chance and the longer we delayed, the greater the risk of being discovered.

Half an hour after the Chinaman departed on the one mile walk to Semadang, Matt and I shut the aircraft door and set off through the six foot lalang grass in the direction of the beach. The first-aid kit was under my arm, the thirty-eight tucked into my waistband under a clean shirt.

It was past one o'clock when the soft chug of a diesel roused me from a catnap and I sat up to see a low, broad-beamed vessel approaching. It seemed to take an age to cover the last quarter mile to the beach at a flat-out speed of close to six knots. The boat was about eighteen feet long and nearly as wide, its heavy clinker hull almost completely devoid of paint. Chong Bee stood in the bow and a wrinkled Indonesian sat in the stern, the heavy wooden tiller tucked under his arm as he manoeuvred the vessel into shallow water. Matt and I stumbled through the shallows and into the boat and the first thing that caught my eye was a huge hand of bananas. Chong Bee wore his nearest expression to a happy grin as he saw me take in the rest of the provisions – tins of steak and kidney pudding, pineapples, dried fish, a carton of Chesterfield filters and, miracle of miracles, a case of Tiger beer.

'Any trouble?' It was a superfluous question but I asked it anyway.

The Chinaman shook his head. 'No, Captain. It went very easily. The boatman has been to Surabaja before and says we will be there by midnight if it does not storm.'

I grunted, made myself comfortable in the bottom of the boat and reached for a can of beer. I flipped the top and handed it to Matt. I poured one down my own throat. It was warm but it was wet, and most of all, it was beer. The first one didn't touch the sides. I opened another and sipped contentedly.

With a bellyfull of steak and kidney and bananas, and half a dozen beers, the world suddenly wasn't a bad place. The boat chugged steadily along the south Java coast a mile off-shore, the boatman unmoving in the stern, his eyes half shut against the glare of the sun. I had been dozing and I looked across to where Matt and Chong Bee were still in the arms of Morpheus, curled up in the wooden stringers of the hull. My watch said it was just past five – another hour or so of daylight, then it would cool down.

I was reaching automatically in my shirt pocket for a cigarette when I remembered that something had awakened me. An alien sound in the steady rumble of the diesel. I was ready to dismiss it; all engines throw off an odd note sometimes. I flicked my lighter at the Chesterfield and sat upright to ease the stiffness in my back.

Past the transom, just over the boatman's right shoulder, a high speed launch was bearing down on us, fast. Standing on the bow, his knees braced around a bollard, was the young Chinese gunman. I had his thirty-eight in my belt, but it wasn't going to help much. He was holding a sub-machine gun and looked as if he knew exactly how to use it. My shouted warning to the boatman was lost in the noise of a loud hailer.

'Itu keppel, beranti la! Beranti!'

The phrase was not as internationally known as 'heave to' – or possibly as polite.

But it meant the same thing.

Chapter Seven

A STARTLED look appeared on the boatman's face; the mechanical voice took him completely by surprise. I guessed the old fellow was slightly deaf, but he had heard the loud hailer, and now he had seen the gun. Fear flashed in his eyes and I saw his hand move to the throttle.

Chong Bee and Matt were awake and I hissed at them, 'Keep down.' I didn't know how much skill I had lost in the past ten years; I didn't even stop to think about it. Once they got us aboard the launch, a very short conversation would stand between us and our sudden demise. So it had to be now. The range was thirty yards and closing as I pushed myself to my feet, my back to the gunman. When I turned to face him the thirty-eight was in my fist and I pulled the trigger.

The second shot was instinct – a pure reflex action. It was already slamming into him as the first bullet found its target, hitting him centre chest. In my heyday I had never gone for a headshot

– even at a range much closer than this. Headwounds are messy, defeating the one big advantage of a thirty-eight – it's neat and clean. Unless tampered with to make it perform otherwise, a standard thirty-eight bullet makes a small, tidy hole. In the hands of an artist, it can be placed with surgical skill. But as the old adage says, 'You don't get nothing for nothing.' The price one has to pay for the precision of a thirty-eight is its lack of hitting power. A flat-nosed forty-five can lift a man clear off his feet and punch a hole in his chest the size of a Jaffa orange, but not so a thirty-eight.

The young Chinese gunman had two thirty-eight bullets in his chest, and despite being out of practice I knew I had placed them less than an inch apart. Yet he was still on his feet and the sub-machine gun was still in his hands. I saw the muzzle raise slightly and my finger was tightening for a third shot when he fell, sideways and backwards. The sub-machine gun dropped beside him onto the polished deck, then it was sliding as the man at the wheel gunned the motors and the launch leapt to life, heeling over in a frantic turn away from us. The machine gun went over the side and the young Chinese followed, head first in slow motion.

The whole episode took mere seconds, yet each one hung suspended in a lifetime. The launch was already seventy yards away and I heard Matt's voice from a long way off. 'Jesus, Pappy.' I turned slowly. Matt was looking at me as if seeing me for the first time. Beside him, Chong Bee was shaking. The boatman was babbling in Indonesian as I tucked the revolver back inside my shirt. I pointed to the distant beach.

'Keppel ambil di sana. Pasir itu. Lakas la.'

He glanced nervously at the launch, now a good hundred yards away, then his eyes were back in my direction and he was licking his lips. I guessed I was no less frightening to the poor little bastard. It wasn't his war and he was caught right in the middle of it. I repeated my instructions and he reached for the throttle and leant on the tiller, pointing us towards the jungle-lined beach. I could feel his nervous eyes still watching me as I slowly sat down and stared at the launch wallowing in the water a hundred yards distant.

'Shut up for God's sake, Chong Bee.' Matt's harsh admonishment said the Chinaman had been jabbering, but my mind was on the launch. It would have to make another move soon; killing the young gunman had only won us a temporary respite. The vessel was about twenty feet in length, with a flying bridge and an enclosed cabin. The shiny black paint of twin Mercury outboards extended from the stern and the recent memory of their throaty roar still rang in my ears. The launch could possibly do close to forty knots and could come up on us very quickly indeed. I glanced over my shoulder. The beach was still a good ten minutes away in our heavy boat but we had to keep heading that way. It was the only chance of evening the odds.

If my brain had been even half awake, the launch would not have come as a surprise. I should have realized that the League would have organized some means of transporting the general once we delivered him to Semadang. The lorry had misled me, but it shouldn't have. The whole of Semadang couldn't boast more than five miles of road, in any direction. After that, there was just thick, impenetrable jungle. Chong Bee must have noticed the launch when he departed the small harbour; it was a pity he hadn't thought to mention it. We could have taken the precaution of staying much closer inshore and, more important, we would have posted a lookout. Now it was too late. The launch only had to come at us flat out and it could be on us in seconds. And they would be more careful next time – a hidden rifleman could pick us off at leisure – a single hand grenade would do the job even more certainly.

My hand tightened instinctively around the butt of the thirty-eight as I watched the nose of the launch suddenly swing in our direction and start closing the gap. But it wasn't coming fast. Fifty yards away it slowed to our speed and kept its distance. A voice sounded through the loud hailer.

'Captain. We want to talk.'

Matt and I exchanged glances and I

motioned him to keep down. The gun was back in my hand as I crawled to the stern and stuck my head up. One man was at the wheel on the flying bridge, another stood in the stern, holding the loud hailer. There didn't appear to be anyone else on board but there could have been a dozen hiding in the cabin.

The voice sounded again. 'We want to negotiate, Captain. We can meet on shore. If you agree to a truce then we will beach fifty yards from you and we can talk – one man from each side. If you agree, raise your hand.'

Matt said, 'Don't trust them, Pappy.'

'I don't.' Even as I said it, I raised one arm over the transom and the voice came booming back. 'Thank you, Captain. You are being sensible.'

What I was being was cunning. This way, we could reach the shore in one piece. After that, with the thick cover of the trees and undergrowth, the odds would be far less one-sided. I passed the thirty-eight to Matt.

'You'll have to cover me, and don't give them a second chance. I'll go talk to that joker – you and Chong Bee make for the trees.'

Matt was shaking his head. 'No, Pappy. I could never shoot like you even when I was in practice. I'll do the talking – you provide the armed guard.' I was on the point of protesting when he said, 'It makes sense, Frank. I can talk to him in his lingo – I speak three Chinese dialects.'

'Alright, Matt.' I nodded slowly. It did make sense although I didn't trust my marksmanship at fifty yards if things shaped up to a double-cross. The launch kept its distance and slowly but surely we chugged towards the beach. The wide hull touched bottom and I went over the side, urging Chong Bee along with me and shouting at the boatman to follow. The launch was nosing gently into the shore sixty yards away as Matt stepped onto the beach and started walking slowly in that direction. Chong Bee reached the trees just ahead of me, his breath coming in painful gasps. I turned to urge on the Indonesian boatman, and stopped dead in my tracks. Then I was running back the way I had come, but after less than half a dozen steps I saw it was useless. The little Indonesian had pushed the boat off the beach. Its prow was already out to sea and even as I saw what was happening, I heard the sound of the diesel starting up and watched the wide vessel mount the first line of breakers. I couldn't blame the boatman for wanting to get the hell out of there, but I couldn't find much to thank him for either. I stumbled back towards the trees and watched one of the Chinese jump from the launch and start walking towards Matt.

'What are we going to do, Captain? They will kill us.'

'Take it easy, Chong Bee. We're not dead yet.'

I was getting used to him by now and maybe scorn wasn't the thing to keep hitting him with. Everyone is afraid of something – with me it was spiders. I was keeping a wary eye for the eight-legged monsters as I edged along the tree line to put myself within working range of Matt if he suddenly needed my help. Chong Bee stumbled along at my heels, unwilling to let me out of his sight.

Matt and the Chinese from the launch

had reached their rendezvous point and the Chinese appeared to be doing most of the talking as he used an arm to gesture, first in the general direction of the sea, then more specifically towards the launch. Then he was listening and after a few seconds I saw him nod his head before turning to walk quickly back to the launch. Matt seemed in no particular hurry as he ambled towards us and I felt my fingers relax their grip on the thirty-eight. The westering sun was low in the sky, silhouetting my co-pilot in a way that made the Captain Kidd image stronger than ever. His feet crunched into the gritty sand, then he was standing in front of me, an enigmatic expression on his blue face.

'We've got a ride out of here, Frank, or we can stay and rot – the choice is ours.'

'Just like that?' I didn't realize I was waving the gun until sunlight glinted off the blue metal. I let it fall to my side.

Matt said, 'No, Pappy, not just like that. They want to talk to Chong Bee – alive. That's why they didn't press home their attack when they had us on toast.

Our Chinese friend might have been killed. It seems he has some information they want so they weren't prepared to risk any more shooting.' Matt's voice had a new low intensity. 'They still aren't. I think we could take them, Frank, if that aim of yours wasn't a fluke.' He was looking at me with a strange, speculative expression.

I turned to Chong Bee. He had gone white and was making odd fish-movements with his mouth. I said quietly, 'Who else have you told about that gold of yours, Chong Bee?'

It was a fair question in the circumstances. I had pieced things together in my mind and come up with the only set of answers which made sense – to me. I hadn't discussed it with Matt although I had made up my mind that I would do so when the opportunity presented itself. I had killed my earlier doubts about my first officer. He *was* just an ex-copper turned pilot, and he had as much larceny in his soul as I did. Which made him very interested in a share of Chong Bee's gold. But there were other interested parties too. Such as the League of the Lotus.

It had to be that way. If the League had only wanted the general there were a dozen other ways they could have gone about abducting him. So the one they were really after was Chong Bee. The general had been necessary to convince Chong Bee he had no choice – co-operate or the general would die, and Chong Bee's life assurance would expire. Somehow the League had found out about Chong Bee's gold which on present day prices was worth nearly half a million dollars. They couldn't risk their ploy in Ambon, stronghold of the rival Society of Jade. So they had chosen remote Semadang. My theory didn't explain why the general had been tortured but I remember the excited conversation between Chong Bee and the two Chinese when we had first landed. Maybe they were arguing; perhaps because Chong Bee was being informed for the first time that he would be remaining in Semadang.

The Chinaman's voice was barely above a whisper. 'I have told no one. No one. Not even my family.'

'Well, they know about it, sport.' I indicated the launch as a new thought jumped into my addled brain. Suddenly I had the answer. 'Your broker, Chong Bee – the man you have been buying the gold from.' He looked at me vacantly. I spat. 'And you're supposed to be smart. I'll lay odds right now that you've bought your entire stock from the one source – and that he's Chinese.' I made no attempt to keep the scorn out of my voice. 'You stupid bastard. Didn't it ever occur to you that a man who keeps buying gold at market price – maybe even black market price as I suspect you've had to pay sometimes – would not be doing so to re-sell. Such a man would be hoarding his gold, and the man who had been supplying him over all those years would keep his own records. Then one day he might start doing some arithmetic and realize just how rich his client was – and how vulnerable.' Chong Bee was staring at me stupidly. 'Maybe your supplier is a member of the League, Chong Bee, or a sympathizer. Or maybe just another greedy man ready to seize whatever chance he can to get some of that gold for himself. The reasons don't matter; the fact is that the League know about your gold and they want it.' The Chinaman continued staring, saying nothing. He was having trouble comprehending, but the reality of what I had said would hit him soon enough. I tucked the thirty-eight under my shirt. 'OK. For the moment we are not without some advantage. The League will hardly expect that you will have told us about the gold, and they shouldn't suspect that we know what they are really after. So let's play it cool – offer to take them to the general as our trump card. And keep our eye on the main chance.'

Chong Bee cringed into the undergrowth and was shaking his head violently. 'No. No. We cannot go on board that boat. They will kill us, I tell you.'

'I'm sure they have that in mind – for me and Matt, but not you. They need you alive to take them to where the gold is hidden. So if things go wrong we are going to have to trust you to bargain for the three of us.'

I caught the look in Matt's eyes and

fought down the similar one trying to find expression in my own. I wouldn't trust Chong Bee an inch in this kind of bargaining, but I had to say something to make him feel better. We sure as hell couldn't stay where we were – the jungle was strictly for the monkeys, and the alternative was a long swim in water owned by the sharks. It was the launch or nothing.

The Chinaman was still shaking as I took him by the arm and gently led him along the beach. Matt walked a few paces in front of us, his good arm held high and waving his cap from side to side in a gesture of surrender.

Chapter Eight

'YOUR gun please, Captain.' The slim Chinaman who had conversed with Matt on the beach was holding out a hand for the thirty-eight. I gave it to him, collecting a queer look from Matt for my trouble, but there was no point in trying to hang on to the weapon. Being plucked off that beach by the League was like being rescued by lions – I knew that, but I also knew they wanted to parley. And not only with Chong Bee. If they had wanted to kill Matt and me, they could have already taken care of that at a dozen points along the way. Two modern rifles clamped down the bridge provided the means. Maybe the League would try to kill us later, but first there would be some talk.

As the man at the wheel gunned the twin Mercs, we were told to wait on deck while a very frightened Chong Bee was hustled below into the cabin. The double doors closed behind him, and the Chinaman rejoined us, leaning against a bulkhead in easy reach of the rifles.

The launch was bigger than I had first imagined. At least twenty-five feet long, it was fashioned on the old air-sea rescue boats, scaled down and with outboards instead of a marine diesel, but very seaworthy. A gold-lettered plate bore the name *Kuching Laut – Sea Cat*. With the motors burbling at not much more than half power we were heading east at close to twenty knots. The easterly course had me puzzled; I was sure they would have taken us back to Semadang but we were headed in exactly the opposite direction.

Sitting in the stern close to the motors, Matt and I were able to converse without being overheard by the Chinaman. I expanded my theory about Chong Bee's gold being the motive for it all. Matt wriggled on his bottom, fiddled with the sling to make it more comfortable and said thoughtfully, 'Perhaps, Pappy, but I don't think so. It's just too much trouble to go to, and in any case, the general was big time. Think of the risk. The GUD will be in on it by now, and those guys don't fool around.'

'GUD?'

I knew very well who the GUD were, but it wouldn't be wise to let Matt know this. It might start him thinking; I still had to explain away my marksmanship with the thirty-eight.

'The Indonesian Secret Intelligence Service, Frank. The Secret Police is one of their departments. The hunt will be on by now and it's not beyond the realms of possibility that they will follow the trail as far as Semadang – and Charlie Delta. Taking on another Tong wouldn't worry the League unduly, but bringing the Secret Police down on their necks is another thing entirely. They wouldn't risk it unless the rewards were high enough, so for my money, the general was number one priority.'

'Don't you think half a million dollars is high enough, Matt?'

'Sure. For many things, Pappy. But not this.'

He could be right. It started me thinking again, but the thoughts were confused and only made my head ache. I wondered what was happening with Chong Bee; he had been gone for the best part of half an hour and had probably volunteered more information by now than the *Encyclopaedia Britannica*. As if in answer, the cabin doors opened abruptly and Chong Bee came up on deck. His features were white. The Chinaman motioned Matt and I towards the cabin doors. I stood up, feeling as if I was about to visit the dentist.

A short, brass-railed companionway

led down into a sumptuously furnished cabin – all teak and plush velvet. Seated in one corner, with a Pekinese resting on one enormous knee, was the fattest Chinaman I had ever laid eyes on. He was gross. That's the only word to describe him and even that couldn't come close. The puffy flesh of his cheeks had pushed his eyes into horizontal slits; his stomach rested in three distinct folds, the lowest of which threatened to engulf the Pekinese. In contrast to the rest of him, his hands were like a child's, small and delicate. A jade ring adorned the index finger of his left hand, which he was using to restrain the dog. The small animal was not enjoying the proximity of that huge overhang and was wriggling to get free.

'Please sit.' A small hand waved us to the port-side settee. A teapot stood on the centre drop-side table, together with two delicate china cups. It appeared that the proper courtesies had been observed during Chong Bee's interrogation, but they had not been enough to quieten his nerves. It was a very frightened man who had just left this same cabin – I wondered what testing lay in store for me and Matt.

'I will come straight to the point, gentlemen.' The small eyes in the flabby face were expressionless. 'You have caused a great deal of trouble; in other circumstances you would suffer the death of a thousand agonies, the extreme punishment of my brotherhood, and one which you well deserve.' Matt fidgeted restlessly beside me. I couldn't quite conjure up a thousand agonies, but with his experience I guessed Matt knew what it was all about. The fat man leaned forward and the Pekinese yelped in protest. A small hand irritably pushed the dog aside and it ran gratefully to the far corner of the settee where it sat watching us with pink eyes.

'There is no point in going over ground already covered; Chong Bee Ng has answered my questions. With General Sartono dead, we must make new plans.' Both tiny hands were now resting on the table. 'Your job for Chong Bee Ng is finished. I am prepared to offer alternative employment, payment for which will be your lives and one hundred thousand dollars.' He sat back on the settee and used two hands to smooth his rumpled shirt over his huge triple belly. 'So! We will talk business? You are charter pilots – accustomed to taking on all kinds of unusual jobs, I am sure. Well, I too have an unusual proposition for you. I want you to hijack a certain aircraft and fly it to a destination we will discuss later . . .'

I caught my reflection in the cabin window. It reminded me of Robert Mitchum in *Fire Down Below*, only *he* had been made-up for the part. What I got was an image of half-closed eyes in a very tired-looking face. I usually wear my eyes wide open and my face doesn't normally look that old. But then, I don't look like Robert Mitchum either; it was a stranger's face staring back at me from the backdrop of total darkness which had now fallen. The past couple of days had made other changes too; I had lost weight. My eyes focussed on my co-pilot, seeking comparison. Matt hadn't fared much better although the customary blueness of his beard helped disguise the deterioration.

Neither of us had bothered to speak in the minute or so since the fat man had left. I could still picture the huge bulk as he had slowly ascended the short companionway and literally squeezed himself through the double doors to the deck. His feet were small like his hands, causing him to move in tiny, mincing steps, the Pekinese following reluctantly at his heels.

Matt ran his good left hand across the blue stubble. 'Quite a turn up, Pappy.' He was watching me, his expression hooded, speculative.

I was thinking about Chong Bee – or Chong Bee Ng as the fat man had called him. Ng, pronounced as a flattened 'Oongg' was a first name, put last in the Chinese custom. What plans did the fat man have for Chong Bee? Nothing had been mentioned about gold or secret societies during our recent one-sided conversation in which the fat man did most of the talking. But plenty of other things had been discussed. What the fat man wanted me and Matt to do made the rescue of Chong Bee's family look like a Sunday outing. It was also highly illegal. But the pay was good.

It was this last item which kept running around my head and I knew it was bothering Matt. He wanted to know how I felt; I wanted the same answers from him. The only person not concerned with the moral issues was the fat man. He had decided that every man had his price and that ours was a hundred grand. I didn't know yet whether he was right about that. It was certainly bloody tempting. It was also bloody dangerous.

The time had come to say something. 'How do you feel about this thing, Matt? Could you go through with it?' I searched his face.

He said, 'We've made a deal with Chong Bee, Pappy. If he tells us we're through, then I'll think seriously about this other offer. It's obvious that Chong Bee hasn't told the whole truth – probably said he hired us as pilots-cum-bodyguards to see him safely home – or safely away from this part of the world. It doesn't matter. But I'm certain Chong Bee didn't mention the gold, and that our fat friend doesn't know about it. I prefer Chong Bee's offer.'

Matt was talking down to me. It was natural enough I suppose; after all, he was the expert in this scene as far as he knew. And I couldn't very well enlighten him. But I didn't think Matt had really thought this thing through. The fat man would be a very difficult proposition to doublecross.

'Have you got something in mind, Matt? The way I read it, we have two choices when we step off this boat; go through with the fat man's job or get ourselves very lost. Either way doesn't leave us much time for Chong Bee. In any event, he's as much a prisoner as we are. Who's to say the League won't just kill him off and send the Society of Jade the bill?'

'I think we have a say in that, Frank. You and I. Look. All that fat bastard has done up to now is intimidate. Play ball and we're rich and alive – do the other thing, we're dead. But how does us being dead help him? The answer is, it doesn't. The fat man is relying on our greed, once we are turned loose, to do his dirty work.

He probably thinks the average pilot would sell his grandmother for half the amount so he's just making sure.' Matt's angry outburst subsided. When he spoke again his tone was much more reasonable. 'It's a matter of trust, Frank. The fat man doesn't have to trust us – the hundred thousand dollars buys him all the loyalty he thinks he needs. On the other hand, we do have to trust him – to come up with the hundred big ones when the job is done. From a Chinaman's point of view this is a very satisfactory business arrangement, but not one he would expect if he was dealing with another Chinaman.

'So we don't accept it either. We haggle with him a bit over guarantees – he will counter with threats. But he knows he can't make this stick and finally he gets the message that we know it too.' Matt wriggled his right arm around in the sling, stretching the stiffness from his fingers. He smiled thinly. 'That will be the crisis, Frank. The fat man will be angry but in typical Chinese fashion, he will also respect you.'

‘Me?’

‘Yes, you Frank. As the captain, you must do the negotiating. He would smell a rat otherwise. Throw your Aussie temper around a bit if you like, but get him to the point where he feels frustration and a grudging admiration. That’s where I put my five eggs in. I will suggest we keep Chong Bee with us as a guarantee we will be paid after the job is done.’

‘He’ll never buy it, Matt. What bloody good is Chong Bee as a guarantee. The fat man couldn’t care less about him.’

‘Exactly. So allowing us to have him won’t cost the fat man a thing. But Chong Bee knows where the general is, and enough to blow the whistle on the League. We threaten to turn Chong Bee over to the police if there’s any sign of a double-cross.’

I was shaking my head. ‘It won’t work, Matt. All you’ll accomplish is to get Chong Bee bumped off a bit earlier. They won’t leave him around to talk.’

‘He won’t talk.’

‘That yellow tub of lard? Come on; he’ll shout his bloody head off at the first opportunity if he thinks it will save his precious hide.'

Matt was wearing a supercilious expression, talking down to me again. 'No, Frank. He won't talk. Not to the police. Chong Bee is under a death sentence; he knows it, and the fat man knows it. The only thing which remain to be settled are the when and the how. Chong Bee is mortally afraid of death, but more so of how he is going to die. The death of a thousand agonies is no myth. With various refinements it is a common Tong retribution. At the moment Chong Bee is somewhere in the five hundred bracket. It could go either way. But the one certain way of hitting the jackpot is to talk to the police. So, what we pretend to believe is the ultimate threat – to the fat man is no threat at all. He'll protest as a matter of form, for the sake of appearance, but secretly he will be pleased.'

'I still don't go for it. One thing you're forgetting is that Chong Bee has already talked to the police – General Sartono, which is what got him in the shit in the first place. If he did it once they'll expect him to do it again. And if the thousand agonies are really what's worrying Chong Bee, he could settle that with a simple suicide. I know he lacks the guts to kill himself, but if he's as scared as you say, even a yellow belly like Chong Bee would take the easy way out.'

'You've been in Hong Kong – haven't you, Frank?' I felt my guts do a slow roll as I tried to see behind the faint smile on Matt's face. Did he know something? Was he guessing? I had never mentioned Hong Kong to Matt – or to anyone else – for the past ten years. It was one place I wanted to forget.

I said slowly, 'I was there once – a long time ago.' I was still searching Matt's face, looking for something. Anything.

'Did you happen to take in the Tiger Balm Gardens?' That tiny hint of a smile was where I'd last seen it. Matt was enjoying himself. I relaxed. I had heard about the Gardens, built by a Chinese millionaire who made a fortune out of a mentholated ointment he called Tiger Balm. For a few cents one could purchase a tin of the magic unguent which was guaranteed to cure headache, toothache, bellyache, or anything in between. The universal panacea. The odd thing was, it seemed to work. The gardens depicted, in one gory tableau after another, the Chinese version of life after death. A smaller establishment in Singapore called Haw Par Villa was an extension of the same theme, although by all accounts Hong Kong was by far the best. I had never visited either.

I shook my head. 'No. I didn't have time for sightseeing, Matt. But I've heard about them. What's it got to do with Chong Bee?'

'Not about him specifically – about suicide. There is a large section set aside to show honest Chinamen just what happens to one of their brethren who takes his own life. Having one's entrails eaten by monkeys is one of the least unpleasant things one can expect. The murder rate in Hong Kong is high by any standards. What is not so well known is that the suicide rate is one of the lowest in the world. Your average Chinese is frightened of the eternal punishment – Chong Bee would be terrified of it. So in spite of everything, suicide is the last thing he would contemplate.' He beetled his black eyebrows in concentration. 'What I'm trying to get through to you Frank is that we have a very strong bargaining position. Because of the people involved, ordinary arguments don't stand up.'

'OK. Let's say I accept *your* argument. You know what will happen don't you? The fat man will get Chong Bee to one side and engage him to spy on *us*.'

'Of course he will.' Matt laughed aloud. 'It's beautiful.'

If Matt was right, and by now I wasn't doubting it for a minute, then I had the answer to other things that had been bugging me. Things I hadn't yet discussed with my co-pilot. I started to feel better. Chong Bee was about as trustworthy as a hungry lecher but his final loyalty would lie with me and Matt because we could offer him life. The fat man could only promise him a more comfortable death. It was worth a try. I would play along with the fat man exactly as Matt had called it.

'OK. Let's get our fat friend down here and start dealing.'

Matt climbed the short companionway and knocked on the closed doors. I stood watching him and thinking about my share of Chong Bee's gold. But I was also thinking about something else. I would earn my money as best I could; do everything in my power to see Chong Bee and his family safe and sound.

But for reasons of my own – reasons which now had a chance if Matt was right, I was going to do the other job too.

The one for the fat man.

PART TWO

Chapter Nine

I WALKED into the shaded lobby still undecided whether my most urgent need was a bath or a beer. I turned right and headed for the bar where I slumped gratefully into a cane chair at a corner table. It had been quite a day.

The long, comfortably-furnished room held half a dozen customers and as many waiters. At 4 pm, the extended-lunch-hour hangers-on had departed and the five o'clock drinkers had yet to arrive. The people here at the moment were probably just thirsty, like me. I ordered a cold beer with a cold beer chaser and lit a cigarette. Two well-to-do Indonesians sat at the far end. A solitary Chinese occupied a table near the door and three tables from me were two European men who looked like seafarers. From time to time they all sneaked admiring glances in the direction of the bar. Me too. From where I was sitting I could only see her back but it was still a pretty sight. Medium-length brown hair, a nicely shaped bottom perched on a high stool, and long, slim, tanned legs. The waiter arrived at my table, obscuring my view, and I was able to concentrate on the two dewy glasses he set down in front of me. I emptied the first in a couple of swallows and sat back to enjoy the second more sedately.

The *Kuching Laut* had docked at Surabaja late the previous night and we had booked into this hotel – me, Matt, Chong Bee . . . and the fat man. We had arranged to meet this morning at nine to go over details, but by then I had already been out at Juanda Aerodrome doing some fast talking with the air traffic people.

I had woken at seven after a decent night's sleep, with my mind back in gear and suddenly worrying about things which I should have worried about earlier. But with everything else that had happened, I hadn't even stopped to consider that to the rest of the world Charlie Delta would be missing presumed lost. I picked up the bedside telephone and put through a panic call to Hudy. He was angry, but I could tell he was also very relieved. He *had* reported Charlie Delta missing, but not until last evening. A search was due to commence this morning. I gave him a yarn about running out of fuel and having to bum a boat ride to Surabaja, assured him the aircraft was OK and that I would inform the authorities. I promised to get Charlie Delta back in circulation and told him not to expect us back in Djakarta for a few days, that I had another charter lined up. That had pleased him. After promising to keep in touch I hung up and then hurriedly put a call through to the aviation authorities at Juanda. I told them we were OK and that I would be out to see them as soon as I had eaten. They told me not to take too long over breakfast.

Ten minutes later, when I walked out of the shower, the telephone was still staring at me from the bedside table. I hesitated for just a moment, decided that the conclusions I had reached late last night still made sense this morning, and picked up the phone. I booked one more call – to Singapore.

The Juanda people were unfriendly at first. I should have contacted the police at Semadang who would have informed the civil aviation authorities of our predicament and everyone would have been saved a lot of trouble. After hours of argument they were still not satisfied but they had calmed down a bit. An Indonesian Navy Caribou was laid on to take me to Semadang, together with enough fuel to return to Surabaja. When I explained that my co-pilot was injured, the Navy had loaned me a young lieutenant who was qualified on the DC3, and from then on things had gone smoothly. Charlie Delta was now sitting safely on the tarmac at Juanda with full tanks, the authorities somewhat mollified. However, I was told that I had not heard the last of it. When I left in the battered taxi which brought me back to the hotel, the bumptious little man who had done most of the talking was still furiously writing his report. On the ride back to town, I wasn't thinking so much about him as Hudy. I wondered what my money-loving employer would say when he received the bill for chartering a Navy Caribou. It wouldn't make him happy but it brought a smile to my lips.

I swallowed the remains of my second beer and decided that although I would dearly like another, I had better go see Matt. I had phoned his room just before leaving for the airport and asked him to hold the fort. He had promised to try and I had agreed not to be any longer than necessary. I didn't feel guilty about the two beers but a third might be straining the friendship. I stood up. So did the girl at the bar.

I hung back, enjoying the sight of her delicious walk as she headed for the door. She had the undivided attention of the whole room, including the waiters, and now that I could see her face I could understand why. I felt an incredible urge to applaud. Instead, I watched her out of sight, let out a regretful sigh and followed.

'Captain Adams?'

She was waiting for me in the lobby. I stopped in my tracks, self-consciously glancing at the desk clerk who was staring at the two of us with unfeigned interest. Up close she was even more beautiful – wide-set brown eyes, classically straight nose and a very full lower lip. The flattened vowel sounds of her voice were comfortably familiar. I tried hard not to swallow like a school boy.

'Yes. I'm Frank Adams.'

Her features relaxed into the trace of a smile. She held out a slim, brown hand.

'Liz Manifold. Southern Cross Travel Bureau. Our Singapore office passed on your enquiry.'

'Ah yes. Good old Southern Cross.'

I forced a smile to my lips but my eyes were darting around the lobby. The clerk was still watching us, so was a middle-aged guest who was collecting his key. But his eyes were only for Miss Manifold. I relaxed, but only a little. What the hell was she doing making contact right out in the open like this?

She kept her smile in place for the audience but her voice was steady. 'Don't worry, Captain. As fellow countrymen, it is natural we should meet; there is no harm in doing it openly. It would be very difficult to do otherwise in a place like Surabaja, I can assure you. So we will have dinner together as old friends. Later, you can lure me up to your room. Shall we say seven-thirty – here in the lobby?' She put a hand to my face, gave me a gentle pat and turned on her heel. Half way to the door she turned and waved. I waved back and she blew me a kiss and was gone.

The desk clerk was looking at me with a mixture of awe and envy. The middle-aged guest was staring out the door she had just gone through. His lips were moist. I crossed jauntily to the desk and asked for my key.

I tapped lightly on Matt's door and went inside. He had been dozing and rose sleepily on one elbow. 'Oh. You came back.' He sounded more hurt than put-out.

I crossed to the shutters and threw them open. Strong sunlight poured into the room and Matt blinked once or twice. He had gotten himself cleaned up in my absence. His trousers were clean and pressed, the shirt was white and he had recently shaved. He had even had a haircut. The sling was no longer in place and as he swung his feet to the floor and reached for a cigarette he looked more human than I remembered seeing him.

'Who's your manicurist? You look positively beautiful.'

'You don't. You even smell terrible. Where've you been?'

'Semadang, among other places. How'd things go with the fat man?'

Matt stood up. 'You've been to Semadang? Charlie Delta . . .?'

'Is safely at Juanda, gassed up and ready to go. Now sit down and relax and tell me what happened with our fat friend this morning. I want to be ready for him.'

'He's gone.' I felt my mouth drop open. Matt sank back onto his bed. 'He left for Djakarta on the noon plane. We are to meet him in Singapore day after tomorrow when he will have everything ready.' A wry smile flitted across Matt's lips. 'He's almost made it too easy for us Pappy, except for one thing. Chong Bee has a room mate. Our friend from the launch.'

A near-full bottle of scotch rested on

the small tray alongside the thermos of ice water supplied by the management. Matt said, 'Help yourself,' as I poured generously into two glasses and reached for the flask. I handed him a glass and sat on the writing chair, catching my reflection in the mirror. I looked tired and dirty – mainly dirty.

'Cheers.' I gulped half my drink and set the glass down. Matt took a slow sip and sat watching me expectantly. I said, half to myself, 'I wonder who the fat man doesn't trust – us or Chong Bee?' My voice trailed off. I stretched my legs, rested my heels on the coir carpet, stared at the floor.

Matt said suddenly, 'Are you alright, Pappy?'

'Yeah. Sure.' I sat upright. 'Just thinking. When did this other guy arrive? I thought he sailed on the launch.'

'The launch is still here Frank. Look! Pardon me for saying so, but shouldn't we be discussing other things – like when do we leave and where do we go after we've picked up Chong Bee's family? I'm for heading straight down your way. There must be airstrips in the north of

Australia we could reach from Ambon. I mean apart from Darwin.'

'Later, Matt. I've got to figure out a way to get rid of our fourth member first. Also, I must have a bath.'

Matt looked ready to burst. I didn't blame him but there were things I couldn't discuss with him until after my dinner date. I was also thinking about the launch. If that was still around it could solve a lot of problems – provide the missing piece which had been worrying me. I stood up.

'Do me a favour, Sunshine. Give me time to have a couple of hours zizz and get cleaned up. I'll meet you back here later and when I turn up, be ready to fly. Stay in your room. I'll get here some time between ten and midnight and I don't want to have to come looking for you.'

'Ten and midnight? What the hell are you up to Frank?' Matt was on his feet again. There was a tinge of red on his blue cheeks; his good fist was clenched tightly. He kept his voice barely under control. 'You disappear for the whole fucking day, tell me sweet bugger all when you do finally get back and now you want me to twiddle my thumbs for a few more hours. While you go off and have a sleep. Bullshit! I say again, Pappy. What are you up to?'

He wasn't going to be put off, and I wasn't about to treat him to long explanations. I took the earthy way out.

'OK Sherlock, calm down. I ran into an old friend from Aussie downstairs – works for a local travel bureau. I've arranged to have dinner with her if you must know – and maybe a bit of something else afterwards. That depends on her, which is why I was offhanded about the time. OK?'

'OK? Are you out of your bloody mind? Christ! You'll have plenty of time for that sort of thing later.' He stopped suddenly as another thought struck him. He said acidly, 'You're bullshitting me.'

'Scouts' honour.' I raised two fingers, stifling a grin. 'Take a peek in the dining room at seven-thirty if you must. Only *don't* bother to come over and introduce her to the Duncan charm because I'll ignore you.' He was beginning to calm down, but still looking at me disbelievingly. I said, 'Look, Matt, assuming we get away tonight, we can't leave before 1 am. We need daylight to land at the other end. In the meantime, Liz has been in Aussie a lot more recently than I have and she is in the travel game. Maybe I can pick up a bit of info which might help if we decide to head that way.'

'Cut the crap. I just think you could have chosen a better time to start feeling horny.' His black eyes bored into me. 'I'll be in the dining room Frank, and if you and Miss Carriage *aren't* there, I'll come looking for you.'

The hotel tailor had done his best for me – a pair of cream linen slacks, batik shirt and an imitation snakeskin belt. The gift shop found me a pair of rope sandals my size, and I discovered Matt's barber. I came out half an hour later smelling of Karate aftershave and rum shampoo.

Waiting in the lobby just before seven-thirty I looked respectable if not resplendent. The clothes were not to my usual taste – I got a couple of 'mutton-dressed-up-as-lamb' thoughts – yet the odd reflections I caught in the glass doors were not displeasing. Maybe I was generally too conservative; perhaps it was time I threw off the old blue serge suit image I had grown up with. I had just never thought much about clothes – I spent half my life in uniform and the other half in whatever was handy at the time. It was time I changed my ideas; I had just been transformed from a dissipated thirty-eight into a young forty; I was enjoying it. Suddenly I got a dose of very cold feet. What if Miss Manifold turned up in evening dress? I was just beginning to feel incongruous when she walked through the door and I relaxed. She had on a Thai silk shirtwaister with a high, fly-away collar. A single row of pearls at her throat said it was past the cocktail hour but otherwise she just looked fresh and clean and very lovely. A cream-coloured clutch purse and high sling-back shoes matched the pearls. The dress was midnight blue.

I took it all in as the vision floated towards me, white teeth flashing and eyes alight with pleasure. I barely felt the kiss she planted on my cheek before one arm was linked intimately into mine and her head was resting on my shoulder as she allowed me to half carry her into the dining room.

By the time we reached our table, every eye in the room was on us, including Matt's. Only for once I didn't notice his eyes, just the mouth hanging wide open. I couldn't blame him; I had only just recovered the use of my jaw muscles.

The waiter beamed as he handed us each a menu. Young love was infectious. I somehow felt the entire room was buzzing at a higher key. We ordered our food and a bottle of wine and then held hands across the table. The waiter danced away and I did my best to remember it was all an act. But her hand felt warm, and funny things were happening in my guts. I was relieved when she broke the silence.

'I hope we're not overdoing it.' She was smiling radiantly.

'All the world loves a lover. Isn't that what you're getting at?

'Partly. But I'm not trying to attract attention for the sake of it. I suspect my cover has been blown.' As a frown started on my face she said, 'Smile, darling. Look happy. The only way I can divert attention from you is to attract it in the most obvious way. If I had tried to make a covert contact you would be under surveillance too. I don't know what this is about yet so I thought this would be the best way. I just hope I can help. I think I could be on my last forty-eight hours before I'm replaced. My own feeling is that I should have stayed out of it but Singapore were definite so it has to be me. There's no one else. Now, do you want to start a lovers' quarrel and get rid of me or are you prepared to chance it? You know what this is all about so the decision must be yours.'

The first thought that rushed into my head was 'a typical Fleming fuck-up.' I didn't realize I had been thinking aloud until I caught the hurt look in Liz's eyes. 'Sorry.' I squeezed her hand. 'Wasn't having a shot at you, just castigating my old arch-enemy – Fleming. I suppose you know him?'

She shook her head. 'No. I'm afraid I don't.' Her voice was cool.

'Then don't worry about it. If I'm heading for disaster, I couldn't think of a nicer companion. I appreciate your sticking your neck out.'

'I hope I'm not sticking yours out too.'

'Forget it. Eat your soup.'

'It's an incredible story.'

'Yes. It is.'

I sat on the edge of my bed. Liz Manifold had chosen the easy chair where she sat with her ankles crossed, a cigarette burning her fingers. I extended the ashtray and she stubbed out the butt.

'Thanks. But tell me, how are you expected to get past airport security at Singapore? They've got every modern gadget there – X-ray, the lot.'

'I don't know. We haven't been briefed on that part yet. But I don't doubt the fat man will have it all worked out when the time comes. What I want to know is, can you do your part? Have everything laid on at the other end?'

'Yes. I think so.' She caught the hard look in my eyes. 'Yes, of course I can. I will. You can rely on it.'

'Good. Now there's something you

can do for me here. I need a hand gun and I need it tonight. Can do?'

She raised one lovely eyebrow and took her time searching my face. Finally she said, 'Alright. At the office. You'll have to give me an hour.'

'I'll come with you.'

She hesitated for several seconds. 'OK. I suppose it will be natural for you to take me home – I live above my office. But we can't go yet – we haven't been up here long enough. My shadow will think it strange if we leave so soon. Have you got a drink?'

'No. But I'll soon fix that.' I picked up the phone and ordered champagne from room service.

I put the phone down and she said coolly, 'Isn't that over-doing it a bit?'

'Depends what you have in mind.' I tried a cheeky grin for size.

'If you've got *that* in mind, Captain Adams, forget it.' Her words were frosty enough to cool the champagne when it arrived.

'Don't be so bloody predictable,' I snapped back. She wasn't wrong, but I had no intention of admitting it.

'What do you mean?'

'I mean that it's a hell of a long time since I've had an hour to kill with a good old Aussie girl. A bit of old home week with someone as pretty as you doesn't come my way too often. When it does, I reckon it's worth a bottle of champers. So you react by thinking with your knickers, that's what I mean.'

'You don't have to be crude.'

I picked up the pack of Chesterfields from the locker and lit one angrily. Liz was staring at me. As I threw the pack down she picked it up and put a cigarette in her mouth, waiting for me to offer her a light. I sulkily extended the lighter. I felt her big brown eyes looking at me as she inhaled then she said softly, 'You're a fraud, Frank Adams.' I turned quickly and she added, 'You're not a bad actor either.'

'What do you mean?'

'I mean you've been wanting to get into my knickers since we first met this evening.'

'Now who's being crude?'

'I am perhaps. But why did you deny it – and with such a performance.'

'Well, why did you put me on the defensive?'

'Because I'm not going to bed with you tonight. It seemed the easiest way of making that clear.'

'Working on the assumption ...' There was a knock on the bedroom door. I crossed to it quickly, accepted the trolley-bucket of iced champagne from the grinning waiter who was trying desperately to see over my shoulder, and closed the door in his face without even tipping him.

'As I was saying, you were no doubt working on the assumption that the woman holds the key to the bedroom door. That's not always the way, you know.' I struggled with the wire surrounding the mushroom cork.

'I know. Especially with a man like you.' She picked up the two champagne glasses and seemed to anticipate the precise moment when the cork would pop. Then she was gathering the bubbles into the glasses with practised skill. 'Cheers.' A high colour was still in her face but her eyes were sparkling. I stared at her, not knowing what was coming next.

'Doesn't it occur to you that a girl has to be on the defensive too. You're a very attractive man, you know, but I'm not interested in one night stands, and that's one of my unbending rules. So as ships that pass in the night we may blow our hooters but there will be no collision.' She held her glass for a refill and looked at me over the bubbles.

'Truce?'

'Truce.' I couldn't help smiling. 'OK, no collision. But we are passing very close. Do you mind if I kiss you?'

'That would be nice.'

The Renault taxi dropped us at a row of buildings in an unlit street near the docks. The headlights which had followed from the hotel went out as I glanced behind; I caught the outline of a small sedan parked forty yards away down the road. The buildings were ominously quiet as Liz inserted her key in a door next to a glass-fronted office with Travel Agent in large letters across the window.

'Don't you find this a bit . . . isolated?'

'I did at first, but I'm used to it now and in any case, I've never had any trouble.'

I followed Liz up a narrow flight of stairs and into a comfortably furnished living room, all rattan and bamboo. I motioned her not to put the main light on and I crossed to the window, pulling a small gap in the matchstick blinds. The Renault taxi was still waiting as instructed; the other car appeared to have gone. Then I caught the faint outline, tucked in behind a lorry on the other side of the street. I released the blind and Liz flicked on the lights.

'How long have you had the tail?'

'A couple of days, but there've been other things. I guess I'll be moving soon.'

'That sounded like regrets.'

'Why not? I've been here nearly two years – there are worse places to live.' She crossed to a camphor wood chest, pulled it away from the wall and inserted a key in an old-fashioned floor safe. She came up with a small automatic. 'Want to tell me why you need this?'

'Not particularly. How far are we from the harbour – or the marina if there is one – where the little boats tie up?'

'No such place. The river is full of sampans and prahus – junks occasionally too. What particularly are you looking for? I might be able to help.'

'A launch, about twenty-five foot named the *Kuching Laut*.'

'The *Sea Cat* – old Woo Tang Sim's boat. Why didn't you say so. That will be outside Woo Tang's godown most likely; there's a small jetty near the silo.'

I was looking at her incredulously. 'This Woo Tang Sim. What does he look like?'

She laughed. 'Tallish for a Chinese. Quite distinguished looking.' She caught my expression and was suddenly serious. 'Was it the *Sea Cat* that brought you here? I see . . . And you thought Tang Sim was your fat man?'

'It was just a stab.' I held out my hand for the automatic. She kept it at her side.

'What do you want with Tang Sim's boat?' That was the second time she had referred to him in the familiar Tang Sim – the equivalent of his Christian name.

'I want to borrow it.'

'At the point of a gun? There's an easier way, Frank. Why not just let me ask him for it.'

This was crazy. Here was I going to all sorts of trouble to get hold of the *Sea Cat* and Liz Manifold could turn around and innocently offer to borrow it. Why not indeed? Christ! I had been toying with the idea of flying Chong Bee's mission on my own so I could leave Matt behind in Surabaja to look after the boat and be ready when we needed it.

I said, 'I'm going to need the launch sometime tomorrow night for a friend of mine. It should have full gas tanks and be provisioned for a week at sea for four people.'

'Where would you want it delivered?'

'You mean you'll do it?'

'It's not such a tall order . . . I'm in the travel business after all. I can tell Tang Sim it is for some special clients. He won't argue. We're good friends. What's more, if it will save you having to use this,' waving the gun, 'then I'm all for it.'

This could be going to work out better than I had dared to hope. Where had we been dropped off late last night? It was a crowded place with river traffic, and taxis on the wharf – not far from the hotel. I described the place to Liz and she said she knew it. 'What time?'

'Well, that's a bit awkward,' I said sheepishly. 'Sometime after dark is all I can tell you.'

'This has nothing to do with the Singapore job does it Frank?' Liz had propped her bottom on a corner of the camphor chest. She was looking at me strangely. 'Just what would I be getting involved in?'

I had trouble meeting her frank expression. I said suddenly, 'Something I have no right to ask you. I'm sorry. I guess I got carried away.' I added bitterly, 'Just give me the gun, Liz. It always was something I had to do myself.'

I was reproaching myself for even thinking Liz would have helped. Our man – woman repartee back at the hotel room had somehow made me look on her as an ally. But she wasn't even a friend in the true sense of the word – just a friendly contact with a job to do. A job that did not include exposing her to Tong evenge.

'I didn't say I wouldn't help. I just isked what it was about.' She was on her 'eet and had come to stand in front of ne. She put a hand on my shoulder, her oig brown eyes looked straight into mine. I enjoyed those kisses, Frank. I like to hink there may be other nights ometime, somewhere. You could get ourself hurt, or worse, if you try to do his thing with a gun.'

I pulled my eyes away. Liz's held a incerity which mine couldn't match. I iad been prepared to use her, and in eturn she was showing real concern. I 'elt like a heel.

To give myself a breathing space, I roped for a cigarette. By the time it was oing, I had made up my mind. I turned o look at her, this time my gaze as lirect as hers.

'I am going to rescue a Chinaman and iis family who are under a Tong death entence. I am not doing it for noble easons. For money – a great deal of noney. I want the *Sea Cat* because it it robably the fastest thing around here nd pursuit would be difficult. It is unlikely that Tang Sim would ever se his boat again but because he is probabl a Tong member himself I don't care to much about that. If he isn't in the Tong then it's just his bad luck. So you see you wouldn't be helping me; I would b using you.'

She stood back, gazing hard at me Turning abruptly, she took a lon cigarette from a lacquered box, lit it from an ornate table lighter and drew deeply She moved to the Singapore cane sette and crossed her long tanned leg characteristically. She said, finally, 'Wh are you, Frank Adams?'

I was still standing. I stayed that way Crossing to the window I stared at th faint willow pattern etched in green o the matchstick blinds.

'I'm a pilot – a Dak pilot. I worke for the Southern Cross organization long time ago – Section T.' I turned t face her, looking for some reaction t this last admission. Nothing. I went bac to studying the blind. 'When this thin started I could only think about savin my own neck. Then I learned about little Chinese girl called Ling Ma an everything changed. Things kind of snowballed after that. I was offered this rescue job at high pay and I was prepared to take it and run – until I met the fat man.'

'And you decided to take him on. Why Frank? Something to do with your Chinese girl. What was her name, Ling Ma? Who is she? Did the fat man hurt her or something?'

'You might say that.' I was facing her. I said suddenly, 'I've got to go. Give me the gun, Liz. Please.' I walked towards her, holding out my hand. She passed the automatic to me, silently. I worked the chamber and automatically flicked the magazine into my palm. 'What is this? It's empty!'

She stubbed her cigarette out in a large stone ashtray and patted the settee beside her. 'Sit down please Frank. I'll get you the bullets, but first, finish your story.' Standing close to her, I could see the hint of freckles under her make-up. She used the long, slim fingers of her right hand to fiddle with a silver scarab ring she wore on her wedding finger. 'Please Frank. It's important to me.' Her brown eyes stared at me frankly.

'Ah, what the hell!' I sat down beside her and reached for another smoke. 'Have you got a drink in this place, Liz?'

'Rum and Coke?'

'Jesus Christ! A bloody Queenslander and I had you pegged for a Miss Victoria. I should have known.'

'Why?' She called over her shoulder from the ornate cocktail cabinet.

'Your freckles. The only place a Melbourne girl collects freckles is on her behind.'

The two rum and Cokes swam in ice with a twist of lemon floating on top. 'Cheers.'

She settled beside me on the settee. I sipped at the drink. 'You were telling me about the fat man. And about Ling Ma.'

'Yeah . . .' My voice was ruminative. So were my thoughts. I got an image of that young kid in her cheongsam and the grotesque streaks of mascara. I started feeling angry again.

I told Liz the story in a cold monotone, trying not to get hot under the collar as I remembered. She let me finish and then was silent for quite a long time.

'I understand, Frank ... yet in some odd way, I don't understand at all. You never knew the girl, yet because you think the fat man killed her, or ordered her killed, you are prepared to take terrible risks to avenge a child you never met. I suppose I have to admit that I *don't* understand. It doesn't make sense.'

'I didn't expect it to. That's why I stopped myself from telling you earlier.'

'But it must make sense to you, Frank.' Liz had sneaked a slim hand into mine and was squeezing it. She put her other hand to my cheek and pulled my head around, making me look at her. 'Tell me the rest of it. The deep part.'

The deep part. That was a good description, and too close to the knuckle. I had never talked about it to anyone, and now Liz was simply saying, 'Tell me.' Maybe it would be good for me to tell someone after all this time. No. Not just someone. Not just a case of confession being good for the soul either. It was Liz doing the asking and I would tell her because I wanted her to know. She was one person who might understand. I emptied my glass and handed it to her.

'Get me another of those Queensland gut-destroyers.'

She patted my cheek, gave me a grateful smile and moved to the cocktail bar. I sat admiring the gentle curves of her bottom in its Thai silk cocoon. By the time she was seated again, and I had my fresh drink, I had steered my mind back through those ten years. I moved away from her slightly so that I could look into her face. I took a long sip of the rum and Coke.

'You know about T Section, Liz?' She nodded, saying nothing. 'I had been with them six years, done four assignments. At the time I am talking about, I had been idle for nearly eight months, waiting for the phone to ring. I'm sure the landlord of my Surfers Paradise holiday flat thought I was a big time criminal from the south. Each month when I surprised him with the rent he used to look at the money as if I'd just printed it myself. Anyway, what I'm getting at is that I was becoming soft and lazy – decadent, and it could have gone on forever. Then one morning the inevitable telegram arrived. I put on my blue suit and was off to St Kilda Road.

'As usual, Fleming briefed me himself. The job was in Hong Kong and there was a panic on. I wouldn't be allowed the usual minimum two weeks to size up my client. The Hong Kong office would give me what they could, confirm identification and I was to be on my way home, job done, within forty-eight hours. That was essential, Fleming told me.'

I reached for a cigarette, realizing I was waffling, wasting time, falling back on the same justification I had used on myself over the past ten years. I forced myself to look at Liz's eyes.

'What I'm trying to say is that it was an unusual job to begin with – hurried. And I was in a frame of mind where the sooner I could get back to my harem and into the swimsuit, the better.'

I was drinking more quickly now, remembering. I took a deep breath. 'I arrived in Hong Kong and everything was arranged. My target was staying at the Peninsula Hotel. I was booked in there too. I liked the set-up. Hotels were good news, plenty of people, lots of rooms, maximum confusion.

'I was promised a pre-view, but after a whole day in the lobby with the local consultant, the target never showed. Time was wasting – and I was getting impatient. To be honest, after eight months of inactivity, I was also a little edgy. I told myself there was no choice, that time was running out; I would have to break precedent. So I disappeared upstairs armed with a name and a room number. I also had a photograph, so I knew by now that my client was . . . a woman.'

The room was very quiet. Liz was watching me through those big brown eyes. I could feel perspiration forming on my forehead. I wiped it away with the back of my hand. Liz smiled.

'Go on, Frank,' in a soft voice.

I swallowed. 'That didn't bother me unduly. My previous four had been men but I was prepared for the fact that one day it could be different. I went to the room I'd been given and tapped on the door. I could hear movement inside so I knew someone was there, but it took a long time to open. I knocked again, getting nervous. I could hear people talking in the corridor round the corner, coming towards me. The door opened. I pushed it wide and stepped inside, closing it behind me. The girl looked younger than her photograph, but I was satisfied with the identification – the same long black hair, same almond eyes.' I forced a thin smile. 'I hadn't had much to do with the East in those days, Liz – I was still at the stage where all Chinese looked alike.'

'You shot the wrong woman.'

'Yes, God help me. That's exactly what I did. She was asking in a frightened voice who I was and what I wanted when she saw the gun in my hand. She turned and ran. I cut off her scream with one shot, and as she fell I saw the long scar on the side of her face. I don't usually hang around once the job is done, but this time I couldn't help myself. I had to know. One look at the photograph and I was sure. When I turned her head to look at her face, her eyes were wide open, staring at me, accusing me. I've been seeing those eyes for the last ten years.'

'It's a horrible story, Frank.'

'Oh, you haven't heard the best of it.' I heard a rattling sound in my throat which could have been a strained laugh. 'The *South China Post* had all the details next morning. It seems that the victim of the Mad Murderer was an off-duty room maid who was there for the purpose of stealing. She was the sole support of a widowed mother and two younger brothers. She was also four months pregnant.'

Liz had sidled along the settee closer to me. She was holding my hand. 'So that was when you quit the organization, and why you're bent on avenging Ling Ma. You're trying to square the account.'

'Something like that. I haven't touched a gun in those ten years until a couple of days ago. Now that I have, I find I can live with it. Provided I use it in the way that fate intends.'

'You mustn't think it's providence pushing you on Frank. You're not God. You mustn't act like an avenging angel.'

I smiled. 'No. I'm not God. I'm not

even an imitation of the Frank Adams I used to be, which is why I'm not setting out to gun the fat man down. But I'm going to fix that fat scum, get him put away where he won't do any more harm for a very long time. And I am prepared to shoot any bastard who gets in my way.'

Chapter Ten

I RODE the rattling elevator cage deep in thought, carrying on from where I had left off in the taxi. Liz's shadow had not bothered to follow me. I had stared hard at the small sedan which I could now identify as a dark red Skoda. There had been no sign of the driver who could have ducked for cover when he saw our lights. I was tempted to stop and scare the shit out of him with the PPK automatic, but I thought better of it. Liz didn't seem too perturbed by his presence so it wasn't up to me to interfere. Just the same, I would have been happier if he wasn't around.

The elevator jerked to a halt at the second floor and I stepped out, heading for Matt's room. He would be coming with me to Ambon after all; Liz had been eager to arrange the launch, had insisted on it. She would cruise on the river from dusk, only making for the town wharf after receiving my signal – a flash of landing lights on final approach. Landing to the west would take me right over the river north of town.

This time Matt was wide awake; he could have been pacing the floor the way he looked. Midnight had come and gone, so had one o'clock. It was nearly two. I was all prepared for another angry outburst, but apparently Matt was above such things now he had seen Miss Manifold. The first five minutes of his conversation can be condensed into: 'Jesus Pappy, she's beautiful. You're a lucky bastard. Has she got a sister?' It was obvious that young Matthew was impressed. I finally managed to steer his mind onto more mundane if somewhat more pressing matters.

'What's the set-up with Chong Bee

and this other joker, Matt? Are they really in the same room?'

'That's the way the fat man spelt it out. Seemed to think we needed help to guard our hostage so he kindly lent us one of his men, leaving you and me free to enjoy the delights of Surabaja. A sign of good faith as the fat man put it, to demonstrate that we really don't need a hostage at all.'

'Well, we haven't exactly got one in these circumstances, have we? I think the time has come to insist on our rights. Get your things together Matt and shoot out to Juanda. Do a preflight and bung in a flight plan for Ambon – two crew, one passenger, ETD 03.30 local. I'll be out there by then with Chong Bee.'

'Are you feeling alright Frank? Why flight plan to Ambon for Christ's sake; might as well give them a bloody signpost? And how are you going to handle the bodyguard? There's no way he's going to give Chong Bee up without a fight. I've only got one good arm but you might need my help just the same.'

'Thanks Matt.' I flipped open the batik shirt to let him see the automatic. 'I can handle things OK.'

'Where did you get that?' His eyes were wide open, staring. Then they narrowed suspiciously. 'There's things about you starting to worry me, Frank. Is there anything you want to tell me?'

'Lots, Matt. But not now, not here. There isn't time.' I threw him a friendly smile, reassuring. 'I'm going to insist that, as Chong Bee is our guarantee against payment, we want control of his whereabouts. So we're going to hide him. If the bodyguard does get on to the fact that we've used the Dak, then Ambon will seem like a red herring. Not only is it the last place he would expect us to go, he will be convinced we've gone off in entirely the opposite direction. Now be a good fellow and do what I've asked. I'll follow as soon as I can.'

I left Matt sulking. Or was he just worried perhaps? In his shoes I'd have been the same I guess. I returned to my room to find my uniform hanging clean and pressed in the closet. The two-hourly laundry service in the Far East was worth its weight in little apples. I changed quickly, stuffed the four-bar epaulettes into a shirt pocket. The roomboy had cleaned away the green, mildewed look; the gold bars were gold again. They smelled of meths. I threw my newly acquired wardrobe into the overnight bag, tucked my cap into the carrying straps and stepped into the corridor. It was deserted as I walked quickly to Chong Bee's room and set the bag down outside.

I could not expect an innocent reaction to my knock at this hour. Just the same, I kept the automatic hidden as I repeated the knock; unarmed I might be a nuisance, but I didn't pose a threat. The slim Chinaman from the launch opened the door a few inches. I said, 'I want to talk to Chong Bee.'

'In the morning.' He started to close the door.

'Now.' I kicked the door wide and stepped inside. He closed it behind me and a revolver appeared in his hand. It looked like the same thirty-eight – that gun was collecting quite a history. I stared at him in surprise.

'What's the gun for? I thought you were supposed to be on our side.'

He gave me a nasty smile. The thirty-eight stayed where it was, pointing at my belly. 'What do you want?'

'I told you. I want to talk to Chong Bee.' I walked across to where my podgy client was sitting up in one of the twin beds. He was wearing what I had come to regard as his permanent expression these days – shit scared. I sat on the end of his bed and innocently reached for a cigarette. The thirty-eight moved menacingly as I put my hand in my pocket. I waved the pack of Chesterfields and said, scornfully, 'Bang, bang. Put that away for God's sake. This is a social call.'

The man was watching me warily. He walked to his own bed and sat down, setting the gun beside him, in easy reach. But not easy enough. This was what I had been waiting for. I fussed with the lighter, trying to stuff it back inside my change pocket, my hand now only inches away from the PPK. It was in my hand before he realized it. He moved instinctively for the thirty-eight. I said quietly, 'Don't.'

His hand stopped millimetres from the

gun. I stood up, menacing with the automatic. 'Move away.' He murdered me with his eyes but he remembered my earlier marksmanship. Slowly, his hand moved away from the thirty-eight and I waved the automatic, indicating he should also move his body. He sidled along the bed and I picked up the revolver, taking a quick look at the chamber. Four bullets remained. I tucked the automatic back in my waistband, feeling more comfortable with the familiar thirty-eight in my fist. 'Get dressed, Chong Bee.'

'You will die for this, Captain.' The bodyguard was getting his courage back.

'Why? I'm not breaking our agreement, just enforcing it. I'm going to move Chong Bee where you and your fat boss can't find him. That way I'm sure we'll get paid. You can tell the fat man that with my compliments. But not just yet – we need a few hours start. Roll over and lie face down on the bed.'

The cord on the roll-up blinds was a strong twine, not as good as rope but it would serve my purpose. I yanked hard and the cord came free, along with about two feet of blind. I made a loop in one end and slipped it around the Chinaman's hands, pulling it tight. Then I had a loop around his legs and the rest was easy. I was able to put the gun down and finish the job properly. When I stepped back the Chinaman was trussed like a chicken – he would get free eventually, but not for three or four hours. That was enough. I went to the bathroom and came back with a face washer. It was small and worn thin from use – ideal. I scrunched it up and forced it into the young Chinaman's mouth with the barrel of the thirty-eight. If he felt like biting, he wasn't going to get my fingers to practise on.

Chong Bee had finished dressing. I switched the lights off as we left the room, picked up my bag from the corridor and headed for the elevator and a taxi. I slipped on my epaulettes on the ride to the airport, and put on my cap. It paid to look official when parading around an aerodrome at three in the morning – especially Juanda, which was eighty per cent military.

Matt had moved Charlie Delta onto

the main apron and was sitting in the cockpit when we arrived. I called the tower to tell them we were ready to start and watched the blue taxiway and yellow runway lights flick on. Five minutes later, run-up complete, I obtained take-off clearance and pulled Charlie Delta up into the darkness. Lights twinkled on the wide river as I gained height and set course for Ambon.

Sitting there with the auto-pilot on, there was nothing much to do for the next three hours or so. It was a good opportunity to brief Matt – it was also about time. I told him what I'd done, and why. There were some awkward moments explaining how I had managed to enlist the aid of Australian Intelligence so quickly, and how I'd known where to make contact. Matt would have lost confidence if I had waffled in a web of lies, so I told a half-truth: that I had served a short stint in Air Force Intelligence whilst in the RAAF, and that naturally I understood the intelligence structure of my own country, and how to make the right contacts.

'Is that where you learned to shoot, Pappy?' I said it was, that I had always been good with a hand gun and that the air force training had polished me. It sounded so bloody plausible I was almost believing it myself. It seemed to convince Matt. What was not so easy to get across was my reason for going after the fat man, and for the trap I had laid. Fortunately, my brain was working overtime.

I said, 'I've figured out the cargo the fat man is after, Matt. It can only be drugs – either a legitimate hospital consignment or he intends to hijack an illegal hoard being transported by courier. Possibly from a rival Tong. Whatever it is, there is only one market for hard drugs close enough to here to make it worthwhile, and that's Australia. My kid sister had a narrow shave with drugs at university – she escaped being an addict by a gnat's whisker.' I treated Matt to my troubled, sincere look. Liz was right – I'm not a bad actor. 'It was me who saved her, Matt. I happened to be available, thank God, and I was in time. But I saw a lot of other kids who weren't so lucky – if I could have got hold of one of those pedlars of filth I would have castrated the bastard – with my teeth if necessary, the same as we do sheep.' I caught my reflection in the windscreen. My face was shining like a crusader's. 'Now I have a chance to fight back – not only to prevent those drugs from hitting campuses in Aussie, but also to get the fat man caught red-handed and see him put away for a long time.'

I had to hand it to me, it was good. I had also acquired a kid sister, which also was not a bad effort for an only child. I must remember to write to her sometime. Matt would have swallowed the whole thing a lot easier if he had known me as a man of sterling character. He was having a job reconciling Crusader Adams with Captain Adams. Nevertheless, he bought it, whether thanks to my hitherto untapped integrity or to his own good nature, I wasn't sure. And I cared less. The main thing was, Matt had got caught up in the crusade himself – he would see it through to the bitter end. I stopped holding my breath. I hadn't realized how much I was counting on him.

Just over half way, I left my seat and went aft to the toilet. Chong Bee was sleeping peacefully on a canvas bench. There had been a marked change in his attitude since we took off: you could almost see the heavy burden drop from his shoulders. I left him with his dreams and went back up front. The false dawn was already a faint lightness in the sky up ahead – the real one would be with us in no time.

Half an hour from destination Chong Bee came into the cockpit. He shouted in my ear, 'I will show you the island, Captain, when we come closer.'

I shook my head. 'We're going straight into Ambon. I think it's safe enough – in any case, we don't have much time. We must be on our way again by three at the latest; that will give you about six hours, give or take.'

Matt said on the intercom, 'You really think Ambon is a good idea, Frank?'

'As good as any other. Chong Bee's got the Society of Jade to worry about – but he'd have that anyway, even if we arrived by submarine. And I don't think the League will have been alerted to expect us; there's no reason.'

'Unless our friend back at the hotel has managed to free himself and give the alarm.'

I had to admit that was a possibility, yet I didn't take it seriously. I had already given Matt my reasons. They were still valid as far as I was concerned.

The airport was its usual sleepy self as we landed just before nine o'clock, local time. I parked at the northern end of the apron next to the Angkasa Air Cargo warehouse. Chong Bee frequently employed Angkasa as clearing and forwarding agents. He had office facilities there if he needed a phone or other services. He disappeared inside the building and I sent Matt to hunt up Pertamina, the refuelling agents. I stepped out into the sunshine and cast a hungry eye on the little restaurant shack eighty yards away. As soon as we had refuelled Charlie Delta we could grab a bite to eat and then catch up on some sleep.

After about ten minutes the fuel

bowser hove into sight with Matt on the running board, hanging on with his good arm. The knife wound had been stitched and dressed back at Surabaja and he was now able to manage without a sling.

'Captain.'

I turned to see Chong Bee hurrying towards me. He couldn't quite manage a run but it was the next best thing. He reached my side, out of breath like he'd just won the Olympic hundred metre dash. He gulped air, grabbed me by the arm and took me aside.

'Captain . . . I have telephoned my wife . . . she will be ready.' He paused. I wondered whether he was waiting for me to say congratulations or something. I said nothing. He obviously had something else on his mind. I waited to hear what it was. Finally, his breath now coming in more evenly-spaced gasps as his lungs recovered, he said, 'I do not think I can manage everything on my own.' His eyes were pleading. 'Would you come with me, Captain?'

I didn't jump at the offer. I had been on the go for over twenty-four hours and my eyes felt like gravel. Charlie Delta would soon become a hotbox, and the 'beds' weren't exactly comfortable, yet I was looking forward to it like it was the Ritz. But I couldn't ignore Chong Bee's cry for help. It had nothing to do with his organizing ability; there were no deficiencies on that score. It was his old enemy, lack of moral fibre – sometimes unkindly described as a yellow streak. The pressures of the day had hardly begun, yet already they were too much for him. He was right; he couldn't manage on his own.

I said resignedly, 'Alright, Chong Bee. I'll come with you.'

The refuelling had already started. Matt was supervising. I climbed aboard and headed for the cockpit, more specifically to my map case where I had stowed the two guns. I picked them both up, weighing them in my hands. I regretted the decision I had to make but there was no doubt that the automatic was less conspicuous. I tucked it under my shirt and dropped the thirty-eight back in the map case. I left the aircraft, told Matt where I was going and why, and asked him not to go away. He said he wouldn't, that some time during the morning he would submit a flight plan so we could be ready to leave as soon as we got back.

Chong Bee's car, a three years old Benz 220, was parked behind Angkasa. I climbed in beside him and we were on our way. He was a lot calmer now he had company.

'What's your plan of action, Chong Bee?'

'We will go to my warehouse first, to collect the cargo. Later, at two o'clock, we will meet my wife in town. She is taking the children to lunch. It will be easier to pick them up off the street than at my house.'

'What about the people watching her?'

He kept his eyes on the road. 'We must be quick, Captain. Quicker than them.'

That sounded nice and simple – logical even. Except that downtown Ambon was not downtown London, or Sydney, or New York. The roads would be jammed with people and bicycle-powered rickshaws called betjaks, and the possibility of a fast getaway, even in a car as powerful as the 220, was not on. Not until we reached the outskirts of town, and it could take us anything up to half an hour to get there.

'Why did you select two o'clock, Chong Bee? Did you think it would be easier at the busiest time of the day?'

'No. It will be more difficult.' He was shaking his head. 'But we cannot get there any earlier. It will take us time to recover the gold.'

I couldn't help smiling. 'What have you done, buried it in an old jam jar?'

Chong Bee failed to see the joke. He said, seriously, 'No, but it is well hidden. There are eleven hundred and ten ounces in my safe – they are easy to get at. But my main fund, the two thousand ounces I prepared for my retirement, are in two briefcases. We must remove part of a wall to reach them.'

The Mercedes wended its way through run-down streets and shanty-town buildings, as Chong Bee drove towards the dock district. We were skirting the town proper so the traffic-jumping crowds of the town centre were not yet in evidence. Just the same, we had been forced to slow down considerably once leaving the main airport road. By the time we reached the large warehouse with CHONG BEE ENTERPRISES above the huge sliding doors, I was feeling quite exhausted.

The warehouse was the size of a small hangar. Stacked cartons took up two thirds of the available floor space, and stairs led up to glass partitioned offices. A wizened old Chinese holding a tally board came across to greet Chong Bee as he drove the Mercedes straight inside the warehouse, pulling up near the stairs. A younger man worked with a fork lift truck at the far end, and two others were loading cartons of soap powder onto an ancient looking lorry. I followed Chong Bee out of the car and was introduced to Mr Lee, the man with the tally board. The two men exchanged greetings in their own language. I followed Chong Bee upstairs.

We walked through the outer office where a young Indonesian woman sat at a typewriter. Chong Bee said a curt, '*Selamat Pagi*' – good morning – and opened the door to his own office. I was right behind him as he entered and stopped dead.

The room was a mess! A gaping hole in one wall was surrounded by chipped fibre board and plaster. Broken wooden laths jutted at odd angles and everything in the room was covered in a film of white dust. A short pickaxe lay guiltily nearby.

'My God!' Chong Bee was trembling as he stumbled to the hole and groped frantically inside. 'It's gone. My gold is gone.' He turned to face me, accusingly, as if it was my fault. His eyes were moist. 'It's gone. All of it.'

I glanced at the heavy Chubb safe behind the desk. It must have been one of the earliest models ever made, an antique with brass curlicues and heavy post corners. It looked solid and imperturbable. Chong Bee followed my gaze. Suddenly he was groping in his pocket. He unlocked a desk drawer and removed a large old fashioned key which he inserted in the safe. A smaller key from his key ring fitted the lower of the two locks and I watched him turn the large key anti-clockwise, the smaller one in the opposite direction. He used both hands to pull open the heavy door and relief flashed in his eyes as he turned briefly towards me. I looked over his shoulder and could see the small, neatly wrapped packages stacked in three rows. Each package was about the size of a bar of soap. I picked one up – it weighed around two pounds.

'So they didn't get it all.' I replaced the package. Chong Bee was looking at me, worry lurking in the back of his eyes along with the distress. I read his mind. 'It looks as though we're both out of pocket.' His eyebrows raised. 'You promised us a third of your gold, Chong Bee. We'll settle for that. But I don't think this is just a case of bad luck. Someone knew about your hiding place and they knew when to move in. I think it's time you questioned your staff.'

'Thank you, Captain.' He was pulling himself together. Maybe the knowledge that he still had a conservative eighty thousand dollars had something to do with it. Matt and I would now get about forty thousand between us. There wouldn't be any airfreight company bearing our name but twenty grand was not to be sneezed at. We could double that if the fat man could be squeezed for a hefty up-front payment before we threw him to the wolves.

Chong Bee walked to the door and called his secretary. 'Asah! *Masok di-sini, silakan.*' Asah came into the room, complete with scribble pad and pencil. She barely spared a glance for the mess in the corner as she looked at her boss expectantly. Chong Bee spoke in Indonesian and her answers were prompt and brief. I was no expert on the lingo but I could follow the gist of the conversation. It appeared that within minutes of Chong Bee leaving for the airport and Semadang, two Chinese technicians arrived to commence installing the new air-conditioner Chong Bee had ordered. They made a lot of noise, were there only a short time and left carrying two heavy bags which she assumed contained their tools. They promised to return after lunch but that was the last she had seen of them. That was three days ago.

Chong Bee dismissed Asah and

started to explain their conversation to me. I said, 'It's OK, I could follow it. What's worrying me is how they knew about the gold and where it was hidden. Did anyone else know about your hiding place? Mr Lee for instance?'

'No. He did not know, I am sure.' His features were drawn. 'Perhaps the builders who designed the false wall. I said it was for insulation which is why I chose that particular wall. It is on the hot side of the building.'

'And the builders were Chinese, I suppose. You bloody people certainly scratch each other's backs. Keeping things in the family is all very well, but it's not always for the best. Never mind – someone knew you had built a hiding place. As for what you were hiding, I still think that can be traced back to your broker. It probably wouldn't take a lot of mind-bending to figure it out exactly, but it's not going to help us if we did know. We're not going to get the gold back.' My eyes wandered around the room. 'Have you got another briefcase?'

He shook his head and spoke Chinese

into a PA system on his desk. I heard the words echo around the warehouse and a minute later a young Chinese appeared at the door with an empty grain sack.

'What about ringing your wife and arranging to meet her a bit earlier, Chong Bee.'

He gave a sad smile and picked up the telephone. Using a thumbnail he unscrewed the plate on the bottom of the instrument, slid it to one side and held it up for me to see. The small bugging device was tucked neatly inside. At my questioning look he said, 'I only make calls from here that I don't mind being overheard. I was going to remove the bug but it seemed more sensible to leave it. Otherwise they might plant another more difficult to find; this way my conversations are never incriminating.'

'What about your house? Maybe that's bugged too.'

'No. It isn't.'

'Then we can use a public phone.'

'Perhaps. But it would be better to leave the arrangements as they stand. My wife will be making preparations –

there is some jewellery at the bank, and some papers.'

I looked at my watch – just past eleven. I didn't relish hanging around the warehouse for three more hours. It was hot and noisy, and somehow ... exposed. I said as much to Chong Bee.

'There is a place we can wait, Captain, owned by a friend of mine.' He smiled as he caught my expression. 'Yes, you are quite right. He is another Chinese but he is discreet. Very discreet.'

Chong Bee's discreet friend owned a brothel, tucked away in a corner of town surrounded by strong-smelling eating houses and food stalls. The proprietor, Ah Ho, was surprised that I only required a room, without companion, but he gave me one just the same. I left him and Chong Bee chatting over cups of tea and sank gratefully onto the hard bed. But not before I sneaked a look out the window at the back yard where our very expensive Mercedes was parked.

At twenty minutes to two I was awakened by a gentle shaking of my shoulder. A young Chinese woman held a cup of weak tea out to me and I hoisted myself up on one arm and took it gratefully. Her eyes offered something else if I was interested. I wasn't – the memory of Liz Manifold had changed my taste for that sort of thing.

Just before two o'clock we were cruising along a main downtown thoroughfare in the restaurant district. At my request, I was doing the driving. Chong Bee pointed suddenly to a small blue sedan. 'My wife's car. Slow down.'

Slow down? Jesus! We were only doing about ten miles an hour, and that between stops. There were people everywhere, as many beggars as solid citizens. The betjaks were the worst, sometimes strung four abreast across the street, bells ringing frantically, drivers shouting abuse at each other. Chong Bee saw his wife and children a fraction of a second before I realized that was who they must be. I was already nosing the Benz into the curb as Chong Bee shouted, 'There they are.'

Madame Chong Bee was a comfortably-built woman on the threshold of middle age. Despite the fact that she was leaving her home and familiar surroundings, her expression was placid as Chong Bee bundled her and the children into the back seat amidst hurried introductions. Perhaps Madame didn't realize she was running for her life or maybe her Christian upbringing had softened the fear of death. Son Richard was about two years older than his sister Jean. The boy seemed over-awed at meeting a real live pilot – I guessed I was going to have young company in the cockpit.

I nosed the 220 back into the slow moving stream of humanity and tried leaning on the horn as a means of improving progress. All it achieved was a bevy of angry stares and bad-tempered shouts. I gave it up and tried something equally impossible like keeping my eyes on the road and in the rear view mirror. We didn't appear to have a tail, but in all that bedlam I couldn't be sure. A pale grey Mercedes with two front seat occupants was about thirty yards behind and the only candidate.

I relaxed. Even if it was hostile, the driver was having as much trouble negotiating the traffic as I was. Just the same, I made sure he didn't gain on us – in fact I made a few yards on him, by sheer bulldozing.

The kids chatted constantly in the back seat, occasionally bringing mother and father into the conversation. I concentrated on the job in hand and gradually we moved out of the dense area so that I was able to do twenty, then thirty miles an hour with only occasional braking. The other Mercedes stayed with us for a couple of miles, then suddenly made a left turn. I let out a slow breath, realized my palms were wet and wiped them one by one on my trousers. The bright chatter continued behind me – just a happy family outing. I couldn't tear my eyes away from the mirror but each successive glance was only more reassuring than the last. As we left the suburbs and finally swung into the winding airport road the only thing within half a mile was an ox-cart laden with firewood. I reached in my shirt pocket for a cigarette.

The *tempat keppel terebang* – the place of ships that fly – was another nine kilometres according to the faded signpost. The narrow tar road wound its way through occasional kampongs of atap huts and well-tended paddy fields. Patches of thick jungly growth clung to small hills which the locals hadn't bothered to cultivate. There were places where the road had been literally hacked through these hillocks. Secondary undergrowth covered old excavation scars and encroached right to the tar on both sides, reducing the road to single lane traffic. I approached these spots with my foot hovering on the brake pedal – it would have been easy to end up with an ox-cart through the windscreen otherwise.

A mile from the airport I was down to twenty miles an hour, winding through a scrub-lined culvert and into a banana plantation where the straggly fronds of some of the older trees reached out like umbrellas. A hundred yards ahead, parked across the road and completely blocking it, was the pale grey Mercedes.

I stamped on the brakes and reversed into the culvert out of sight of the other car. I could have asked Chong Bee about alternative routes to the aerodrome, but I hadn't thought to do so and now it was too late. Our pursuers had followed us long enough to establish our destination and then taken to the bush. I had noticed an occasional dirt road without paying much attention. I interrupted Chong Bee who was making hurried explanations to his wife in their own language.

'Take the wheel, Chong Bee. One of two things is going to happen in the next five minutes – either that car is going to come looking for us or you are going to start driving towards it.' I let him glimpse the PPK under my shirt before he could start raising objections. The alarm which flashed in his eyes died quickly as he saw the gun. I breathed a sigh of relief – I didn't want his wife and kids to recognize the other Chong Bee I had become familiar with over the past few days. It could start an epidemic.

'If they come to us, I'll be ready for them. If they don't, then I want you to drive slowly in their direction in exactly five minutes. Pull up twenty yards short and regardless of what happens – *stay in the car*. OK?'

'Alright, Captain.' His eyes had the trusting look of a spaniel as I jumped out of the 220 and headed into the scrubby undergrowth. Through the open window I could hear excited conversation starting up again, the kids' voices in there too. I watched Chong Bee slide behind the driving wheel, then I forced my way through a tangled mass of tall lalang and thick ferns. I skirted the hill, staying on the right side of the road but hidden from it. Two minutes later, hot and panting, I arrived at the edge of the bananas from where I could see the grey Mercedes.

It was as I had seen it, straddling the road eighty yards ahead, the two men standing alongside and talking earnestly. One was gesticulating towards the airport, which made me think there was probably yet another back road and he was worried we might have doubled back. Maybe the simplest way to handle things would be to shoot out two tyres and then go looking for the back road. I considered it for two whole seconds and then dismissed the idea. One of the men could run to the airport within six or seven minutes and summon reinforcements by phone. Or the two of them could just wait in ambush near the airport and shoot *our* tyres out. So I was going to have to take care of them here and now.

I ran along a line of banana trees, fending off the drooping serrated leaves and wishing once again I didn't smoke so much. Twenty yards from their position I slowed down and began to move more carefully. The PPK was now in my hand and I realized that if I had to do any shooting I was going to have to aim the thing. The weight and balance was all wrong for the instinctive way I could handle a thirty-eight – my usual move-and-squeeze technique.

I crept five yards closer and stopped. The men had reached some sort of agreement because I could see they were about to get inside the car. Once they did, the advantage would be back with them; I had to make my move now. But I couldn't risk trying to bail up the two of them from where I was; if they went for their guns, one of them might get lucky. At the very least, if they took a dive for the bananas, one of them had a chance of making it. So it was just bad luck on the man closest to me. I took careful aim with the PPK and shot him in the left knee.

The sharp crack of the little automatic was still ringing in my ears as I saw him go down, the startled expression on his face disappearing suddenly as he screamed in pain. The other man was reaching for his weapon as I burst through the trees and snapped off another quick shot, aimed high and right, a warning shot. It wasn't as high as I thought. The bullet whanged off the Mercedes roof, making a nasty scar in the shiny paintwork. The man glanced behind briefly and lost any advantage he might have had. By the time his attention was back where it should be, I was standing four feet in front of him the automatic trained on his belly.

He let his hand fall to his side. I smiled sweetly. 'Don't let me stop you. Take your gun out slowly and drop it on the road.' I turned to where the other man was writhing, nursing his shattered knee and moaning in pain. 'You too, my friend. Just put your gun down and kick it over here.'

Two forty-fives clattered onto the bitumen – large, ugly guns with a kick like a mule and designed only to kill. If I had shot our friend in the knee with one of those it would have just about taken his leg off. He would now be a cripple, but at least he'd still have his own ten toes to wriggle. I picked up one of the forty-fives and kicked the other one off the side of the road. When the standing man got over his surprise he might risk a move against the PPK, but not against one of the other monsters. I slipped the automatic back inside my waistband and let him look into the business end of the cannon in my fist, knowing from now on I would be instantly obeyed.

The man said, 'What is Chong Bee paying you, Captain? We will pay more.'

'Gold – or lead?' I waved the gun. 'Forget it. Just help your friend into the car – the front seat. Then you climb in behind the wheel, nice and slowly.'

The injured man screamed again as his companion lifted him none too gently and helped him into the Mercedes. I got into the back seat behind the driver. As he started the engine, I said, 'Just drive straight ahead into the trees.' It was going to put some nasty scratches on the paint job, and the plantation owner wasn't going to like it when he saw a dozen damaged trees, but that was too bad. As the man hesitated I prodded the back of his neck with the muzzle of the revolver. 'Hit that accelerator hard, buster, and get going. They put a nice big engine in this model so don't try and be funny or I'll hit you over the head and drive the bloody thing myself.'

Ten seconds later we were as many yards off the road, and as far as we were going to get. The short, lurching ride had taken us into a shallow gully, banana fronds all around and the bonnet hard up against the thick, plaited bole of a mature banana tree. The driver had done a good job; my threat about hitting him over the head did the trick. It was no time for niceties. I hit him anyway and as he slumped in his seat I reached over and switched off the ignition, removing the keys. The right hand door refused to budge; I forced open the left and climbed out. The forty-five was still in my hand. I aimed at the nearside front tyre and pulled the trigger. There was a loud bang as the large gun tried to jump out of my hand, but the tyre went down with a rush, leaving behind a ragged hole. The effect was pleasing. I repeated the process on the rear tyre and then threw the gun far into the trees, sending the car keys sailing after it.

Chong Bee was cruising slowly in the 220 as I regained the road, his eyes peering anxiously. They posed a question as I climbed into the front passenger seat and I shook my head.

'No. I didn't shoot them, just a couple of their tyres. They won't be following in a hurry, but just the same, don't waste any time. There could be others we don't know about.'

Chong Bee didn't need any second bidding. He took a worried glance at his wife and gunned the Benz towards the airport, driving too fast for the narrow road but not getting any argument from me. The sooner we were away from Ambon, the better.

Two minutes later the car squealed

into the Angkasa car park and then we were hurrying around the building to Charlie Delta. Chong Bee and I struggled with the heavy grain sack and Madame clutched a huge handbag to her chest. Matt was waiting near the rear door.

'Everything ready?'

He nodded, relief on his face as he helped the two youngsters up the metal steps. Madame reluctantly parted with the handbag before climbing aboard, setting it down just inside the door. The bag was back in her hands almost before she was properly inside the aircraft and I indulged myself in a wry smile. If she was so concerned about the valuable things in her handbag, I wondered what she would think about what was inside the grain sack. I was last up the steps. I unclipped them, pulled them inside and closed the doors.

Matt had everything ready for a fast start-up as I reached the cockpit. I smiled gratefully, and he said, 'Had some trouble, Pappy?'

'Some. There could be more on the way so let's get the hell out of here.'

Both engines were hardly turning before Matt had the radios switched on and was asking for taxi and take-off clearance.

'Charlie Delta, hold your position,' came booming back from the tower. Matt and I exchanged glances and I watched horrified, as a blue and white police car nosed onto the taxiway, heading in our direction. Another car followed – a white Ford with no markings – but a short antenna protruded from the roof. I got a brief, half-crazy idea of grabbing full power and trying to out-run them, but fortunately discretion got the better of insanity. I resignedly pulled the mixtures into idle-cut-off and clambered out of my seat as the engines died.

Chong Bee was struggling to unfasten his seat belt. I said, 'Stay where you are, and keep calm. It's the police. You and your family are legitimate passengers so just sit tight and keep your mouth shut. Tell your family not to worry.'

I hurried towards the rear door, pausing as I saw the heavy grain bag lying there. I opened the toilet, dragged the gold inside and closed the door. Then I unlatched the main doors and pushed them open.

Both cars had halted about ten yards away. The drivers were still inside their respective vehicles but a uniformed inspector was climbing out of the police car and a dapper, well-dressed man had vacated the Ford. He was holding an overnight bag.

The inspector saluted. 'Sorry to delay you, Captain. This is Mr Sangeron, an official of our Government who has urgent business in Surabaja. Could we prevail upon you to give him a lift? Unfortunately, there is not another scheduled service until tomorrow and that would be too late. Mr Sangeron's business is . . . most urgent.'

Sangeron hadn't said a word. He was keeping in the background, but one look told me he was no shrinking violet. He had GUD written all over him; so the hunt for the general had already begun. What an odd coincidence that Mr Sangeron should want to travel on *my* aeroplane!

Yet I couldn't refuse. If I tried then the

police would suddenly find that I had infringed some minor rule – failed to comply with some 'irritating formality' as they would put it. The result would be a visit to the police station and a lot of flak. I hit the inspector with my prize-winning smile. 'It will be a pleasure, Inspector. Always glad to help a government official; it's no trouble. We have plenty of room.'

'Thank you, Captain.' The deep cultured tones came from Sangeron's lips. I slotted the steps into place and helped him aboard. Just before closing the door I said to the inspector, 'Would you mind asking the tower to amend my flight plan and passenger manifest.'

The inspector's voice was friendly. 'That has already been done, Captain. We were sure you would not refuse so we . . . took the liberty.'

I closed the door, showed Sangeron to a seat far enough away from Chong Bee to discourage conversation, and walked into the cockpit, closing the cabin door behind me. I told Matt about our extra passenger and who I thought he was. Matt just pursed his lips and began the start-up drill once again. This time there was no delay. Taxi and take-off clearance were right where we needed them. I turned to Matt.

'You want to do this leg, Sunshine?'

He tapped his sore shoulder and shook his head. I nodded, pushed the throttles and we were on our way. As we lifted off the strip Matt said, 'Airborne at fifty-one.'

In terms of local time that was fifteen fifty-one – nine minutes to four. Allowing for the prevailing westerly, it should put us at Surabaja around eight-thirty in the evening – in good time, if everything else had been arranged. Sometime during the flight I was going to have to brief Chong Bee about the next stage of his journey. It would come as a shock to him, and if I knew Chong Bee he wasn't going to like it. But it was the only way.

I started thinking about the *Sea Cat*, and about Liz.

Mostly about Liz.

Chapter Eleven

THE night air was so clear I could see pinpricks of light twinkling on the river from forty miles away. Some came from houseboats and junks; others from stilted huts at the end of bamboo fish-traps, burning carbide lamps as old as the Bible. Many slender necks emitted a flame which even a hundred watt globe could not match for brightness. Sometimes a small cluster of these lamps betrayed the presence of a jungle village – a nest of fireflies in a carpet of blackness. Then there were the coastal settlements, signposts to a primitive, peaceful life where the evening conversation may never sparkle with the brilliance of a carbide flame, but it seldom lacked contentment. It was easy to wonder about those people – envy them even.

The lights up ahead grew in the brightness and number and soon the reflections of the river itself could be seen. Liz would be down there somewhere. I craned my neck, looking for a tell-tale red or green navigation light which would betray something more sophisticated than a sampan. It was a crazy exercise. What I was really looking for was a glimpse of Liz – from three thousand feet, in the dark. I hadn't known she had made such an impact on me, yet she had been in my thoughts throughout the flight from Ambon. I had been engaged in conversation with Chong Bee some of the time. Sangeron had also visited the flight deck – and virtually determined my next move. But first, there was Liz. I kept telling myself it was the *Sea Cat* I was worried about – would Liz be there with the boat, on time? It was essential to this whole crazy gamble. Yet I finally had to come to terms with myself – it was Liz I wanted to see first and foremost, as if I hadn't already got enough on my plate to keep a regiment busy. For a confirmed bachelor it didn't make much sense, but somehow my desire for this woman went deeper than my loins – much deeper. It scared me. It also delighted me.

Charlie Delta was now at two thousand feet over the river, right on glidepath for the long runway with its funnel of yellow flares. I flicked the landing lights on and off. Ten seconds later I repeated the process and left them on, calling to Matt for flaps and gear as I continued towards the waiting threshold. If Liz was on the river, she would have seen my signal. So would anyone else who happened to be looking up at the time. This last thought niggled at me as I taxied towards the brightly-lit apron. Fortunately, no one bothered to marshal an off-schedule charter flight so I was able to select my own parking bay. I swung Charlie Delta to put the passenger exit door in shadow, leaving Matt to do the shut-down. I hurried aft.

Sangeron had identified himself as a policeman – not as a secret policeman or an intelligence agent – but then he hadn't needed to. Just being a representative of the law should have been enough to ensure the co-operation of two innocent pilots – which of course, we were. In answer to his questions, I had acknowledged that we were normally based in Djakarta. Yes, I would be proceeding there from Surabaja, but not immediately. Due to the number of hours

Matt and I had already been on duty we were obliged to take a rest period in Surabaja – a minimum of eight hours.

It turned out that eight hours in Surabaja was almost exactly the time Sangeron needed to complete his business, after which he must proceed to Djakarta himself. As our timetables coincided so conveniently, could he impose on us further? I assured him he could, provided he did not mind leaving at some unearthly hour in the morning. As I came up to him in the fuselage of Charlie Delta and announced, 'Five am, Mr Sangeron, don't be late,' he understood immediately.

'Thank you, Captain Adams. I will be here before five. I appreciate your help.' He turned to the others. 'Goodbye Mr and Mrs Chong. I hope we shall meet again.'

Chong Bee's expression didn't radiate the same hope as the Indonesian made his exit from the aircraft, but the Chinaman's spoken farewell was polite. I waited until Sangeron had gone. 'OK, stay here until I come back. I want to make sure there is no welcoming committee and then I'll drum up some transport. Wait inside the aircraft. Don't even stick your big toe out that door.'

Chong Bee nodded sullenly. He was still brooding about the impending boat ride which he was now aware of. I had briefed him and he hadn't liked it one bit – had accused me of breaking our agreement by not flying him immediately to safety. In a way, he was right, but I didn't let it bother me. If it had come down to a straight choice between helping him or going after the fat man, Chong Bee would have come off second best. He would have to play it the way I called it. I had lost my temper at one stage – told him if he didn't shut up and do as he was told there would be more things broken than his version of our agreement – his neck for instance. I had then managed to reason with him, point out that now the police were involved, further movement in Charlie Delta could be difficult, and delay dangerous. Arrangements had been made to get the Chong Bees out of Surabaja that night, quietly and unobtrusively. It was the best way. The launch would have plenty of fuel and provisions for a week. Navigation would be no problem. All he had to do was follow the Java coast until he recognized Semadang – then head south to our island and wait. Within three to four days I would be there to pick them up.

I left Chong Bee still feeling miserable and jumped to the tarmac, heading for the corner of the terminal complex nearest the control tower. Anyone watching our arrival would be doing so from the far end of the building in the public enclosure. It was empty – so was the not very elegant restaurant where two waiters stood disconsolately under a squeaky ceiling fan.

A solitary taxi waited hopefully near the exit. A strong smell of clove-scented tobacco hit me as I jumped into the back seat and jolted the driver out of his reverie. One mile from the airport I told him to pull over at a coffee stall where a group of coolie class Indonesians were feeding. A decrepit lorry was parked nearby and I immediately identified the driver. He was wearing a grubby singlet and an old felt hat, living proof that he was in work, and therefore a cut above his companions. Despite the lack of other signs of affluence I suspected he would possess an essential piece of paper – an airport pass. If he didn't, then I was going to have to look elsewhere, but I thought it unlikely. He would hardly be plying his trade this close to Juanda without the means to gain access to air cargo. At Juanda, that meant driving right onto the apron alongside the aircraft, which was exactly as I wanted it. I didn't have to ask about the pass. In my pilot's uniform, with its obvious airport connotations, the piece of paper was waved ceremoniously under my nose and I was quoted a price approximately double the going rate. But it was still cheap by any standards. I climbed into the lorry and told the taxi driver to follow.

It all went smoothly – the lorry driver didn't even realize that the bulk of his cargo was human as he pulled away from Charlie Delta. The man had been more than content to remain in his cab. As I had loaded the grain sack onto the back of the truck, Chong Bee and his family followed on their hands and knees, Madame clutching determinedly at her enormous handbag. Matt and I shared the lorry to where the taxi was parked and instructed the lorry driver to head for the quay Liz had named. We jumped into the taxi and followed.

Bouncing along in the back seat of the old Chevy, we kept the single tail light of the lorry in sight, and I relaxed. The thirty-eight was back in my waistband. Matt was wearing the PPK in his – it was the most convenient way to return it to Liz.

'So far so good, Pappy,' Matt said through his cigarette. 'Is there anything we haven't thought of? I've got this feeling in my guts and I don't think it's just hunger.'

I turned to look at him, but all I could see on that unlit road was the glow of his cigarette on a blank background. I couldn't see his eyes – the reliable signpost to what he was thinking, so I didn't know whether he was worried or just speculating.

'Once we get them on board the *Sea Cat* you'll feel better, Matt. I'm sure Liz will have done her bit. Anyway, we'll soon know.'

'One way or the other,' Matt replied sardonically.

I recognized the quay where we had disembarked from the *Sea Cat* two nights earlier. It was even busier than I remembered, but then, it was also much earlier in the evening. There were people everywhere. I left Matt in the cab and walked across to where the lorry was parked. I called in English through the wooden tailgate for Chong Bee to stay down until he got the word. His hoarse reply reassured me – he was too bloody frightened to do anything else.

I walked to the edge of the quay, my eyes on the river, searching for the *Kuching Laut*. Liz should be holding off, waiting for our arrival, ready for a quick pick-up and away. But there was no sign of the *Sea Cat*, just a bedlam of noise, and lights that twinkled in every direction. I moved into a more brightly lit area. If Liz was watching from a darkened deck then maybe she could see me. I was attracting enough attention anyway; in my gold braid I felt like a bloody Christmas tree. I was surrounded by pedlars, offering everything from aphrodisiacs to dried fish.

'*Tidah mau— pergis la. Pergis.*' I fought them off, all except one, a young boy who pulled at my shirt and yelled, '*Keppel, Tuan? Ada keppel di sini.*' It took several seconds to sink in what the kid was saying – he was asking did I need a boat? Maybe I did! If I went out onto the river I would have more chance of spotting the familiar shape of the *Sea Cat*. The issue was suddenly beyond doubt – I *did* need a boat and I needed it in a hurry. A winking green light, way out in midstream and a good hundred and fifty yards away, had penetrated my subconscious. Dit dit dit, dah di dah dit – dit dit dit, dah di dah dit. It was repeating the letters SC – Southern Cross. Liz was there and for some reason she couldn't come in. I grabbed the boy by the hand and yelled at him above the din.

'*Baik. la. Saya mau keppel, sekarang la. Lakas.*' It was a mixture of bad Indonesian and kitchen Malay but the boy understood and led me quickly along the wharf to where a small prahu was tied up near a set of broken steps.

We moved onto the river in slow, pushing strokes, the boy's young muscles coping effortlessly with the task as phosphorus dripped prettily from the paddle blade. The green light was still repeating its signal – I could imagine a worried Liz flicking the navigation switch and wondering whether her message was getting through. 'I'm coming, Liz,' I muttered under my breath as the letters SC continued to wink at me. Southern Cross . . . *Sea Cat*.

The starboard profile of the hull was now discernible, low in the water forty yards away. I whispered to the boy, '*Pergis plan-plan, pusing. Baik?*'

He nodded, his reply also a whisper. '*Baik, Tuan.*'

Following my instructions he was now dipping the paddle with soft, easy strokes, pulling the blade slowly from the water without trailing the tell-tale phosphorus. Gradually and silently we made our way around the *Sea Cat*. Approaching from her port side she was better silhouetted against the lights of the town. As the prahu slid towards the waiting hull I put my finger to my lips and whispered, '*Nanti di sini* – wait here.' The boy nodded, saying nothing.

The thirty-eight was in my fist as I jumped silently onto the afterdeck. I was not expecting to find anyone but Liz aboard, but that was no excuse to be careless. I could see the shape of her head outlined against the sky as she sat in the flying bridge, staring anxiously towards shore. The soft clicking of the nav light switch ceased abruptly and I saw her stand up and stretch, turning towards me. She hadn't seen me and I was wondering how to make my presence known without alarming her when she descended suddenly onto the deck. The cabin doors opened and she threw the light switch.

'So. You're awake.'

The sound of her voice startled me – I had been about to show myself. I remained stock still and watched her descend to the cabin below as a muttered reply sounded – a man's voice.

I crossed quietly to the open doorway

and peered inside. Seated on the settee where the fat man had been two days earlier was a man with the most terribly pockmarked face I had ever seen. His features were swarthy, but because of the disfiguration it was impossible to pick out his nationality: he could have been Indonesian or Chinese – or something in between, Eurasian even. There was a nasty bruise at the side of his neck and his hands were tied above his head, secured to a brass porthole grummet which had been screwed tight. Liz stood looking at him, hands on hips, businesslike, competent. I coughed and she turned, one hand flying to her mouth in an instinctive feminine gesture that even her training had failed to erase. I found the movement endearing.

'Frank!' She moved towards me as I descended the steps. A hand came out to me. I grasped it and held tight.

'Hi, Liz. You seem to have things under control.'

I was staring at the man's bruise. She followed my gaze and glanced ruefully at her feet, stifling a smile.

'Seems everyone is kung fu fighting

these days, Frank, just like the song said.' Her mouth hardened. 'This is the gentleman who's been following me. He sneaked aboard somehow and I had to deal with him. I couldn't risk coming ashore; he has help. I saw someone else drive off in the Skoda. I thought it was him.' She brushed a hand through her bouncy hair. 'I'm glad you're here.'

'Do you think you can manage on your own a bit longer, Liz? My party is ready on the quay but I think you should pick us up a bit further downstream – somewhere quieter.'

She was shaking her head. 'There isn't anywhere, Frank, anywhere suitable that is. It's either the public wharves or private godowns – with locked gates and watchmen if you choose the latter. I know this place is noisy, but it's still the safest.'

'What about him?'

The pockmarked man was watching me closely, his eyes beginning to show signs of nervousness.

Liz turned to stare at him. 'I've been waiting for you to get here, Frank. I thought that between us we might persuade him to tell us his life story. Condensed of course, like into about five minutes' straight conversation.'

Key words in Liz's phrasing caused long lost bells to ring in my head. She was playing the ASIO* version of the good guy – bad guy technique. I was to be the heavy. It had been years since I had sat through what I had then thought of as so many childish, repetitive lectures. But I hadn't forgotten them, simply because they had been repeated to the point of indelibility. Liz had suffered them too and was now inviting me to play.

I raised the gun. 'He doesn't look like much of a talker to me. Let's just get rid of him – the water's deep here; he won't be found for days, perhaps not at all.'

'That's too final, Frank. Maybe he deserves to die – maybe not. You people always want to shoot first, but I look at things differently. What if it was one of us sitting there instead of him? Wouldn't we want the chance to talk – and live? I know I would.'

* Australian Secret Intelligence Organization

I pointed the gun at his head and rasped, 'What about it, buster? Have you got anything to say or is the lady talking bullshit?'

'I talk.' His eyes were darting nervously from one to the other, his lips moist. 'You no kill, I talk. I talk good. You no kill . . .'

The poor quality of his English startled me. It was coolie class and I was about to write him off as a cheap crook. But then I realized he was probably fluent in Dutch, a European language that I couldn't even manage in kitchen coolie. I lowered the thirty-eight, exchanged glances with Liz and said quietly, 'OK, talk. Begin with who you work for and why you have been following this lady for the past three days.'

Liz sat in the bow as the prahu moved steadily towards the quay. I was amidships, softly coaxing the boatboy to make use of whatever cover there was as he steered us towards the broken steps. We bumped under the stone wall and I sprang ashore, looping the painter loosely through an iron ring.

'I'll be as quick as I can. You'll be safe here for the time being.'

Liz nodded and I ran up the steps, my gold braid now back in my pocket, my cap lying in the bottom of the prahu. I had pulled open the buttons of my shirt almost to the waist, hoping to pass for a sailor in a town accustomed to sailors. With no tattoos to fall back on, I had to rely on a not very hairy chest to convey the image of a tough nautical background. I probably wasn't fooling anybody but at least I felt a little less like a sore thumb as I hurried to where Matt was staring anxiously.

I called to him and waved. 'Matt!' Here.'

He said something to the taxi driver and crossed the road. 'Where's the launch? Is everything OK?' He was agitated and I couldn't blame him. He had spent more than half his time since this thing started waiting around for me and wondering what the hell I was up to. Well, now there was something for him to do. I hoped it would please him.

'Things are nearly under control Matt

but I want you to look after Liz.' Even with his blue face in shadow, I saw his eyes light up. 'She's waiting along the wharf. I want you to take her back to the hotel.'

'Fine.' He nodded eagerly. Then his conscience seemed to grab him. 'Will you be OK Frank – managing Chong Bee I mean?'

'I'll be alright, provided you do what I tell you. Liz is being followed – a red Skoda which should be parked around here somewhere.' As Matt turned his head I said, 'Don't bother looking for it now for Christ's sake – it will find you – just as soon as you show up with Liz on your arm. What I want you to do is make *sure* the Skoda follows you – I don't want it hanging around here taking an interest in what I'm doing. So before you head for the pub, get the taxi driver to double back through the square over there. That way I can make sure the Skoda's with you before I try to move Chong Bee. OK?'

'Do you want me to shake the tail then, Frank?'

'Not the way you mean, Matt. I want

him parked outside the hotel, and you and Liz inside. That way I know exactly where he is. When the cab drops you off, send it back here to wait for me – and keep your clammy hands off my girl.'

He returned my grin. 'Your girl, Pappy? We'll see how she feels about that after she's met the brains of this team.'

I stayed half hidden in a doorway as the cab drove off with Matt and Liz in the back seat. There was no sign of the Skoda so I had to bide my time. I knew it would not be far away – it should be on to them by now. About three minutes passed before I recognized the Chevy as it nosed once more across the square. Thirty yards behind, its lights dimmed, was the Skoda. I grunted in satisfaction and stayed right where I was, waiting for the cruncher. If I had made a mistake then things were still far from safe – I was playing my instincts to the limit, making my own odds.

I didn't have long to wait. Eighty yards behind the Skoda, travelling easily, was a light coloured Ford, the tell-tale stubby antenna protruding from its roof. The professionals were on the job. I couldn't identify Sangeron as one of the front seat passengers, but I would have made book on it. I threw down my cigarette, stubbed it out with my heel and walked leisurely to where the lorry was parked.

The family Chong Bee was lying flat and looking scared as I flicked the chains and lowered the tailboard. I said cheerfully, 'Alright, you can come down now, it's quite safe.'

The ride in back of the dirty lorry had done them good. They no longer looked too overdressed for the type of Chinese who make a habit of travelling that way. Madame Chong Bee had recently come down in the world – with her hair dishevelled and dust all over her clothes she looked like tired old fishwife as she stumbled along the quay clutching her precious handbag. The kids just looked like kids anywhere, and Chong Bee like any other Chinaman. Nobody took a blind bit of notice. I paid the lorry driver his hundred rupiahs and dragged the heavy grain sack onto my shoulder. As I struggled with it along the wharf I really felt like a sailor. I was also trying to work out just how many pounds eleven hundred ounces came to. By the time I reached the steps where the prahu was waiting, the sack felt like a hell of a lot more than seventy, although my calculations said it was a little less. I dropped the bag gratefully in the bottom of the boat and followed the others aboard.

'You'd better give me some money, Chong Bee. I've been spending it on your behalf like it was going out of style – now I'm just about broke. You won't need rupiahs where you're going – give me what you have.'

He pulled a money clip from his back pocket and handed me a wad of fifties that would have choked an emu.

'My wife has more if you need it, Captain.'

Madame made to delve into her handbag, but I stopped her.

'No – this is fine.' Fine? Jesus. I had been worried about having enough to pay my hotel bill. With what Chong Bee had just given me I could damn near buy the bloody place.

Liz's visitor was still tied up where we had left him. Chong Bee wanted to ask questions but I shut him up.

'He'll be coming with me, so don't worry.' I took the Chinaman to one side. 'Now, you know what you have to do.' He nodded unhappily. I said harshly, 'Look! You won't be on your own for long – three or four days at the most and I will be back to collect you. But you *are* on your own for the moment and that woman out there and those kids are relying on you. So am I. If you do what I've told you, you'll be OK – the worst is over now. Just don't waste any time. You can be there by mid-morning if you keep going. Now, will you be OK?'

I was having second thoughts. The moment had come and I wondered whether I should have ever considered leaving this part of the job to Chong Bee. The trip to the island was simple and straight-forward – a kid could do it. But would Chong Bee wait quietly without his cold feet getting the better of him? Despite all that had happened I felt that right now was the biggest risk of the whole operation – trusting Chong Bee to keep his head.

He guessed what was going through my mind. I saw him moisten his lips. 'I know I am a coward – it has always been that way, but I have raised and provided for a family despite that. And I will protect them now.' He managed a thin smile. 'Don't worry, Captain. I may not be a braver man when you see me again, but I will be there, waiting. My whole life is right here on this boat. It has not always been in other's hands.'

Despite my best efforts, the doubt showed on my face and Chong Bee said suddenly, 'There is an old Chinese proverb, Captain. 'He who walks backwards has his head on the ground." I must forget what I have been and concentrate on what I must be – for the next few days anyway.' He reached for my hand and took it firmly. 'We will be alright.'

I looked at the round face, at the slanted eyes trying hard to match the smile on his lips, and I felt better. Chong Bee didn't lack courage – he just didn't know what it was or what it should feel like. He was feeling it now but he couldn't recognize it, and I couldn't tell him. He wouldn't believe me. I returned his handshake. 'OK – it's your ball. I'll see you.'

A few minutes later I sat in the prahu and watched the *Kuching Laut* slip moorings and head down river with a slow rumble from the outboards. Chong Bee would have to keep the speed down for most of the night, but as long as he stayed awake there was no problem. I recalled that on our trip up this same river the shallows were well buoyed and village lights were plentiful. I waved the *Sea Cat* out of sight and turned to my passenger.

I had lowered him into the prahu, still tied up, setting him down amidships. The presence of the Indonesian boatboy came as a predictable surprise and I heard him cajoling the boy in his own language. A few quick words designed to throw Frank Adams overboard when the time presented itself. The boy had agreed in a frightened whisper and I relaxed. Halim – the boatboy – and I had held an earlier conversation which not only concerned our passenger, but had anticipated him pretty well. With a captor who apparently did not understand Indonesian, and plans already afoot to make good his escape, my passenger sat quietly waiting for the moment to arrive. Whilst he was doing that, he wouldn't be too worried about doing anything else – like paying particular attention to where we were heading. Until it was too late.

The harsh clanging of the bell finally broke into whatever his subconscious was savouring, and he glanced around. The main channel marker buoy was still fifty yards away but already the noise was deafening. Halim sat in the bow, digging the paddle with firm strokes, pulling us towards the noise and its accompanying winking light. My passenger was now decidedly edgy, looking nervously over his shoulder and shouting at the boatboy. When his eyes fell on me again I was holding the thirty-eight. He misunderstood.

'No. No kill. You promise. No kill . . .' He was screaming. I switched the gun to my left hand, took a firm grip on the rope with my right and stood up, bracing my knees against the seat. I jerked him to his feet, pulling sideways at the same time, throwing him off balance. The prahu rocked madly and because I had to do something or end up in the water with my captive, I dropped the gun and grabbed desperately at the port gunwale. I fell back onto my seat and the rocking subsided. The water in mid-channel had become decidedly choppy and Halim was having a hard time making the last few yards to the buoy, the drag of the man in the water was not helping. I could hear him trying to shout between mouthfuls of salt water. He would have been better off keeping his mouth shut. Somehow, Halim got us alongside the buoy and I managed to secure my end of the rope to a metal hawser. Now it was up to the man himself. If he kept his head he could climb up onto the buoy and spend a restless but comparatively safe night. One thing was for sure, it was no good him trying to shout for help above the noise of the bell. He was there until daylight when someone would no doubt see his plight and pick him up.

That was OK – I didn't care what he could get up to once this night was over, but if he didn't stop that stupid bloody screaming, he wouldn't live to see the morning. The buoy offered safety only if he took it. If he stayed in the water then he was a candidate for all sorts of unpleasant things and I wasn't thinking about sharks or drowning. These waters were host to a particular type of flesh-eating crab. Still, if one of them got hold of his behind I guessed he would find a way up onto the buoy soon enough.

The noise of the bell gradually grew less strident and I stopped thinking about the pockmarked passenger. I had given him a chance – it was up to him now. I lit a cigarette and groped in the bottom of the prahu for the thirty-eight, stuffing it back inside my shirt. That gun was starting to feel like an old friend.

When we reached the broken steps at the quay I pulled two fifty rupiah notes from Chong Bee's clip. It represented more money than Halim would earn in three months. His eyes lit up as I held out the notes. I said, '*Tengah* – half.' He thought I was teasing and his face dropped. In my best Indonesian I told him I was not offering him half of what he could see – that the hundred was only half what he would receive if he kept quiet about the night's work. I explained that when I woke up in the morning, if I could use my binoculars and still see the man on the buoy at daybreak, then one hour later Halim could come to my hotel desk where an envelope would be waiting for him. It would contain another hundred rupiahs.

I passed him the money. He looked at it for fully ten seconds, then tucked the two notes away in his dirty trousers. He held out his hand in a solemn gesture, his voice showing a hint of emotion. '*Terima kasi, Tuan. Terima kasi bunyak.*' I returned the handshake and looked into eyes that were too sad for one so young. '*Salamat malam, Halim. Terima kasi.*'

'*Selamat malam, Tuan,*' he almost whispered. '*Selamat malam, Tuan . . . besar.*'

I climbed into the waiting taxi feeling very humble, Halim's words ringing in my ears. *Tuan besar* he had called me – noble lord – big man on campus. For the equivalent of fifty bucks, American, I had corrupted a fifteen-year-old boy and been thanked for it, honoured for it. What a stinking, dirty system. What a stinking, dirty world. And what a set of standards to hand on to the young – or were they already their standards? Whatever Halim's life had been up to now, it was not encumbered by standards, good or bad. He had learned to survive, without rules. At least his eyes were clear and his muscles strong, and there were no puncture marks on his arms. Maybe he wasn't so badly off.

Chapter Twelve

I ENTERED the hotel through the back entrance after making sure the red Skoda was still on guard at the front. There had been no sign of the security police vehicle as I circled the block in the taxi, but I hadn't expected there to be. If Sangeron had left a man on duty, he wouldn't be where I would see him.

The back stairs entered the lobby behind the elevator and close to the bar, which was crowded. I became one of the crowd. I probably needed a good meal more than a beer but that would only be my stomach's opinion – the rest of me said beer. I sank two quick ones and was ready for a third when I felt a tap on the shoulder.

'Good evening, Captain.'

I turned abruptly, knowing it would be Sangeron. The expression in his eyes when he had left Charlie Delta earlier in the evening had promised unfinished business between us. I had tried to put it out of my mind, but I knew it would be coming. It wasn't Sangeron. The man wasn't even Indonesian. I stared at the intruder, remembering Liz's description. 'He's tallish for a Chinese – quite distinguished looking.'

'Mr Woo Tang isn't it?'

It was his turn to look surprised. He smothered it well and, keeping a hand on my arm, tried to steer me away from the bar. 'Can we talk, Captain? To our . . . mutual advantage?'

'I've already talked to one of your

boys tonight, Woo Tang. Last I saw of him he was on the river. Or was it in the river? I'm damned if I can remember.'

His eyes narrowed and his grey moustache bristled. It was the moustache which gave him his distinguished appearance; right now it was giving him away. Something was bugging Woo Tang Sim.

'We must *talk*, Captain,' he hissed. He was still gripping firmly at my elbow.

I pushed his arm away and followed his quick glance towards the doorway. The slim Chinese from the launch was standing there, watching us. Woo Tang signalled with his eyes and the man laconically detached himself from the wall and started slowly in our direction. There was a bland, neutral expression on his face which had me instantly on guard. No one looks *that* bored unless they are brimming with self-confidence. I looked quickly over my shoulder towards the other doorway, the one I had come in by. By the time my eyes reached Woo Tang again they had been around the room and counted a half dozen more bored-looking Chinamen.

'OK. So what do we talk about?'

'Not here.' Woo Tang waved the slim Chinese to keep his distance. 'We can go to your room.'

The slim man made to follow us into the elevator. I said, 'If he goes along, I don't.'

'Only as far as the floor, Captain. He will ensure our privacy.'

I shrugged and let the man into the car. He stood respectfully in one corner as we climbed to the third floor, showing no resentment that I had left him bound hand and foot in this very hotel only hours earlier. Woo Tang had the right influence on the younger man. Godfatherly one might say.

Woo Tang followed me into the bedroom and closed the door. He looked around carefully, his eyes coming to rest on the bathroom door. 'Do you mind?'

I shrugged again, walked into the empty bathroom and came out again. 'OK. I've enjoyed our little game. Now what is it you want?'

'Do you mind if I sit down?'

'I don't mind if you bloody fall down – so long as you make this quick and get out of my room.'

Woo Tang lowered himself into the single armchair and placed his well-manicured hands on his knees. It was an elegant gesture; everything about him was elegant. 'I find your rudeness excusable, Captain.'

'That's generous of you. I find myself unable to excuse yours.' His moustache twitched once as I glowered at him. I could sense his annoyance and I had to admire his self-control. Something was seething inside but whatever it was, he would air it like a gentleman. I wasn't made of the same stuff – and if he thought his cool manner was going to intimidate me he had come to the wrong shop. I said acidly, 'Why have your thugs been following Miss Manifold?'

The Chinaman's eyes narrowed briefly, then a faint smile crossed his lips. 'That is information we may be able to bargain with, Captain. Shall we wait and see?' He sat back, composed, enjoying his small victory. I turned away abruptly and reached for a cigarette, not wanting him to sense my satisfaction. The pockmarked man had named Woo Tang as his boss, but had been unable to elaborate on why he had been instructed to keep Liz under surveillance. Now Woo Tang was willing to use that information as a lever and I was content to let him believe he had something to bargain with. He didn't. Liz had been recalled – would be leaving for Djakarta on the noon plane with a connection to Sydney the same night. So whatever Woo Tang's motives had been, they were now academic. I spared a brief thought for the pockmarked man clinging wetly to the buoy as I lit a cigarette.

When I turned towards Woo Tang again my eyes were hard and I said fiercely, 'Shall we stop fencing. Get to the bloody point will you.'

'Very well, Captain, the point it shall be. You have an agreement with the fat one . . .' As my mouth opened Woo Tang made an impatient gesture with his hand. 'I am familiar with the details.' His eyes narrowed. 'But I suspect our fat friend has misled you – as he has me. There is only one piece of information I want from you Captain Adams – your final destination. In return for that one item, I am prepared to fill in the gaps which I am certain he omitted to tell you.'

'Such as?'

Woo Tang smiled thinly. 'Such as why you were selected for this operation for one thing.' I took a firm pull on the cigarette. Woo Tang had not missed the fractional widening of my eyes. He said softly, 'Come now, Captain. You didn't really think you and your co-pilot happened into this by accident, did you? Ex-Superintendent Duncan has been on our files for a long time – almost as long as yourself in fact. It was the woman in Hong Kong you *didn't* kill whom we can thank for that information. She is one of us, although I don't suppose you knew that.'

I could feel the blood draining from my face and I was breathing so fast I thought I would pass out. Despite what Matt had told me, I had continued to think of the Tongs as slant-eyed Freemasons, which I now realized was about as bright as thinking of the Mafia as a church social club. I had a lot to learn. Woo Tang was still talking in the same soft voice. It sounded to me more like the hissing of an angry python. I reached desperately for another cigarette, the Chinaman's words penetrating deep into my numbed brain.

'The reasons for your participation will soon become apparent. As will some other, shall we say, rather more *unpleasant* certainties. However, if you co-operate with me I will guarantee your survival – and your payment. Should the fat one suffer an unfortunate accident and fail to survive the venture – I will double the fee.' The softness left his voice suddenly and he said intensely, 'Now. Can we talk business like sensible men.' He paused. 'Perhaps before we do, I should point out something. If we reach agreement and you fail, for any reason, to carry out your part of the bargain, I will guarantee your untimely and unpleasant death within the year. *My* Section T people will find *you*, wherever you are. That I promise.'

My head had stopped spinning. An awful certainty had taken its place as I realized for the first time what I was up against. Just how far did the tentacles of the League reach? I had thought of them as small-time: a localized pocket of limited power. But the ramifications now were frightening. If they had taken on the GUD by kidnapping the general, it was because they were powerful enough to do it. And I had thought they were just little crooks with big ambitions.

'You seem to have all the answers, Woo Tang. What happens if we fail to reach an agreement, as you put it?'

'If I were you, Captain, I wouldn't even contemplate *that* possibility.' His eyes looked innocently at me and I suppressed a shudder. At least I had the answer to why Liz had been followed. If the Chinaman knew of my ASIO connection then it was inconceivable that he didn't also know about Liz. The tail on her had begun three days ago – the day we *should* have arrived in Surabaja. Liz had been watched to discover whether a certain pilot made contact with her, and when. My mind was just starting to feel smug at that brilliant deduction when it did a back somersault. *If Woo Tang knew of my connection with Liz then he also knew I was planning a doublecross*. Yet the Chinaman was still prepared to negotiate. Why? There could be no logical reason as far as I could see unless . . . *Unless that contingency had been allowed for from the very beginning*.

Now I *was* worried, bloody worried. In choosing Matt and me for this job the League could expect one of two reactions. Either we would turn crook and take the hundred grand, or we would blow the whistle. And if it made no difference to them *which* way we jumped, I had a right to worry. It meant we had not been chosen for the special abilities of our backgrounds, but for the backgrounds themselves. We were to be sacrificed on someone's political altar, a pair of Judas goats with wings. It had to be a political manoeuvre – something designed to embarrass either the Australian or British governments. Perhaps both. Woo Tang was right, the reasons were becoming apparent. What was not so easy to understand was why I was being allowed to know those reasons. Woo Tang wanted the fat man dead, but that was not just a case of thieves falling out. The elegant Chinaman was planning his own doublecross. But why? A power struggle within the Tong? It was a possibility, but a slim one. By putting me in the picture Woo Tang had jeopardized the whole operation – something not likely to make him the people's choice within the League. Yet he was willing to take the risk.

I saw his moustache bristle impatiently; he was anxious to get on with it. So was I, but for different reasons. I needed desperately to talk to Liz – have her open her communications channel and let the people in Canberra know what was happening. Matt also had a right to let his people in on it, but I would check that out with Liz first. Maybe she would want to keep this in the ASIO family.

'Well, Captain?' Woo Tang's voice held only a trace of the impatience which I knew was eating at his insides. His self-control was admirable. I sat on the edge of the bed and managed to keep my voice calm.

'You mentioned some guarantees . . .'

Matt's evil intentions with Liz had apparently died a quick and natural death. He was sound asleep on one of the twin beds as I tapped lightly on his door and Liz let me into the room. I glanced once more at the sleeping form, then whispered to Liz to come with me. We left quietly and a minute later we were back in my room. From somewhere close by the sound of a clock striking two drifted through the open shutters.

I briefed Liz on my conversation with Woo Tang. Her face hardened and once or twice she got up from her seat on the corner of the bed and paced the room. She interrupted only once, to ask for a cigarette. Even after it was apparent I had finished, she was silent for several seconds, deep in thought. She stood up, crossed to the open shutters, and stared into the night. When she finally turned to look at me her face had regained its beautiful lines. Standing with her feet apart, hands clasped, she looked very competent.

'I agree, Frank. There has to be a political motive but I'm damned if I can see what it is. Woo Tang must know his threat to liquidate you won't stand up – you can get all the protection you need. He must *know* that, so what is he up to? What are any of them up to?'

I smiled weakly. 'We have some of the answers. Surely between us we can come up with the remainder.'

'Can we?' Her voice was sharp. 'Well I don't share your optimism. Someone is being taken for a great big ride. Maybe it's us – then again, maybe it isn't. Let's go back over it and you'll see what I mean. You and Matt were deliberately chosen for a certain job by a powerful Tong. The Tong knows about your backgrounds but they can't predict how you will react, so they cover the three alternatives.'

'Three?'

'Yes. General Sartono was their insurance for the third eventuality.' As I stared at her she continued. 'Look! Supposing you had decided to blow the whistle here in Indonesia. One certain way to stop you would be to produce the general. Seeing a leading member of the Secret Police in the League's power would achieve two things. Demonstrate that the League was not to be fooled with, and that the local authorities were not competent. This would leave you with only two choices – go along quietly, or contact people you could trust.'

Liz used both hands to smooth her bouncy hair. She said ruminatively, 'It's almost as if they wanted you to come to ASIO – planned it that way. But why, damn them? Why?'

'Don't crease your brow like that Liz. You'll get wrinkles.' Her eyes flashed angrily, then her features relaxed in a wan smile. I said, 'We know some of the why. They want me and Matt to hijack an aeroplane and fly it to a place they have yet to name. We don't know which aeroplane, or what they want from it – just that we take over after Singapore. By having you followed, they know that I planned to doublecross them and despite Woo Tang's threat, he knows I *still* intend to do that. So maybe that's what they *want* us to do. The way I figure it, whatever it is on that plane, it is going to cause embarrassment to our government when we land in Australia. If we try to fly it anywhere else, the chief hijacker, an Australian, will still have the desired political effect. Yet if we don't do the job we'll never know what they were after. Or what alternative plans they have in mind if we don't go through with it.' I lit two cigarettes and passed one to Liz. I said resignedly, 'Or maybe I'm figuring it entirely back to front. What if the League have deliberately let us into the picture to make sure there's *no* doublecross. That could make sense.'

'It makes nonsense. If they really want that aircraft, or whatever's going to be on it, they could hijack it in the normal way. They don't need pilots for that. No! They have gone to a lot of trouble to get you and Matt on board that plane, and to get ASIO involved. There has to be another reason – and I'm damned if I can even come close to what it might be. It's almost as if the whole thing is a red herring, a distraction.'

'That's it!' I jumped to my feet. Considering how tired I felt it was a bloody good effort. I said excitedly, 'That has to be it. While we are getting our balls in a knot, running around like hairy goats, they are going to hijack another plane. The one they are really after.'

Liz gave me a motherly smile. 'I already thought of that, but it doesn't come any easier to swallow either.' She sat in the armchair and crossed her tanned legs. 'Whether the League planned the ASIO involvement or not, they now know we *are* involved, and it was a risk they always had to take even if they didn't plan it. The least they will expect is a tightening of security – particularly at Singapore International Airport. Why would they do that if they were planning another hijacking?'

I let out a slow breath. Liz was right. My eyes felt like gravel. I had to fly in less than three hours and I was desperate for some sleep. Not that I would enjoy waking up much – I had a five o'clock date with Sangeron and I wasn't looking forward to it. But that was three hours away. In the meantime I should relax.

I fell back onto the bed and let my eyelids close. It was a delicious feeling. Suddenly they were wide open again and I was back on my feet. Liz wasn't right – she was wrong – dead bloody wrong.

There was a startled expression on her face as I said urgently, 'What day is it?'

She stared at me stupidly. I yelled again, 'What day is it? I've lost track – tell me it isn't the fourteenth.' Even as I said it I knew I was being stupid. Of course it was the fourteenth – it had been for nearly three hours. Liz suddenly looked as though she had been slapped in the face. A hand flew to her mouth.

'My God!'

'Yes,' I said sourly. 'Clever bastards aren't they. Matt and I arrive in Singapore at eight tonight. Meanwhile, you will be on your way to Australia and it will all be over.'

'What time are they leaving?'

'The Notice to Airmen I got said Singapore International will be closed from twelve to one and Djakarta from three till six. The people here always go a bit overboard on VIP travel so they close the airport for a bit longer.'

'I must get a message through to Singapore.'

'No!' Liz blanched. I said, a little more softly, 'You'd never get it through. They'll be out there, waiting for you.

You leave here when we do – which is right now. If these winds are holding up we can make Singapore in six hours.'

Liz hesitated for just a moment, then she nodded. I grabbed her hand and raced along the corridor to Matt's room He was sound asleep. I shook him roughly by his good shoulder. 'Wake up Matt. We're flying.' He slowly rubbed his eyes and I said harshly, 'Shake it, sport We've got a Mayday.' That did it Suddenly he was awake and moving like I always knew he could if he ever tried.

We left the hotel by the back entrance and had to cross three streets before we found a taxi.

Liz said, 'My bag is packed. Can we call for it?' I was about to protest, then changed my mind. It wouldn't delay us more than a few minutes.

'OK.'

She smiled gratefully.

Matt said, 'What's the panic, Pappy?'

I glanced in Liz's direction, then back at Matt. 'The panic, old son, is that today is the fourteenth, the day the OPEC conference is due to convene in Djakarta. The delegates are at presen overnighting in Singapore. At noon or thereabouts a chartered jet is bringing them to Djakarta. That is the aircraft the League is going to hijack.'

'Jesus Christ!'

'That sums it up alright. On that one aircraft will be sixty odd of the most important people from the richest countries in the world. What's your guess at the ransom? Fifty million? A hundred? They can afford it.'

'Jesus Christ!' Matt was a nice guy but he did suffer from a limited vocabulary at times. Not that I could blame him. The Oil Producing Exporting Countries were meeting in Djakarta to hoist yet one more rise in petrol prices onto an already overburdened world. Word had it there was some dissension in the camp about the percentage the rise should be, but I couldn't see that argument going on too long if the League got away with kidnapping a bevy of top ministers. The ransom would be the biggest in history by far, and the man in the street in Washington and London and Tokyo would foot the bill.

I glanced through the rear window for

signs of a tail. There wasn't one. Just the same, I couldn't relax. Two streets away from where Liz lived I told the driver to stop. I held out my hand to Liz. 'Give me the keys.'

She was about to protest but changed her mind. She dived into her purse for the key ring. 'In the bedroom, Frank. A green suitcase and if you can be bothered, there's a white vanity case beside it.'

'I can be bothered.' I squeezed her hand and slid out of the car, keeping to the shadows. Apart from the odd person sleeping in a doorway, the streets were deserted. I turned the corner into Liz's street and ducked silently between parked cars as I made my way towards the travel agency. Faint moonlight glinted from the car windows as I went from car to car, quietly and quickly. I saw the open driver's side window from twenty feet away and I caught myself smiling grimly as I took the thirty-eight from my waistband. No one leaves their car unlocked in Surabaja at night – unless they're sitting in it. My man was in a light doze, his head on the seat-rest as I pressed the muzzle against his neck and said quietly, *'Selemat malam'* – good evening.

He sat up with a start and I stood back, pulling open the car door. I waved the gun. *'Datang.'* He stared at me with frightened eyes but he did as he was told and got out of the car. I pushed him along in front of me, opened the door to Liz's flat and bustled him up the stairs. I flicked on the light and as he glanced around, taking in the surroundings, I reversed the thirty-eight and hit him sharply over the right ear. Two minutes later I switched off the light and descended the stairs. I threw the two cases onto the back seat of the stranger's car, climbed in and turned the ignition. He wouldn't be needing transport for a while. I hoped he was comfortable in Liz's wardrobe. It had looked a little cramped to me.

I pulled in alongside the taxi and paid off the driver. Why waste any more of Chong Bee's money on taxi fares when Woo Tang had so thoughtfully provided transport?

There would be no customs and immigration people around at this hour so there was no point in putting in a flight plan for Singapore. They wouldn't let us go. Matt disappeared up the tower stairs with a flight plan to Djakarta worked out in his head. Ten minutes later I watched as he crossed the tarmac towards Charlie Delta. I was already in the cockpit, ready for a fast start-up. But Matt wasn't alone. Walking beside him keeping step, was the jaunty figure of Sangeron. I heard the rear door slam shut as I turned in my seat, and the GUD man followed Matt onto the flight deck. There was a thin smile on Sangeron's lips.

'A good thing I was here early Captain. Had you forgotten about me perhaps?'

I returned the smile. 'Not at all, sir But my company wants me in Djakarta before six for another charter. I didn't know how to contact you.'

He pursed his lips, staring at me thoughtfully. 'No. Of course not Anyway, no harm done.' He walked back into the cabin. Hell! Why did he have to turn up right now? But there was nothing I could do. I just hoped he had his passport with him.

At eight thousand feet I levelled out and switched in the auto-pilot. I said over the intercom, 'Watch the office for me Matt. I've got to get some bloody sleep or my head will drop off.' I passed him the thirty-eight. 'Keep this beside you, just in case.'

Sangeron was seated halfway along the fuselage on the port side, his eyes closed in a catnap. Liz sat opposite and she too was dozing. I stood in front of her and tapped her on the knee. She opened her eyes and I indicated in Sangeron's direction. I picked up her handbag, took out the PPK and dropped it in her lap. She nodded.

Sangeron was still dozing as I walked past him and lay down on the canvas seats near the rear door. As a bed, the mis-shapen seats weren't worth two bob but I was never so grateful for a place to lie down. My last thought before I dozed off was a fervent hope that I could trust Matt's navigation.

Chapter Thirteen

I WOKE up with a start. Sunlight was streaming through the windows and as I swung my feet to the floor I glanced at my watch. A few minutes to nine: I had been out cold for nearly five hours. My head felt remarkably clear – so clear that as I remembered the night's events I started to doubt the whole business. The conclusions we had reached at 3 am suddenly didn't make as much sense in the harsh light of day.

Liz was holding the PPK lightly in her lap and as I turned in her direction she gave me a faint smile. Sangeron's face wore a quite different expression. As I caught his eyes they bore into me with intense dislike – or was it distrust? It didn't matter, either way it was a policeman's look. I paused briefly near Liz.

'Any trouble?'

She shook her head. 'No. But I think our friend across there is anxious to talk to you.'

'He'll have to wait.' I spared Sangeron one quick glance and strode towards the cockpit.

Matt was quietly smoking, the auto-pilot doing the work. I glanced at the direction finder; the needle was swinging aimlessly around the dial. We were obviously out of range of any beacons but I noticed the set was tuned to the St John frequency. Matt must be expecting to be in range of Singapore soon.

'Morning, Pappy. I thought you'd died.'

'I did. Where are we?'

Matt gave me one of *those* smiles. It was the classic unanswerable question, especially when flying over water. But the alternative was a long-winded reference to last-known positional fixes and despite Matt's attempt at humour, he knew what I meant. 'We should pick up St John in the next twenty minutes if the winds are holding. I got a visual fix an hour ago and my latest ETA is one six – another seventy minutes, give or take.'

I nodded and glanced up at the magnetic compass. The heading was about right – so was the timing. All we could do was sit it out for a while, but dead-reckoning navigation is like that.

Matt offered me a cigarette. 'I've been thinking, Pappy – are you sure about this OPEC thing? Couldn't it be just a wild guess?'

It was a good question. I wasn't bloody sure, although I *had* been at three o'clock that morning. Thinking about Sangeron then had given me the idea. Telling myself I could relax for a while before question-time, it had suddenly struck me that was what the League was up to. Focussing all attention on me and Matt as the hijackers, so they could strike in the 'calm before the storm', when everyone was off guard. With Matt and myself still in Indonesia, not due in Singapore until the Garuda flight landed at 8 pm, no one would be panicking. They would be making preparations, sure, but in the relaxed atmosphere of people who know time is on their side.

The pending OPEC conference had been making newspaper headlines for a couple of weeks – journalists trying to outdo each other, speculating what the outcome would be in terms to cost per litre to the average motorist. So the conference was no secret. As a pilot, I had received formal notification by circular. Due to the VIP nature of the flight, Singapore and Djakarta airfields would be closed to other traffic for specified times. It was standard procedure. Now that I was able to give it more thought I realized the security surrounding the OPEC flight would be top class anyway. With no other movements in or out of the airport around departure time, the security bods would have nothing else to concentrate on and would give the OPEC ministers their full attention. But would they be alert in the manner of people expecting trouble, or would they just go through the motions? I had to assume the latter. The trouble with security people is that at times they tend to feel too secure.

I said to Matt, 'No, I'm not sure – but I don't feel it's a wild guess either.' I gave him a slightly amended version of the conversation with Woo Tang. Matt looked thoughtful. When I had finished, he reached for another cigarette and made a pantomime of stretching the fingers of his game arm.

'I think you're dead right about our

proposed hijacking being a blind, Frank. Did Woo Tang talk to you at all about your experience?'

I looked at him sharply. 'No.'

'And neither did the fat man, did he? Yet I can't see them wanting us to hijack just another DC3. I got the impression it would be a jet but neither you nor I have ever flown jets. We could probably manage an old DC4 if it came to a push – maybe even a DC6 or a Constellation, but without special training we'd kill ourselves if we tried it with a jet.' Matt's eyes narrowed impishly. 'Maybe the League thinks we are something special and can fly anything – but I don't think so. And it's inconceivable they wouldn't know that a guy needs training on each new aircraft type. Yet they didn't even ask whether we had that training or not. Which for my money means they never intended us to fly this mission in the first place.'

Sunlight gleamed dully off Matt's blue jowls. The expression in his eyes betrayed a humour his bland expression failed to disguise. He managed to keep his voice matter-of-fact. 'I could go along with this whole business, including the trouble the League have gone to laying their red herring, if it wasn't for one thing. As an ex-superintendent of police, I'm pretty small time, and your air force intelligence experience twenty years ago is even smaller. Maybe you and I were the best available on short notice but if I had been planning this operation I'd have wanted a CIA man at least.' Butter wouldn't have melted in Matt's mouth as he followed up innocently, 'What's the equivalent of the CIA down your way, Frank? ASIO isn't it? Now if you had been an ASIO man it would have made the whole thing feasible, and I'd be left with no doubts that they are after the OPEC plane.' He drew deliberately on his cigarette and turned his head to gaze vacantly out the starboard window.

'You son of a bitch,' I muttered under my breath. 'Have you known all along – or just since Liz came on the scene?' I said aloud, 'I think a man's past is his own bloody business. I've never questioned you about your time in the fuzz.'

'No. That's true.' Matt was still

window-gazing. He turned towards me slowly, his expression serious. 'So I won't pry either. But unless something else comes along in a hurry, I suggest we go hell-for-leather on this OPEC thing. I just know we're on the right track.'

'Want to tell me why?' I knew I had gone fish-eyed again but there wasn't a damn thing I could do about that. I was born sceptical.

'Because I no longer think this is a Tong ploy – its too big. Someone is backing them.'

'The communists?'

If I hadn't known my co-pilot better than to take dumb insolence too far, I would have sworn the look he gave me was pitying. Then the scorn in his voice left me in no doubt.

'Why has it *always* to be the bloody communists? They don't have a monopoly of skulduggery. OK – it might be the commies, but those are Arabs on that plane. It could be Israelis, CIA – even one of our own countries. We all have an axe to grind with the Arabs one way or another, which means we all have a motive.' As he caught me staring, Matt said, 'Look! We don't *know* it's money the hi-jackers are after – it could be a political ransom. And don't make the mistake of thinking all Chinese are reds. The kind of Tong we are up against contains some of the most devoted bloody capitalists in the world. They'll work for anyone who can lay cash on the barrel.'

I forgot that the tone of Matt's voice should be making me angry. What he was saying made too much bloody sense. I found his suggestion about a big-time backer particularly easy to swallow. The League's knowledge of my ASIO connection was embarrassing, but if they were being fed that kind of information from a foreign intelligence agency it was easier to live with. And easier to understand. In Section T we were never given a reason – just the assignment. And we were only told enough about the client to make the hit a certainty. In my case, I had tried to bully information out of Fleming after the Hong Kong débâcle, but it hadn't worked. He gave the impression that another Section T man would finish the job I had botched, and that was that. So Woo Tang could have been lying through his teeth when he said the woman was a Tong member and still alive. Now I came to think of it, he had to be lying. Fleming would not have left the job half done.

I couldn't go along entirely with Matt's thinking. Money was still a powerful motive in a caper like this. Christ! I could think of half a dozen countries which could balance their current budget with a windfall of fifty million – and leave a forty-nine-and-a-half million surplus. But at least I felt better about what we were doing: our mad dash to Singapore would not be a waste of time. Before we got there, however, I had a couple of things to take care of.

I spoke into the intercom. 'Go and stretch your legs for half an hour Matt; keep Liz company. And tell Mr Sangeron if he's not too busy I would like to see him.'

Sangeron did not like being sent for like an errant schoolboy, but I had a distinct advantage on the flight deck. Surrounded by a host of gauges and levers which seldom fail to confuse the layman, Sangeron was reminded that it was *my* office. I invited him to jump into Matt's seat and put on the headphones.

'Before we get down to other matters Mr Sangeron, I want to point out that you have not been kidnapped. You boarded this aeroplane of your own free will and all that has changed is the destination. When we land at Singapore you are free to go. Should you need money, it will be available, and you will be provided with a flight ticket to Djakarta.' I ignored the odd expression in his eyes. 'I am not obliged to answer your questions but I will – within reason. To begin with, General Sartono is dead and the people responsible are the League of the Lotus. Now, go ahead and ask away. If I don't like some of your questions, I won't answer them. On the other hand, I will volunteer quite a lot of other information, so that should make us even.'

On an island the size of Singapore there is no need for a domestic air service so all flights arriving at Paya Lebar are international. To cope with this, together with a huge volume of tourist traffic, customs and immigration are streamlined for fast, efficient service. The overworked air traffic control service is also efficient, but if occasionally an aircraft arrives from Indonesia without prior flight-plan notification, it is not treated as any great event. Indonesian air traffic control is not as inefficient as its Singapore counterpart likes to think it is, but any slight lapse by the Indonesians is greeted with smug satisfaction by the Singaporeans.

Thirty miles out, Matt called Singapore on VHF, gave them our estimated time of arrival and reported our long-range HF radio unserviceable. The inevitable question was asked – had we filed a flight plan? Matt answered, 'Affirmative.'

There was a slight pause, then Singapore came booming through the headphones. 'Roger Charlie Delta. You are cleared to St John seven thousand feet, no delay expected.' It was as simple as that.

Charlie Delta was not an unfamiliar

sight at Singapore International – I had brought her here many times. But with all those shiny jets on the apron, her presence there was aesthetically unacceptable. Air traffic control ordered us to park in the space reserved for old pelicans, at the south-west corner of the airfield near the Singapore Flying Club, out of sight of the main terminal. This suited Sangeron admirably. He had no passport to enter the country legally so the procedure was to wait ten minutes, walk laconically through one of the hangars to the far side of the airport and use the Flying Club telephone to order a taxi. Liz had provided him with a telephone number. I told him to book into the Ming Court Hotel where I would contact him in the next few hours.

We left Sangeron sitting in Charlie Delta and the three of us made our way to the main immigration hall. On the way I ordered fuel from the Shell depot. I had gone overboard to co-operate with Sangeron. It occurred to me that I might need him. More to the point, what I needed like a hole in the head was his bloodhounds on my trail. I still had to go back into Indonesia for Chong Bee, Charlie Delta would be gassed up and ready to go and it might be advantageous to have Sangeron along. There was no harm in keeping him on ice.

Liz had to produce her passport. Matt and I waved our pilot licences at immigration and climbed into the back of an Austin diesel taxi. Liz was nestling between us in a matter of seconds and we were on our way.

I had last seen Arthur Hughes at the ASIO training school sixteen years ago – or to be more correct, at the Portsea Army Officers' Training Camp where we had completed our unarmed combat and assault courses together. Since then, Arthur had come up in the world. He was manager of Opalcraft Exports and this made him the senior resident ASIO agent in Singapore. He had also grown fatter and was almost bald, but recognition was there and his handshake was warm.

'Been a long time, Frank, although you'd never know it looking at you. The years haven't treated me as kindly.'

'That's because you worry too much, Arthur,' I smiled. 'I should have known it was an old classmate at this end. I didn't expect help to turn up as quickly as it did.' I glanced affectionately at Liz. 'But I'm not complaining.'

Matt was standing awkwardly near the door. I introduced him. 'This is my co-pilot, ex-Chief Superintendent Matthew Duncan, late of Special Branch, Malaya.' Hughes's eyes narrowed and I said quickly, 'Matt is in this for better or worse so I brought him along to meet you. But I should warn you – he's a helluva poor security risk.'

Hughes hesitated for the briefest moment, then shot out his hand. 'Glad to meet you, Matt.' Arthur turned to me. 'Can you excuse Miss Manifold and me for a few minutes?'

I nodded and grabbed Matt by the arm. 'Come on, Sunshine. They want to talk shop and our money's no good in this emporium.'

Arthur smiled gratefully. I followed Matt into the small waiting room where a pretty Eurasian girl sat behind a typewriter. I picked up a magazine from the coffee table, settled myself on the settee and learnt something about opals.

Liz was out of the room in five minutes flat. Arthur Hughes stood in the doorway.

'Come in please, Frank.'

I glanced anxiously at my watch. We had gained an hour on Eastern Indonesian Time but it was still a few minutes past ten in Singapore. If we were to do something constructive out at the airport it was time to get going. I walked quickly into Arthur's office and closed the door, hoping to convey some of my own sense of urgency. But Arthur seemed in no particular hurry.

'Sit down, Frank.' Hughes went to his chair and pushed a lacquered cigarette box across the desk. 'Smoke?'

'Listen, Arthur, shouldn't we be making a move to the airport or something?' I made no attempt to hide my agitation.

Hughes had a superior smile on his face and I remembered why I hadn't liked him at training school. It's funny how you can greet a man like a long lost brother after many years, forgetting that in the old days you hated each other's guts. That smirk brought it all back – I hadn't liked Arthur much then, and if he kept that bloody supercilious grin on his face, he wasn't going to get my current vote.

'There's no panic Frank – the OPEC delegation is already in Djakarta. Safe and sound I might add.'

I knew I was gaping like a codfish but I couldn't help myself. Arthur's smile remained fixed. 'They never came through Singapore at all – refuelled at Bangkok and went straight through to Kamayoran last night. An expensive security risk – they paid for seventy rooms at the Singapore Hilton they never intended using. Still, they can afford it. Bloody Arabs – they invent hijacking as an art form but make damn sure it doesn't catch them napping.'

'You mean it was planned that way?'

'Obviously.' As he caught my expression Arthur allowed himself a chuckle. It was more genuine than his smile and I involuntarily softened towards him. ‘Christ! You didn’t think *we* had prior notice did you? The first I knew of their real plans was after they were safely in Djakarta.’

I relaxed and took a cigarette from the open box. Arthur had not been treating me as a man who had just made a colossal fool of himself. If the Arabs’ security was so good that not even ASIO knew their intentions, then the League of the Lotus would not have known either. I suddenly felt a whole lot better. Arthur could not accuse me of going off half-cocked. Not he and his supercilious smile together.

‘So the League is in for a disappointment,’ I said through a cloud of smoke.

‘Perhaps.’ His expression was serious. ‘Perhaps not.’ Arthur helped himself to a cigarette. The piercing look in his eyes was something new he had picked up along the way. I met the direct gaze and he said, suddenly, ‘Tell me a little more about your co-pilot.’

‘Matt?’

Arthur was smiling again. ‘Don’t look so startled, Frank. I naturally want to have a chat with him. Just fill in some background for me.'

The Eurasian secretary fed Liz and me cups of coffee and had a reassuring smile ready each time she caught my eye. I kept staring at the closed door of Hughes's office, then back at my watch. Matt had been in there one hell of a time – more than an hour, and there was still no sign of the door opening.

'What the hell are they up to?' I muttered to Liz.

'I'm sure we'll find out in good time, Frank.' She squeezed my hand. 'Stop worrying.' Her smile was sweet, but it didn't quite reach her eyes. If Liz knew something, she wasn't telling.

A buzzer sounded on the secretary's desk. The girl coughed politely. 'Would you go in now please, Captain. And Miss Manifold too.'

Hughes stood up as we went through the door. Matt half rose but sank quickly back into the padded chair as Liz waved him to remain where he was. When she and I were seated, Hughes returned to his chair and spread his hands on the desk, palms down – a gesture of command.

'Sorry to keep you so long – we have had a very interesting discussion.' Arthur's eyes darted from one to the other of us. 'We'll get to that in a minute. First, we'd better get down to immediate business. I think it is generally agreed that the League's target could have been the OPEC plane but that in the circumstances, we cannot be sure. In fact we *dare* not assume it. This means we have to go back to the original timetable.' Arthur was staring at me intently. 'The fat man expects you to arrive at eight tonight on the Garuda flight, Frank. I think you and Matt should be on that plane.' I opened my mouth to protest but Arthur beat me to it. 'You can make it alright.' He glanced quickly at Matt, then his eyes were back on me. 'If you take off at twelve forty-five – in one hour – you can reach Djakarta in time to make the connection. I understand your seats are booked and the tickets are at the airport so there's no worry on that score. You can tell the Djakarta people that you had to make an emergency landing on the way from Surabaja to repair a fuel leak – anything, and that you were out of radio range. They won't know you've been in Singapore until ATC here query your lack of a flight plan, and that will take days.' I looked in Matt's direction. He *had* been talking a lot it seemed. Arthur continued, 'As for Mr Sangeron, you can leave him to me for the time being. I think I can tell him enough to keep him interested – and to reassure him whose side we're on.'

I wanted to say something, but I also wanted someone to translate the meaningful glances which Arthur and Matt kept throwing each other's way. Arthur read my mind.

'Alright Frank, I'll get to the guts of it in just a minute. In the meantime, if you're not on that Garuda flight the opposition could smell a rat and we may never get to the bottom of this thing. So will you agree to go back to Djakarta?'

I could easily have refused. But then, I had never been forced to go along with this business in the first place. My reasons for doing so had been entirely my own and if they had since become obscured by other motives, they were still valid. Deep down they counted most. So I was stuck with it to the bitter end and I had to admit Arthur was right. If we had to fall back on the fat man's programme to discover the next step, then that was what we must do. And if that meant being seen disembarking the Garuda flight at eight tonight then I had to be on that aeroplane. I shrugged resignedly and nodded.

Arthur slapped the desk. 'Good. Then we'd better not waste too much time. The reason I spent so long talking to Matt will become obvious to you shortly. His experience of the Chinese is rather special so I wanted to quiz him about certain details which you may not have noticed.' His expression was warm and the smile sincere as he added, 'This is no reflection on you Frank – but Superintendent Duncan has had a lot to do with these people. Anyway, we've had our little chat and I think you will be more than interested in the outcome.'

Arthur spoke for five minutes. I listened at first with disbelief, then with awe. I caught myself blushing once or twice, then anger crept into my bones and kept right on going. I turned the full force of it on Matt as Hughes finished talking. I had risen in my chair and was glowering at Matt, fists clenched.

'Why the hell didn't you say something? Did you get a charge out of seeing me win prick-of-the-year award?'

Matt's eyes were hard. 'Cool it, Pappy. How *could* I tell you? I've only just put it together myself. One at a time, the little inconsistencies with Chong Bee didn't mean much.' He added, deprecatingly, 'Maybe they should have, but they didn't. Not until Mr Hughes got me thinking the right way. Now it sticks out like a sore thumb that our favourite Chinaman might be playing ducks and drakes, and if anyone feels embarrassed, it should be me. So you take that temper of yours and stuff it.'

'Gentlemen.' Arthur's tone was reproving but there was a twinkle in his eye. 'Don't go fighting between yourselves. Just be thankful we're partly aware of what this is all about. At least we can now guess why ASIO is involved.' He stood up suddenly. 'I'll drive you to the airport. With a little luck we'll soon know the rest of it.'

PART THREE

Chapter Fourteen

I SANK gratefully into the window seat of the 707 and let out a slow breath. Matt dropped beside me and adjusted his seat belt.

'They're on the ball tonight, Pappy.'

I grunted, staring out the window through heavy drops of rain at the lighted terminal. The storm was still a mile away, but moving towards the airport, and a gaggle of umbrellas was making its way to the front steps of the Boeing and the first class seats. Matt's remark had been aimed at the security staff. They *had* seemed a little more thorough than usual tonight. Not that they could take things much further. A full body search was routine at Djakarta and hand luggage was emptied onto a table, with each item scrutinized before being put back. Matt and I had undergone the same ritual. It was annoying but reassuring at the same time.

I glanced up at the parapet which ran along the front of the terminal. At about ten yard intervals Indonesian soldiers stood in the now steadily falling rain, sub-machine guns pointing down from shoulder slings towards the apron. On the level below was a visitors' area – a wide platform backed by French doors leading into the restaurant. A few hardy souls stood in the rain eager to wave farewell to passengers on our aircraft but Liz was not among them. We had said our goodbyes – for a few days until we met again in Darwin. She had travelled here with us on Charlie Delta, ready to pick up her Qantas flight south. It had seemed simpler that way.

Matt's voice broke into my private thoughts once again. 'Do you think Sant saw us?'

I turned to look at him. My resentment was dying slowly but it was taking its time. I said quietly, 'No. I don't think he could have.'

Santi was Hudy's airport manager general factotum and right hand man. He was also a pain in the arse. He had a little office at the back of the terminal which he shared with a taxi-truck operator. The office was always full of sundry hangers-on who stank the place up with their tobacco while Santi sat behind an oversized desk and played God. It was more than a hour since I had landed Charlie Delta and parked her at the far end of the apron. Santi would know of our arrival but he considered it more dignified to have us report to *his* office than for him to meet the aircraft. We hadn't gone to see him. Matt and I had headed straight for the Garuda counter to collect our tickets. Standing in the small queue, we had both spotted Santi's greasy hair bobbing over the crowd further along the terminal. As soon as the tickets were in our hot little hands we disappeared into the immigration hall. Santi would be expecting me to drop in on him with the flight reports and technical log, but it wouldn't be the first time I had detoured via the upstairs bar and taken a couple of hours over a few drinks first. On one memorable occasion he had intruded on me there, and over a foaming glass of beer I had made it quite clear that if he ever did that again, I would screw his head off at the elbows. Santi had believed me, and our relationship was forever cemented in mutual hatred. If he had any inkling that Matt and I might be on this plane we would certainly know it by now. Santi would have drummed up some nasty excuse to have us pulled off the aircraft – just to be cussed if for no other reason.

We had taken precautions even after we were safely inside the departure lounge, staying away from the bar and spending a lot of time in and around the men's room. On a wet night such as this Santi would use the international departure route as a short cut to the apron if he decided to come looking for us. He hadn't showed, and we made it aboard the Boeing without attracting attention.

The jet engines started with a low whine and the piped music was interrupted by a female voice welcoming us aboard and drawing our attention to the safety regulations of a 707. The aircraft moved slowly away from the ramp and lined up on the long north runway, then we were rolling. The storm was very close and the large aircraft bumped through the lower levels of the atmosphere on its way to thirty-plus thousand feet where we would be above the weather. The no smoking signs went off. I accepted a cigarette from Matt and turned my face back to the window.

Maybe it wasn't Matt's fault, but I still felt a deep resentment that he could have told Arthur Hughes so much and me so little. I felt that Hughes had been too ready to jump to conclusions. On the other hand, I didn't have to rush into any hasty decisions. It would all come out in the wash and in the meantime, I could afford to wait and see. There was a ninety per cent chance that I *had* made a bloody fool of myself. But I had to give the remaining ten per cent some sort of chance too.

The seat belt signs went off as the Boeing climbed into smoother air and there was a scurry of activity in the aisle as the stewardesses started the dinner service. The pre-cooked meals, pre-wrapped in aluminium foil, were presented to us. I caught the aroma of food as Matt unwrapped his package. I hurriedly did the same. It was a delightful Eastern menu – a delicious mixture of Indonesian fried rice and rendang beef.

There was a sudden click from the concealed loudspeakers and I smiled through a mouthful of food as I got a picture of Shelley Bermann's 'silver-haired, father-image captain' about to make his obligatory, public relations announcement. A pause of several seconds ensued before a strained voice broke the silence.

'Ladies and gentlemen, this is the captain.' There was a further pause. I unconsciously put down my spoon as I wondered what was to follow. 'I'm sorry to inform you that due to unforeseen circumstances we are proceeding to Palembang, where I hope we will not be delayed very long. We will be landing in about twenty minutes from now so could you please assist the cabin staff by handing in your trays. Those of you who have not yet eaten will be served on the ground. We apologize for the inconvenience. Should anyone wish to send a message to friends or relatives meeting you in Singapore, please advise the cabin staff after landing.' There was another pause then the captain said quickly, 'Thank you, ladies and gentlemen.'

The speaker clicked off and the engine note changed as the power reduced for the descent. Matt and I were looking at each other open-mouthed. A red light glowed on one of the cabin interphones and a stewardess picked it up. Her face was drawn. She replaced the instrument and I watched as she said something to the other two girls, then all three of them headed aft.

Matt broke the silence. 'Are you thinking what I'm thinking, Pappy?'

'In spades.'

My mouth had suddenly gone dry. Palembang was a Fokker Friendship-size aerodrome, way too short for a 707. If the captain was good enough then he might get us in there in one piece, but he'd never get out again. Not unless he dumped all the passengers and freight, and most of his fuel. Even then it would be touch and go. Palembang was not an airfield *any* 707 skipper would go into voluntarily, whatever the emergency. The level of conversation in the cabin had risen noticeably. I glanced at the other passengers within range. Some of them looked puzzled, others annoyed, but none of them looked scared. They should have.

The fasten-seat-belts sign had illuminated again but I ignored it and stood up. 'Let me out, Matt. I'm going to take a look-see.' He hesitated for a moment as if he didn't approve of the idea, then he shifted his knees sideways and I stepped over him into the aisle. The three stewardesses were talking earnestly in the rear galley. As one of them saw me she gestured frantically for me to return to my seat. I ignored her and strode towards the front of the aircraft.

Near the forward galley a curtain was drawn across the aisle to provide the first class passengers with a privacy they had paid for. I stepped through the curtain, let it fall behind me – and looked straight into the business end of a large automatic pistol. The small hand holding the gun moved fractionally, then a pair of oriental eyes narrowed into a smile as the fat man said matter-of-factly, 'Ah! Captain Adams. Good of you to join us.'

He was standing against the forward bulkhead. Behind him, the door to the flight deck stood ajar, the faint glow from the instrument panel breaking the darkness. Half of the sixteen first class seats were occupied and I felt hostile eyes on me as the passengers turned to inspect the newcomer.

The fat man did not come as a complete surprise – I had been expecting something like this. What did have me puzzled, though, was how he had managed to smuggle weapons aboard at a place like Djakarta, where security is tighter than a duck's arse. I glanced at the torn foil wrappings on the cabin floor, and then I understood. The Djakarta security system was not foolproof after all: there *was* a loophole, and the fat man had found it – guns à la carte. Now that I could see it, it was simple. Why hadn't somebody thought of it before? Not more than a dozen of the larger, first class dinner trays would have come aboard – each foil-wrapped tray capable of hiding a weapon. In fact, *all* of them must have been packed that way. The fat man and his accomplices could not guarantee beforehand which dinner trays would be served to them, but they *could* guarantee being served first, by booking the front row of seats. For some reason best known to themselves, airline cabin staff always serve passengers from front to rear. The fat man was standing near the empty port-side front seats. The double seat opposite was also empty and my eyes wandered back to the door. How many were up on the flight deck – one, two? I decided there would have to be two of them holding the crew at gunpoint. Five unwrapped dinner trays still rested on the trolley at my side and my fingers itched to get at one. I missed the comfortable feel of the thirty-eight nestling against my belly, but I had known I could never get the gun aboard the 707 so I had stowed it in the roof lining of Charlie Delta. Not that I ever expected to see the old Dakota again – it had been more of a sentimental gesture. Now, with those other guns so close, my nakedness was almost painful.

I ruefully returned the fat man's smile. 'I see the timetable has been changed – or was it always meant to be this way?' His head dipped sideways, the gesture of a man well pleased with himself. I kept my voice conversational. 'Well! You seem to have things under control. I won't stay.'

I turned and disappeared through the curtain before he could stop me. But *not* before I had caught a glimpse of the two people sitting in row three. The worried hostess was waiting for me on the far side of the curtain. She had deemed it wiser not to follow into first class and I didn't blame her. I tossed her a smile and headed back towards my seat. There was a confident expression on my face for the benefit of the other passengers, but when I threw my leg across Matt and sat down, I was sweating. I reached quickly for a cigarette, conscious that Matt's impatience had reached boiling point. I took a couple of quick puffs and turned slowly to my co-pilot.

'Its the fat man alright, and he has help.' I let out a deep breath. 'He also has a reason – a bloody good one. Things are finally starting to make sense.'

Matt was looking at me expectantly, waiting for me to continue. I turned away from him and drew deliberately on my cigarette.

'Go on then, Pappy. What else?'

Despite the slow churning in my guts, I was half enjoying the situation. I said nastily, 'Ask your friend Arthur Hughes – he has all the answers.'

'Come on, Frank.' Matt's eyes were smouldering with the hurt look of a little boy. 'I told you the way things happened. If I'd had any idea myself I would have said something. I didn't – that's the truth.'

I fussed deliberately with the cigarette, twirling it in my fingers, realizing *I* was being childish. But Hughes and Matt had filled me with so many self doubts over the past few hours that I was enjoying my revenge. I couldn't keep it up, though we would be landing in a few minutes, and even as I thought it, the no smoking signs came on and I reluctantly ground my cigarette into the ashtray.

'Alright, Matt. I'll believe you. I don't think it makes a lot of difference now anyway.' I dropped the smugness from my voice. I had had my day in court – no sense overdoing it. I said, seriously, 'A certain royal gentleman is on board, together with his young wife.' Matt looked at me vacantly. I added, 'They have been honeymooning in Fiji.' Matt still wore an expression of non-comprehension. I said angrily, 'Don't you ever read the bloody papers? Have I got to draw pictures for Chrissakes?'

'Yes, maybe you should.' Matt's blue face was scowling at me.

'Prince Constantin and his bride.'

'The blue-collar prince?'

The penny had dropped. I said sarcastically, 'So you *have* heard of him. Bully for you.' A cluster of lights caught my attention through the port window as the Boeing went into a slow turn – Palembang.

Prince Constantin was the communists' dream of royalty, the working man's prince. He had fallen in with a left-wing crowd at Oxford and, using the Students' Union as a mouthpiece, had given forth with his ideas of the role of royalty in the welfare state. He would have nothing to do with royal yachts, special aircraft, red carpets. He was the original democrat, the blue-collar prince as he had become popularly known – popular amongst the proletariat that is. To his own family he was an embarrassment; to the world's security services, he was a royal pain. The prince liked to travel as an ordinary man on scheduled air services. But even scheduled air services had to land somewhere, and when they did so with the prince on board, the security people at the destination country were faced with an immediate headache. He refused to accept the protection of bodyguards or secret service men, and in return the security people refused to let the prince get himself killed or abducted on their territory. So it became a war of nerves, the prince going to endless trouble to throw his tail, and the security service having to assign twice as many men to the job to keep him safe. Many countries around the world watched the prince climb on board a departing aircraft and let out a deep sigh of relief.

Regardless of his blue-collar image, when he had decided to marry, it was not into poverty, despite the aspirations of many a working-class bride-to-be. The prince announced to a disillusioned world that he would marry Nanala Orinassus, the only daughter of Greek shipping magnate, Avis Orinassus, one of the six richest men in the world. The *New Yorker* labelled it an ideal love-match, the *Daily Worker* called the prince a traitor to his principles. The prince himself rode blithely through the storm of mixed criticism, enjoying the controversy he had created.

But when he announced that he and Nanala would honeymoon in Fiji and Australia, the Australian Government replied that he would be ten times welcome, but that they would suffer none of his eccentricities. Prince Constantin would accept the protection of the Australian Government in the normal way, or he had better decide on another venue. The newspapers were gleefully sharpening their pencils to report on the ensuing row, when old Avis Orinassus had stepped in. As a married man, with new responsibilities, Prince Constantin's views had matured. He would be glad to accept the protection of the Australian Government, in fact he would be grateful for it. There were a few journalistic chuckles at the evidence of the new, firm hand in the prince's life. Then a few weeks later, *Time* reported that the old man had made a deal with the Australians to protect the newlyweds throughout their sojourn in the South Pacific. The report was neither confirmed nor denied. I remembered thinking at the time that ASIO would be in it up to their necks, and would only release their interest after the prince was safely on his way northbound from Singapore. If a deal had been made, the Australians would consider Singapore to be within their area of responsibility. After that, it was someone else's headache.

The Boeing was now on finals for the short runway. I tensed into my seat, feeling sorry for the captain. This was going to be a close one. But I was also feeling another kind of excitement. If I was right in my thinking then there would be an ASIO man on board right now. If I could only make contact . . .

The 707 slammed its wheels into the gravel runway and there was an immediate shuddering throughout the aircraft as the crew selected full reverse thrust. The Indonesian skipper did a good job – a fine job. I heard the faint pop of one of the main tyres bursting, then we were slowing down until finally the aircraft turned off the very end of the runway at walking pace and taxied slowly towards the apron. I pressed my nose against the window and turned to Matt.

'Get ready to go to work, Sunshine.' He raised one eyebrow and I jerked a thumb at the window. 'Take a look.' He leaned across me for a moment and then he was back in his seat. Standing at the edge of the apron, rear door open, was the familiar shape of a Dakota, its silver paint glinting dully in the artificial light of the terminal.

I said blandly, 'Seems the fat man knew what he was doing after all.'

Chapter Fifteen

THE Dakota was much more luxurious than Charlie Delta in every way. Padded VIP seating in the carpeted cabin was surrounded by teak veneer; half way along the fuselage was a refrigerated cocktail cabinet. The cockpit was rather less luxurious but there was a newness about everything – even some of the instrument clocks looked new, and the radio equipment was the latest design. The army registration explained why the fat man had needed two outside pilots – what it did not explain was how he had acquired the aircraft, or why the well-armed military personnel on the apron stood silently by, doing nothing. The fat man and his two accomplices, a man and a woman, had led the prince and his wife on board at gunpoint. Matt and I followed, throwing each other disbelieving looks.

I had walked the length of the Boeing before disembarking, studying the puzzled faces of the passengers, trying to identify the ASIO man I was sure was on board. I had been unsuccessful. Now, sitting in the left-hand pilot seat of the Dakota, I realized that it didn't matter. Whoever he was, he would be on the phone to Singapore or Djakarta within minutes. Hughes would soon know what had happened – even if there wasn't a damn thing he could do about it.

The Chinese woman stood between the two pilot seats as Matt and I went through the start-up drill. Five minutes later I was cleared for take-off and I opened the throttles and headed up into the darkness. It was a strange feeling. For the first time in my life I was airborne without having the first idea where I was going. Matt raised the gear and the flaps and I turned to the woman.

'OK. Where to?'

'Remove your headphones, Captain.' Even above the noise of the engines, the strange lisp in her voice was unmistakable. I did as she asked and the corners of her mouth turned up in a satisfied smile. 'Turn off the radio.'

I thought about faking it, but the new Collins equipment was unfamiliar to me. If I hesitated too long looking for the right knob she would become suspicious.

I reached across and switched the set off.

'Good. Now please turn onto a course of three hundred and twenty degree magnetic and climb to eight thousand feet. At top of climb, adjust your power for a true airspeed of one hundred and forty knots.'

Her voice was precise despite the lisp and I looked at her with new interest She had used all the right words – the young lady knew quite a lot about aeroplanes. I was suddenly glad I hadn't tried fooling around with the radio. She tapped Matt on the shoulder with the automatic. As he turned around annoyed, she motioned him to stand. He gave me a funny look, but I kept my face expressionless. He reluctantly climbed out of his seat and I overheard her tell him to go back into the cabin She climbed into Matt's vacant seat, put on the headset and motioned me to do the same. She flicked the intercom switch.

'You seem to have about eight degree of drift, Captain. Please adjust you heading to track three two zero. Her voice was coming to me without the accompanying roar of two Pratt and Whitneys, and I could detect the faintly nasal, American twang behind the lisp. I glanced at the automatic direction finder. She was right – we did have eight degrees of port drift.

I leaned on the wheel and straightened up on the new heading. My voice was friendly as I asked, 'Where did you learn about flying?'

Her black eyebrows seemed to straighten, accentuating the slant of her almond eyes. 'Please don't waste time on idle conversation.' She glanced at her wristwatch. 'Maintain this heading for another twelve minutes, then commence a five-hundred-feet-a-minute descent at one twenty knots.'

She had it all worked out. I tried to get a mental picture of just where we were going – somewhere in central Sumatra was the nearest I could manage, but I couldn't come up with a town. As far as I knew, there was just thick jungle ahead; the only towns I could think of were on the coast. But it never occurred to me to doubt the young lady's navigation – her instructions were too precise.

I commenced descent, watching the altimeter slowly unwind as we headed down into the blackness. As we approached five thousand feet my hands instinctively held back on the wheel – there were hills down there somewhere central Sumatra was riddled with them.

'Keep going down, Captain.' I risked a sideways glance. The girl was peering ahead in concentration, but her features were untroubled. I dragged my eyes back to the instruments and she suddenly said 'There.'

I looked up. About four miles away twenty degrees to starboard, the double lines of a flarepath glimmered faintly The lights flickered in the manner o paraffin goosenecks as we drew closer The girl was back in her seat, relaxed.

'Approach from the south east Captain. You will probably be downwind but there are hills at the other end.'

'OK, no sweat. You'd better go fetch my co-pilot.'

'It will not be necessary – I can assis you.'

I glanced at her sideways. Her lef

hand was hovering above the two levers. I said matter-of-factly, 'Give me fifteen degrees of flap.'

There was the faint hiss of hydraulics as I felt the slight nose-up trim-change and her voice sounded, competently, 'Flaps fifteen.'

She was very good. Landing gear and flap increments were right where I called for them. I felt like introducing her to Hudy. She would be a lot more fun to fly with than Matt – especially on overnights. I slid the Dak onto the runway and then had to work overtime on the rudders to keep straight on the bumpy surface. It may have been an airstrip once, but there had been a lot of neglect in the meantime. Clumps of weed and grass showed up in the landing lights. I taxied the aircraft to the far end of the strip where a cluster of tin huts stood rusty and forlorn, and I realized where I was – an abandoned oil camp.

A hurricane lamp burned in one of the huts and two men stood nearby. From their stature I knew they were Chinese long before I could confirm it in their features. Matt walked onto the flight deck as the engines died. He lookec oddly at the girl still sitting in his seat then at the gear and flap levers in the split parked position.

'Been giving flying lessons, Pappy?'

I was about to retort to his sarcasm when the girl stood up abruptly. The gur was held tightly in her hand. She wavec it towards the rear of the aircraft 'Alright. We will go.'

Matt was in the mood for conversation - I wanted to sleep. And why not? I hadn' had much to do with Morpheus's lovin arms over the past few days and there was, staring at a freshly made bed in th glow of a hurricane lamp. Matt and had been taken straight to this tin hu which contained two beds and an ol card table on which rested a pitcher o water and two glasses. We had bee shown the latrine out back, given hurricane lamp and bade goodnight. A quick inspection disclosed no guard o our shack. It was a different story at th hut where the hostages had been taker Two men had been posted to watch th newly-weds.

'Leave it till the morning, Sunshine; I'm too bloody tired to think.' I couldn't be bothered with Matt's questions and speculations – the white sheets were just too damned tempting. The peculiar smell of new mosquito nets hung in the room. I finished undressing, pulled aside the stiff netting and climbed into bed. It was heaven.

'Put the light out, sweetheart. If anyone dares wake me before noon – I'll fuck the cook and fire the butler.'

My battered old Rolex said it was just after seven when the door opened and sunlight streamed into the hut. A young Chinese stood at the foot of the bed, a carbine slung from his shoulder. 'Blekkefast – velly soon.' He wore a friendly grin and was obviously proud of his English. 'You come soon. Blekkefast.' He rubbed his stomach, gestured to the door and went through it, leaving it open.

Matt was sitting up in bed. He pulled aside his mosquito net, lit a cigarette and threw the packet near my bed. I reached through the net and picked it up, then ruffled through my trousers for my lighter, a battle-scarred Dunhill as old as the Rolex. Both were relics of more affluent days – Fleming days. In the strong sunlight, Matt's face was the same blue as the tobacco smoke.

Blowing out a mouthful of smoke, Matt said, 'What do you make of all this, Frank? They're not exactly being unfriendly, are they?'

'Why should they be – we're on the payroll. But don't get too carried away. We don't have a guard on us, but there will sure as hell be one on the Dak so we ain't going anywhere until they say so. In the meantime, eat, drink and be merry.'

'You're taking all this very . . . stoically, if I may say so, Captain Adams.' Matt was watching me speculatively. I jumped out of bed and reached for my trousers.

'The game's the thing my lad. Didn't they teach you anything at school?' I picked up my shirt. 'The fat man may have a prince, but both queens are still on the board and if we run into trouble, there's always the scientific way out – we can cheat.' I grabbed a towel and headed for the door and the ablution hut. 'Come on; get out of that bed. You heard the man – it's time for blekkefast.'

I followed Matt into the mess hut feeling a lot less jocose than I was pretending to be. Little niggling thoughts at the back of my mind kept trying to surface and I was just as determined not to let them. Flights of fancy belong in bedrooms and opium dens and there were some things I refused to believe – refused even to think about.

Three card tables made up the dining room, each one set for breakfast on the beer-stained, faded green baize. The fat man sat at one table and was already digging into a bowl of rice and smoked fish. He beckoned Matt and I to join him as grease dribbled down his chins towards the white napkin at his neck. I dropped into a chair and lit a cigarette. When it was going, I said, matter-of-factly, 'Are your guests joining us for breakfast?'

'Later, Captain.'

'And how long are *we* going to be here – at this place, I mean?'

'A few days – a few weeks. However long it takes.' He looked at me slyly. 'Are your quarters not comfortable, perhaps?' A young Chinese arrived at the table and set down two more bowls of the rice and fish, together with a pot of coffee. The fat man waved a deprecating hand. 'I hope you enjoy Chinese food – this is a very simple dish I'm afraid, but no doubt lunch will be more interesting.'

'What are we having – royal pudding?' My gaze was direct. The fat man's eyes opened fractionally wider and he set his chopsticks down slowly on the table in front of him.

'You are very well informed, Captain Adams.' He returned my frank stare. 'Sometimes knowledge is a dangerous thing. What else do you know?'

'Not as much as I'd like to. I wonder what the army has to do with all this, for instance, and how you managed to persuade the military commander in Palembang to lend you his aircraft.'

The fat man's stern expression stayed on his face for several seconds, then slowly his features relaxed into a smile.

A Machiavellian smile. 'Ah! Such a simple thing, my friend, and it has you in a quandary. I must say I am surprised.'

'Why?'

'No reason. Perhaps I am being unfair.' He toyed with the greasy chopsticks. 'Would it help if I told you the name of the military commandant? Colonel Sartono.' The fat man was looking at me wickedly. As he saw the light dawn on my face he said quickly, 'Not that it is entirely a family affair, you understand. General Sartono was a secret policeman, but first he was a soldier – a hero. The army will do much to ensure his safe return – it was not *necessary* to involve the General's younger brother. Just a convenient coincidence.'

'You bastard.'

'No, Captain.' The fat man's voice was full of crisp authority. 'I am a pragmatist. It makes no difference to our dead departed general what we say of him now. Yet even in death he is serving a useful purpose. How many men are privileged thus?'

I picked up one of the dessert spoons

which had been thoughtfully provided for the 'round eyes', gave Matt an odd look and dug into the rice. At last the mystery of why General Sartono had been kidnapped was solved. And I could now understand why his death had been no great inconvenience to the Tong – so long as the army thought he was still alive, and that by co-operating, they could still save him.

I said laconically, 'I hope you are going to show more concern for the prince and his bride. No doubt her father will pay your ransom – but he won't settle for damaged goods.'

The fat man was in high humour despite my nit-picking. 'Oh, yes. He will pay – it is already agreed.'

He saw my raised eyebrows and chuckled. 'These things do not take long where one's own flesh and blood are concerned. It is not like dealing with a government. There one invites procrastination. Entebbe was a good lesson, and an example. So we do not make the same mistakes – our whereabouts are unknown and we are dealing with a man who is anxious to pay our price.'

'Haven't you forgotten something?' I tried to sound nasty – the fat man's smugness was getting on my nerves. He looked at me quizzically. I said, 'What do you think will happen when you don't produce General Sartono alive and well? You'll have the army *and* the secret police on your necks, and they won't give up easily. If I were you, I'd start running right now.'

'Ah, but you are not me, Captain Adams. I suggest you eat your breakfast – a man who worries as much as you should not do so on an empty stomach. It is bad for your health.' He suppressed another chuckle and slurped noisily at a cup of tea. He stood up abruptly. 'Now, if you will excuse me I have some work to do. You are free to wander about, only I should not stray too far if I were you. This is tiger country.'

It sounded funny hearing him use the phrase – tiger country. In Australia that was slang for any area of rugged bush, but the fat man meant it literally. The Sumatra tiger shares honours with his Siberian cousin for being the biggest cat in the world. Pound for pound there is little to choose between them – they are both ferocious and incredibly strong. I have heard stories of a Sumatra tiger jumping an eight foot wall with a full grown bull by the neck, and I believe them. Tigers measuring two feet across their diamond-shaped heads are not uncommon in this part of the world. As I watched the fat man walk through the door I complimented him on his psychology. Matt and I would not be taking up bush-walking to pass the time.

But there was another walk I wanted to take and ten minutes later we strolled into the hot sunlight and turned right, towards the airstrip. For a moment I thought the DC3 was gone, then I saw it, parked with its tail in the trees and covered in leafy branches. Someone had been busy, but I pondered the reason for camouflage. Having co-operated so far, the army would hardly be searching now. After all, they had allowed the horse to bolt. Maybe the fat man was being extra cautious. There was no guard on the machine and I exchanged puzzled glances with Matt – it didn't make sense.

Then, as we came closer, we could see the padlock on the rear door. Somehow, the sight of the lock made me feel better – anything less would have been out of character for the fat man. He hadn't made too many mistakes up to now, apart from believing that his hundred grand had bought me and Matt. On reflection, he hadn't made a mistake there either. The way he had organized things, he didn't have to trust us. By removing opportunity, he had effectively removed temptation. As I turned back in the direction of the huts I got the feeling that no matter what we did, the fat man was going to get away with the whole damned business. The thought made me angry.

Matt's mind was working in the same direction, except *he* wasn't getting his balls in a knot about it. He said quietly, thoughtfully, 'This is a very well planned operation, Pappy. I wonder who's behind it.'

I turned to look at him, and kicked aimlessly at a clump of weed for the benefit of anyone watching. I handed him a cigarette. 'So you still think this is a power-play, Matt?'

His expression was calm. He lit the cigarette and gazed thoughtfully at the sky. We could have been discussing a test match. 'It has to be. There isn't a Tong in existence with this kind of sophistication.' His dark eyes gazed at me intently. 'Think about it Pappy – go over things in your mind one by one – this binge has the professional touch at every turn.

'To begin with, they know all about you and me. I can understand them getting on to me – I locked enough of the bastards up in my time – but you are a very different proposition. I don't know what your job was with ASIO. After all this time, you wouldn't appear on too many intelligence files around the world. Whoever dug you up has you on a current file somewhere – and I can assure you it's not the League of the Lotus. It has to be one of the big boys and there are only half a dozen countries in the world with that kind of organization.'

'I could have appeared on a list somewhere, Matt. A certain amount of exchange information goes on from time to time, but because no one is entirely honest, there is always some padding. The name of a defunct agent could be thrown in for good measure – maybe it was my name in this case. That widens the field to just about any bloody country in the world that runs an intelligence service.'

'Have it your own way, Pappy, but I don't believe it happened like that. It gets back to sophistication, and that leads right back to the big boys – Britain, America, Russia, France – take your pick.'

Matt was right. I had put some of my worries aside by convincing myself that it *was* just a chance appearance on an exchange list which had led the Tong to me. But for Matt's money, the Tong were only mercenaries who worked for the highest bidder. The fat man acted like an entrepreneur but that could just be his ego working overtime; it was possible he didn't even know who his employers were. I suddenly felt completely bloody helpless, and that made me angry again. Whoever was behind this operation had not only used an ex-ASIO agent – they had played it in such a way that ASIO would know about it. Someone was thumbing their bloody nose at us – and they weren't going to get away with it. The thought made me feel better, but not for long. How the hell was I going to stop them?

I pulled myself together and smiled ruefully at Matt. 'OK, we're caught in a big squeeze – I'll buy that much. Any ideas?'

'About who it is, you mean?' Matt shook his head. 'None. But some good brains have been at work. The Russians are good at chess, but so are the French.'

'Don't leave out the Yanks. They've got Fischer. And although it pains me to say it, there are one or two bright Poms around too. So we're back at square one.'

'Maybe. That business of smuggling guns aboard in the dinner trays tends to make me discard the French. The way they feel about food, it would be sacrilege.' Matt grinned. 'In fact, that's more like a dirty Aussie trick – like bodyline bowling.' He was suddenly serious. 'I don't even think they are after money. There's political capital to be made out of this operation and I keep thinking about all those ships Avis Orinassus owns. If this is a political ploy, then the punchline would come on the other side of the world and we wouldn't be any the wiser. That's the beauty of this whole operation; the pay-off could be guns for the IRA or butter for Nicaragua. Whatever it is, old Avis will play ball if it's within his power, as it must be, and we'll only know about it after it's all over. And we may never know who was behind it in the first place.' Matt's blue face had a sheepish smile. 'I guess I'm still a copper at heart. This operation could set the pattern for similar ones in the future, and that worries me. Crooks are great imitators. When they see this caper succeed they'll be on the bandwagon before you can shout, "Crime doesn't pay".'

'They haven't succeeded yet,' I spat.

Matt looked at me pityingly. 'Well, let's say they have a ten goal lead, Pappy. I don't think they can be beaten, and they don't think so either.' He put a hand on my arm. 'Let's you and I just make sure we live long enough to read all about it afterwards in the papers. I think that's the best we can do.' His forehead creased into a worried frown. 'And I'm not even sure we can do that.'

Chapter Sixteen

IT wasn't good enough. Not by a bloody long chalk was it good enough. I had come into this thing all fired up to fix the fat man's wagon. There was no way I could just sit back and watch him get away with it.

I sat in the darkened hut, watching night descend and listening to the insect noises as they gathered into a crescendo. Matt was dozing on top of his bed which was why I had not lit the hurricane lamp. The day had passed uneventfully, the newly-weds once again being kept out of sight at lunchtime. Maybe they would show for dinner, although I doubted it; the fat man obviously did not want them conversing with the likes of me and Matt. Or maybe it was His Highness's idea not to mingle with the hired help. The girl hijacker certainly felt that way. I had twice tried to engage her in conversation during the day – once at lunch, the other time when I had seen her walking by. I had received the proverbial brush-off. Even the fat man was far less talkative over lunch than he had been at breakfast. Matt and I were suddenly pariahs.

I was glad Matt was sleeping. He had shattered my confidence quite a bit and I was glad of the opportunity to do some thinking on my own account. Maybe Arthur Hughes had no knowledge of our whereabouts, but once he knew the prince and the lovely Nanala were involved, this would lead immediately to Avis Orinassus. I had it figured that with ASIO on the job, old Avis would co-operate. But then I considered why the hell should he? He would be worried about his daughter – *only* about his daughter. He couldn't care whether the Nicaraguans had enough butter, or the IRA enough guns, and he wouldn't have much sympathy for those who did care if he thought it would jeopardize Nanala's chances. In fact, the wealthy Greek would probably go to great pains to keep the law out of it, and I didn't blame him. Over the years many kidnappers had been caught, but a lot of victims had also died because of police interference. Avis could afford to pay the ransom, *whatever* it was. He had nothing to gain by letting ASIO, or anyone else, become involved. On the other hand, he had *everything* to lose. This effectively put the ball back in my court. If the operation was to be sabotaged, it had to be at this end, and Matt and myself were the only ones who could do it. I didn't yet know how. I was long on ambition and short of ideas as I stood up, stretched my muscles and quietly walked outside into the night. For the moment, everything came back to basics. I needed a gun.

It was spitting with rain as I made my way to the rear of the hut and skirted the tree line. The tall lalang grass soaked my trousers, but it also provided cover as I passed first behind the dining shack, then the one being used by the hijackers. The shutters were closed and I was almost out of earshot when I heard the familiar, low whine of an alternating-current vibrator. Someone in the command hut was using a radio transmitter.

Crouched against the side of the hut, I could hear the radio operator's words quite distinctly, but it wasn't worth a damn. The man was speaking Chinese. I heard the fat man break in once; the girl also added a comment or two, but they were using their own language. I thought of waking Matt, but decided against it. He could translate but two of us stood more chance of being discovered. In any event, the radio conversation would probably be finished before we could return. I quietly went back into the lalang.

I skirted the hostages' hut, keeping well in the shadows. What I was hoping to do was surprise one of the guards, overpower him and take his weapon. I couldn't make up my mind whether it was optimism or foolishness egging me on – more likely desperation. I stayed close to the trees for as long as I could, making my way past the hut to where I could see the front door. A rear shutter was open and I caught a glimpse of the prince as he crossed the room. One man lounged outside the door; his face glistened in the glow of a cigarette as he stood in the rain. There was no sign of his companion. I slowly left the cover of the trees and ran to his side of the hut, keeping low. I reached the tin wall, breathing hard. I was now soaked through and could not suppress a shudder as I felt a sudden chill. I straightened up and peered around a corner to the back of the hut – all clear. If I was going to act, I should do it now. Delay would only set me thinking and I might realize how bloody stupid it was trying to take on an armed man with my bare hands. I glanced around for a weapon, a piece of wood, anything. Something hard pressed into my back and I felt my blood run cold.

'Stand still, Captain.' The voice was light, effeminate. I cursed under my breath. The open rear shutter should have told me someone would be keeping watch at the back in case the newly-weds decided to escape via the window and take to the jungle. The muzzle was still pressing into my spine. I had a chance. Whoever was holding that gun was untrained. Lesson one of the basic manual – never put a gun into a man's back; he can turn and knock it off-target in less time than it takes to pull a trigger. I had seen it demonstrated; had even practised it – with an unloaded gun.

I slowly raised my arms and half turned to look at my adversary. I kept the turn going, suddenly dropped my left arm and swung it viciously. There was a second part to the exercise which I had never practised – was not even convinced would work. If the young Chinaman had been even half-trained it wouldn't have succeeded, but before he realized what was happening, I had my right hand clamped over the automatic, my index finger jammed into the trigger guard, squeezing his knuckle against the hard metal. He let out a muffled whimper. Why he didn't yell his bloody head off and bring help running I'll never know, but he'd left it too late for that. My left hand sliced wickedly into his windpipe; he gasped once; I took his weight and lowered him slowly to the ground. I gently released his fingers stood up, caught my breath and suddenly felt ten feet tall. I was my own man again.

Matt was still sleeping. I shook him roughly by the shoulder and as his eyes opened, I stuck the gun under his nose.

'On your feet, Sunshine. We're back in the game.'

He scrambled out of the net and reached for his shirt. Enough light was filtering into the darkened room for him to see but he had trouble finding his shoes. I flicked my lighter and saw his eyes come back to the automatic.

'The fat man gave you that, I suppose.'

'I talked him out of it. I always was a smooth-talking bastard. Come on, get dressed. We're getting out of here.'

I had it in mind that if we could get to Palembang and advise the army their precious general was dead, they could move in on the fat man and his bunch.

Matt and I reached the hostages' hut without being seen. I was under the window, about to call softly to the prince, when the door opened and the Chinese guard stood in the opening.

'Dinner. You come dinner now.'

The man started for the open window and I scurried away on all fours and fell flat in the lalang.

'Ching Wa . . .' The man was calling to his companion who was lying near the corner of the hut, still unconscious. If the guard poked his head out of the window and looked to his left, he must see him. I eased the automatic into a shooting position and took aim, my finger already tightening on the trigger when I heard an answering call in Chinese. The man at the window laughed, yelled a rejoinder and I saw him turn and walk away. I let my breath out slowly and turned my head in the direction of the answering Chinese voice – Matt's voice, pitched an octave higher to handle the Chinese diction, and good enough to fool the guard above the sound of the falling rain. I stood up and Matt was quickly at my side.

'That was quick thinking. What did you tell him?'

'Not to disturb a man with his

trousers down.'

I ran to the corner of the hut. The newly-weds and their escort had almost reached the dining room.

'Shit.' I let out the oath and I meant it. 'I wanted them with us.'

'You're not thinking of leaving without them, Pappy?' Matt's voice had just a trace of sarcasm. I matched it.

'What would you rather do, boy scout? Wait until second sitting when it's our turn to eat and everyone knows we've gone?' I pointed at the unconscious Chinese. 'And what about him? He could come out of it soon. Then what?' I shook my head. 'We're going to have to play this another way. It's risking the prince's life, not to mention his sexy looking spouse, but we have no choice. We've got to stop these bastards and that's number one priority as far as I'm concerned. Wait here. I'm going to recce the other huts; we need the key to the Dak.'

The command hut was quiet. I listened at the window before I risked approaching the front door. It stood ajar. I eased it open slowly and looked inside.

The fat man's male accomplice sat at a radio receiver, one headphone carelessly in place, the other pushed forward. He had his feet on the table and was idly thumbing a magazine. I deftly moved across the room. The man heard me at the last second and turned abruptly, but the reversed automatic was already descending towards his head. He slumped in the chair and I urgently searched for a key – any key. A lady's handbag was on one edge of the table. I grabbed it, emptied the contents onto the metal surface, and found what I was looking for. I picked up the key and was halfway to the door when a thought struck me. I went back to the radio desk, pulled open the metal drawer and suddenly I was two-gun Adams. Good. It was time Matt took his turn as a heavy in this operation. I turned again to the door, just in time to see the female hijacker backing away.

'Hold it.' I levelled one of the guns and moved quickly towards her. I had the other automatic reversed as I reached her side, but I couldn't do it. Before Hong Kong I hadn't been conscious of any scruples about hitting a woman. But I had them now. My hand froze half way. I looked at her for several seconds, stuffed the spare gun into my belt and grabbed her roughly by the arm.

'Let's go.'

She came meekly enough, but not quietly. 'You are being stupid Captain Adams. You cannot stop what has already begun. You would be safer here.'

'Shut up.' I pushed her ahead of me, not sure what I was going to do with her. Matt expressed surprise but did not come up with any bright ideas. All he did was ask, 'Why are you bringing her along, Frank.'

'She could be useful,' I answered too quickly. I wasn't going to tell him I had chickened out. But unless I was prepared to hit the young lady over the head, there was no alternative but to take her with us. So it was settled.

I handed Matt the spare automatic and slipped the key into the padlock.

'What about those branches, Frank?'

I looked up. Against the backdrop of wet darkness, the Dak was an odd mixture of twisted shapes. It looked like some science-fiction insect with too many antennae.

'Most of the stuff will fall off when we start to move. Just have a quick look at the control surfaces but don't waste any time.'

I hoisted the girl into the aircraft and scrambled up behind her. Matt would also have to manage without the steps. I flicked the Dunhill and pushed the girl up the sloping fuselage to the cockpit. I located the master switch and turned on the rheostat-controlled panel lights. The dome light would be too bright and could be seen from outside so I left it alone. I grabbed one of the webbing straps from the luggage bay and tied the girl's wrists to an upright stanchion. It wouldn't hold her indefinitely – just long enough for us to get airborne. After that, she wouldn't be going anywhere.

I heard Matt call out. The automatic was in my hand as I hurried down the cabin, nerves on edge. Matt was standing outside the door.

'Sorry, Pappy. Can't make it.'

I stuffed the gun in my belt, relief flooding over me. I had forgotten about his injured shoulder which would not yet be strong enough to take his weight. I took hold of his good hand and pulled him aboard.

'Everything OK?'

He nodded.

'Right. Then let's get this bloody fire hazard into the air.'

That take-off is one I won't forget in a hurry. Matt primed both engines ready for a quick start-up. I wanted both motors turning within seconds of each other; the take-off would be a mad dash into the air with no preliminaries. The fat man and his cronies were less than seventy yards away – they would be on the job, shooting, in no time once they heard the noise. I gave Matt the nod. Number two engine started with a roar, but number one took its own sweet time. I counted the seconds, fifteen of them, before the engine suddenly decided to burst into life. Every second seemed an eternity. I could see people running from the huts as I switched on the landing lights; the aircraft lurched onto the runway and I pushed the throttles to full power.

The small windscreen wipers could not cope with the rain which was now falling heavily. Sheet lightning had joined the fray; the night equatorial storms were right on cue. One could set one's clock by them in these latitudes. With no flarepath to mark the limits of the airstrip, I had to rely on the landing lights in poor visibility on a bad surface. It was a nightmare. I couldn't set my gyro and follow it because I didn't know the exact magnetic bearing of the strip, so I had to rely on the proverbial mark one eyeball. The lightning was mostly a distraction, but in the last seconds of the take-off, it saved our lives. A distant flash from the south east outlined a bank of trees dead in our path at the same instant as I lifted the Dakota clear of the ground. I grabbed a bootful of left rudder, swung the wheel hard to port and pulled it back in my guts with all my strength.

'Gear up.' I almost screamed the command but I was too late. Matt had snatched at the lever without waiting to be told. There was a bump and the whole aircraft shuddered. I thought I had lost her, then slowly, excruciatingly, the old gooney bird stopped shaking and got on with the job she was born to. We were flying.

Matt's blue face was a sickly yellow as I turned to look in his direction. 'Thanks, Sunshine. Glad you were awake.'

He gave me a sick smile and reached quickly for the cigarettes – his hands were shaking. Mine gripped the control yoke so tightly that the knuckles shone white in the panel lights. I forced my fingers to relax slowly, then wiped my wet hands on my trouser legs.

The cigarette tasted very good. In twenty years of flying, that was the closest I had come to buying the farm. I had heard other pilots describe their close shaves as a time of reflection – a kind of 'what the hell am I doing here when I could be home in bed' syndrome. Me, I just felt stunned. It was several minutes before I could pull my mind back to reality. When I did, I saw we had already climbed through eight thousand feet, both engines still screaming at full take-off power. I eased back on the throttle and pitch levers, put the mixtures into auto-lean and set up a south-easterly course as I let the aircraft slowly settle back to seven thousand feet – our correct quadrantal height.

'Do you need the landing charts for Palembang, Frank?' Matt had pulled himself together and was thinking like a pilot again. I was relieved; I wanted him to take over for a while.

'Keep them handy, Matt. I'll let you know in a couple of minutes. Watch the office for me; I'm going back to have a chat with Lotus Blossom, or whatever her name is.'

The girl was tied where I had left her. She had made no attempt to struggle free and as I flicked on the dome light she stared at me impassively, as if she was bored to death. I unfastened the strap around her wrists and steered her into the main cabin towards a pair of facing seats. I gestured her into one of the heavily upholstered chairs and lowered myself into the other, keeping the automatic tucked in my belt in full view.

'Right young lady, you and I are going to have a heart to heart talk.' I tried to sound tough. Her almond eyes stared at me blankly. She had a pretty face, spoiled by an over-flat nose. Beneath her make-up I could discern one or two smallpox scars but they were not deep; she could not have had the disease too badly. I guessed her age at late twenties but I could have been flattering her by five years. It was impossible to tell.

'Here's the situation,' I said. 'Talk to me, now, and I'll drive this aeroplane straight to Djakarta, where you will be free to go. Play hard to get, I'll land at Palembang and turn you over to the army. I will naturally tell them General Sartono is dead.' I saw a flicker of life on her deadpan face – a chink in the inscrutable armour. I pressed home my small advantage. 'But don't try and sell me a bill of goods; if I think you're not being fair dinkum, I'll throw you to the wolves.'

A smile flitted briefly across her mouth. 'I understand, Captain, but there are things you should understand too. First, you cannot bargain with me for my life; I am under a blood oath which I took willingly, and which I will never break.' I mistook the light in her eyes for fanaticism, but the eyes were not burning; they were twinkling. For some reason, she found the situation amusing. I felt the beginnings of annoyance. She continued, lightly, 'However, my freedom would be useful so I will tell you certain things. But they will make no difference. I have already explained, you cannot stop what has begun.'

'You think that knowing the whereabouts of the hostages will make a difference, Captain. It won't. My people still control their destiny – their life or death. Any attempt at rescue will bring about their sudden demise, so the girl's father will not cancel our arrangement. The camp was well chosen. It can only be approached from the air; the jungle is impenetrable so a surprise attack is not possible. There is a radio installation, and now that you have taken such precipitate action, the only voice they will accept as genuine is my own.' She looked at me intently. 'Even you cannot return, Captain, without me to handle your radio communication. If any other aircraft attempts to land, the prince and princess will be murdered. So you see, there is nothing you can do. You should have stayed where you were. In three weeks' time everything will be settled. You would have been paid for your services; you were never meant to come to any harm.' She patted her long black hair into place – the natural gesture of a woman discussing nothing particularly serious. Her eyes were friendly. 'It is still not too late to turn back. I will explain your behaviour as an unfortunate impulse – and you will get your money. In the circumstances, it is a generous offer, I think you'll agree, particularly as you can do nothing else. If you continue this foolishness, the only loser will be you – a hundred thousand tax free dollars. Think about that for a moment, Captain Adams. It is a lot to give up – for no good reason.'

I did think about it. To be honest, I thought about it very hard despite my incredulity at the way the roles had been reversed. The Chinese woman had taken control and left me feeling helpless. And there was something else, something I had seen in the radio shack which compounded the feeling of helplessness. My mind refused to accept the evidence of my eyes, but sooner or later it would have to. I was only putting off the inevitable.

I reached for a cigarette in defeat; the simple movement brought me back to reality. The damned woman had me under her spell. I shook it off – *nothing* was foolproof, nothing.

I said sardonically, 'We're not going back. What is so important about three weeks' time?'

Surprise flashed briefly on her face. She tried another smile which didn't quite come off, then one of her hands lifted in resignation. 'You are a foolish man, Captain, but perhaps it is a foolishness I understand. There is nothing more zealous than a zealot.' This time the smile managed to make it. 'So be it. We are motivated by different things, you and I. Your reasons elude me, but no doubt they are noble in your own eyes. It is an impasse. What happens in three weeks' time will benefit a lot of people – it will inconvenience others. That is an inevitability of life which my race understands more readily than yours. It will not help if you know the details, on the other hand, it could do a great deal of harm. All I will tell you is that a certain ship is on the water, bound for a certain place. Its journey will not change the world, just a small part of it. To bring about that change, I would gladly die a thousand deaths. So you see, Captain there is nothing you can threaten me with.'

I stared at her. She *was* a fanatic, yet in some odd way, she didn't strike me as a radical. There was a sincerity in her quiet voice which disturbed me, but something was missing. I suddenly realized what it was.

I said, sarcastically, 'Since when has the League of the Lotus taken up noble causes?'

Her eyes widened. It was her turn to look surprised and the thought pleased me. She would not have expected me to identify the Tong by name. No doubt that was supposed to be their secret. She stared at me for several seconds before replying. I was feeling smug as I watched her grope for words, then suddenly, she took the wind right out of my sails.

'Is *that* who you think we are?' She pursed her lips. 'Ah! I think I understand now.'

I knew I was gaping. I pulled myself together. 'What are you handing me? Are you trying to pretend you're *not* with the League?'

'No, Captain Adams. I am not trying to pretend anything. But the League of the Lotus is a secret society, a Tong; they have nothing to do with us. Where did you get such an idea?'

'Where did I get such an idea?' I looked at her incredulously; this couldn't be happening. I heard myself saying angrily, 'Stop it. Of course you're with the League. This whole business is a League caper. It has been from the beginning.'

'No, Captain.' She was shaking her head. I could swear the expression in her eyes was sympathy.

I half rose in my seat, feeling angry to the point of explosion. If *she* was telling the truth, then there was something I had to have out with Matt – he was the one who had filled me with all that League stuff. The early doubts I had about my co-pilot were suddenly alive again, glaring at me. He had been clever, bloody clever. Well I would fix his wagon good and bloody proper.

I suddenly sat down again, my mind bringing me up with a jolt. I was going off half-cocked. It wasn't Matt who had introduced the League – all he had done was explain who they were. It was Chong Bee. I broke out in a cold sweat. It looked as though Arthur Hughes was right; Chong Bee had played me for a sucker from the word go. I had refused to believe it, despite the series of 'little inconsistencies' Hughes had referred to. Matt had assured me that they had only become significant under Hughes's prompting. I tried to remember what they were.

There had been the business of the teacups in the cabin of the *Kuching Laut*. According to Matt, that Chinese courtesy was inconsistent with the circumstances of Chong Bee's interview. And the fat man had used Chong Bee's full name – Chong Bee Ng. He had used it twice so it was no slip of the tongue. But it *was* a mark of high respect among Chinese. There were other things too, but I had dismissed them.

I could not deny that Chong Bee had survived thus far, despite the odds stacked against him, but I couldn't forget that the rescue of his family had been genuine enough, and I had seen the evidence of his stolen gold hoard. So there were arguments for and against Chong Bee. The scales had just tipped against him.

I looked hard at the young woman. She could be leading me up the garden path, but if she was, I couldn't see any logical reason for it. In fact, she had to be telling the truth. Hers was not the self interest of a mercenary but the dedication of a fanatic; this was inconsistent with the League's reputation.

I stood up. 'When we reach Djakarta, disappear. If you cross my path again, I'll kill you. I can't keep you prisoner without creating problems for myself so you are lucky. But take some good advice. Keep out of my way.' I closed the door behind me and re-entered the flight deck. Matt had the auto-pilot on and he sat looking at me expectantly. 'Forget Palembang. Get the charts for Kamayoran. Work out an ETA as soon as you can.'

'Djakarta?' He looked puzzled. 'Why not Singapore, Frank? We've got enough fuel; it would be a safer bet.'

'Djakarta, sonny boy, and don't argue. We wouldn't get away with that no-flight-plan lark a second time, and in any case, Singapore is no good to us. Use a civil call-sign and tell them we're from Medan or somewhere – they won't worry about a domestic arrival. We can park at the southern end so they won't wake up to the army paintwork until the morning. Now just be a good fellow and do what I tell you.'

'OK, Pappy.' He let the resentment die out of his eyes. 'It's your funeral.'

How nearly right he was!

Chapter Seventeen

I TOOK a taxi straight to my flat; a one-up one-down apartment in a row of wooden buildings owned by Hudy. Matt insisted on coming with me. On the way, he also insisted on making conversation. He kept the questions coming as I unlocked the front door, switched on the light and scanned the comfortable surroundings. I would have to leave most of my possessions behind, but there were some things I could take along – the world-band Sanyo radio, one or two ivory pieces and a pair of matched Balinese heads. I gathered the items together, set them on a cane coffee table, and ran upstairs to the bedroom. Matt followed me. I threw my suitcase on the bed and rummaged through drawers and cupboards. There were several items of clothing I was reluctant to leave, yet most of them were out of date. I had had a brief taste of less conservative attire. I packed mainly underwear and slacks, leaving my old-fashioned best blue suit hanging in the closet. Matt was prattling on, most of it going over my head as I searched through drawers. I turned suddenly.

'Haven't you got some packing to do? I suggest you go and do it.'

'Have you been listening to me, Frank?' He stood, feet apart, belligerent.

'Yes, I heard you. But in case you haven't got the message, we're getting the hell out of here. Why don't we talk later?'

'Because later won't do Pappy. We'll talk now.' I had returned to my packing with a gesture of dismissal. Matt's tone brought me up abruptly. I turned to face him – it was Superintendent Matt standing there, his face grim, eyes blazing. He said softly, 'We'll talk now, Frank.'

I stared at him, ready to put him in his place, but I didn't do it. I could sense a crisis. I sat on the edge of the bed and reached deliberately for a cigarette. 'OK, Sherlock. Get it off your chest.'

My placating tone was wasted on him. Matt still had fire in his eyes. 'Alright, Pappy. Then let me begin by saying I don't like being taken for a bloody ride.' My eyebrows raised involuntarily, but that only seemed to antagonize him. His jaw set hard. 'We came into this business apparently by accident, but since then you have been leading me in any direction that suited you. I went along with you because I believed you thought the fat man was a drug merchant and because I don't like drugs either. Then, when you thought they were after the OPEC plane I went along with that too because we couldn't be *sure* OPEC was the target. Your ASIO background came as a bit of a shock, but no real surprise, and when we left Singapore to catch that Boeing, I could still sympathize with your motives. But I don't know what your motives are, and I realize I never did know. The kidnapping obviously didn't move you. If it had, you'd have made a sincere effort to rescue those two people. We each had a gun by then, and that girl was our prisoner. So we had a good chance of pulling it off, but you never even made the effort. Then the girl tells you she's not with a Tong and you get all uptight about that, and to cap it off, you let the bitch go.'

Matt's anger gathered momentum. I

didn't butt in – didn't even try to stop him. In a way, I had it coming. Not from the beginning, as Matt was suggesting, but certainly since leaving the oil camp. I had seen something in that radio shack which had made my guts turn over; its significance hit me like a slap in the mouth. I could not ignore it yet I had still refused to admit it. Slowly I had come to accept it, but I had not given Matt so much as a hint. And because I had not been entirely honest with him, I could hardly begrudge him this angry outburst. But if Matt thought he was being taken for a ride, he should have looked harder in my direction where he would have seen the sucker of the century. Strangely, I was not angry. There is something beautiful about the way professionals work – even if it was a ruthless bunch of bastards who had planned this operation. If it had been me behind a desk thousands of miles away, working out the details, I too would have made use of whatever was offering. And if I had needed a pilot, I would have made the same choice.

Matt was still talking. 'The Chong Bee

operation was straightforward. We should have left it at that and taken our money, regardless of whether or not your Mr Hughes thinks Chong Bee is on the level. But that didn't suit you, and the only reason which makes sense to me is that you are not ex-ASIO; you're ASIO *now* and have been all along.' Matt was still spitting his words. 'I can understand a man doing his job. You have the right to take off in any direction you like if it's for something you believe in. But you took me along with you, Frank. You had no right to do that.'

'Have you finished?' Matt was staring at me defiantly. I ground my cigarette butt into the floor and stood up. 'OK, I admit I haven't been entirely honest with you, but you are dead wrong about other things. I am not an agent – for ASIO or anyone else; I'm just a dumb airframe driver the same as you. But I used to be an ASIO man and I have to apologize to you for that because if it weren't for that fact, we would never have become involved in this bloody caper.' I returned to the bed and sat on it. 'I made a mistake a long time ago, Matt. I foolishly hoped that by going after the fat man, I could put things right with myself. I say foolishly, because I am no longer sure the fat man is the one I am after. Not that my high-flown motives were necessary to the operation. If I hadn't contacted ASIO, they would have contacted me.'

Matt's eyes were still hot, but now they looked interested. 'Are you suggesting what I think you are?'

'Unfortunately, yes. When I was in that radio shack I happened to glance at the log. The writing was in Chinese, all except the date-time-groups and the call-signs.' I reached for another smoke. Matt took one too. I said quietly, 'There were things I was trained never to forget. Two messages were sent from that radio to a call-sign I know as well as my own name – the main ASIO communications centre in Melbourne.' I stared hard at my co-pilot. 'I couldn't figure it at first. I told myself that my country would never become involved with an international criminal operation. That was strictly CIA territory.' I smiled, deprecatingly. 'But after my chat with Lotus Blossom I began to understand. Australia might not sanction international crime, but it could very easily become involved in a political "adventure". I suspect the girl and the fat man are involved in some sort of coup which Australia would like to see succeed, but which they cannot approve of publicly. Hence this operation. The way ASIO works, they would know the last time I had a tooth filled, despite it being ten years since I left them. So knowing my whereabouts is what probably prompted them to play it the way they did. They would have checked you out quickly and decided you were OK too.'

'You mean ASIO planned it from the beginning?'

'That's exactly what I mean. And they are still in control. Don't look so surprised, Matt. It was you who first suggested there was a pro-organization behind it.'

'What are you going to do?'

'Let them bloody well get on with it, *without* our help. They had it all worked out nicely. If I hadn't contacted them, then the beautiful Liz Manifold would have contacted me – would probably have appealed to my sense of patriotism. But I spilled my guts about my reasons for wanting to help, and she didn't have to lift a finger. No wonder she was so willing to assist with Woo Tang's boat; she had me on toast and wanted to keep me that way.'

Matt stroked his jaw. 'That's right; I had forgotten about Woo Tang. Where does he fit in?'

'I don't know. In fact there's a few things I don't know, but I suspect that if we ask him nicely, Chong Bee will have some answers.' I stood up abruptly. 'Now, go and get packed and we'll see if Chong Bee is waiting on our island. In case you've forgotten, that podgy bastard owes us some money. I think it's time to collect.'

'Alright, Frank.' Matt wore a worried expression. 'I hope you have been honest with me this time, because if you haven't . . .'

I looked at him sharply. 'If I haven't, then I've been fooling myself as well. I've told you more than I should because I didn't want you to think you were the only dumb bastard in this crew. We've both been taken for a ride, but the ride's over. From now on we look after ourselves. I'm disappointed about the lovely Liz – I had plans for her. But she's the *only* thing I'm going to lose out of this caper. Go and grab your bits and pieces and we'll get going. A two hours' ride in Charlie Delta and we can start feeling rich.'

I snapped the suitcase shut and followed Matt down the stairs. Standing near the coffee table, idly handling one of my ivory knick-knacks, was Sangeron. Another man stood just inside the door, holding a sub-machine gun.

'Good evening, Captain.' The GUD man's sibilant voice cut the air like a knife. His eyes fell on the suitcase. 'You weren't thinking of leaving us were you?' He snapped his fingers and the man near the door moved forward a pace, bringing the gun to bear. Sangeron pointed to the automatic tucked in my belt. 'You'd better give me that, Captain. Yours too Mr Duncan. They don't like it down at headquarters if I put armed men in the cells. It upsets the other prisoners.'

I pulled the gun gingerly from my waist, holding the weapon with two fingers as I set it down on the coffee table, and stood back. I didn't want to give Sangeron's assistant any excuse to go berserk; the expression in his eyes said it wouldn't take much. Matt's gun clattered onto the table next to mine.

'Good.' Sangeron picked up the two weapons and balanced them in his hands. 'We will go.'

'Are we under arrest? If so, what's the charge?' It's difficult to sound innocent when you've just been found in illegal possession of firearms, but I did manage to sound righteously indignant. More to the point, I left Sangeron's policeman image intact. Sooner or later his intelligence identity would evolve, but I wanted *him* to be the one to disclose it. The machine gun in the hands of his companion was a broad hint; an SMG is not a normal police weapon, but I preferred to be naïve. I probably wasn't fooling the GUD man for a moment, but the game had certain rules.

Sangeron raised an eyebrow in feigned amusement. 'The charge, Captain? When the list is complete, I think we could legally hang you half a dozen times. It's a pity we can only do it once.' He gestured towards the open front door. 'Please.'

'I would prefer to talk here if you don't mind.' At the sound of Matt's voice I turned quickly. He had sat himself down in a cane armchair and was nonchalantly lighting a cigarette. I tried unsuccessfully to stifle my amazement. The expression on Sangeron's face was comical. Matt continued, confidently: 'Ask your goon with the gun to wait outside, Mr Sangeron; I don't think you would want him to hear this.'

Sangeron's face was something to see. He was fighting a battle between incredulity and doubt. Matt leisurely reached for an ashtray; the directness of his gaze would have intimidated an archbishop. He said quietly, 'Patrice Lumumba will still be there when we've finished talking, Mr Sangeron.'

That did it. Sangeron's eyes widened briefly, then he turned to his assistant and instructed him in Indonesian to wait outside the door, but to remain alert.

Seven hundred Patrice Lumumba was the head office of the Indonesian immigration service. That was what the sign over the front door said, but the rear half of the brownstone building was where the GUD had its headquarters. Matt had thrown the ball straight at Sangeron. The Indonesian closed the front door behind his assistant and sat himself in the other armchair. This left me the settee. I crossed to it and sat down, looking from Matt to Sangeron. His expression said he thought Matt was bluffing. I *knew* he was bluffing, but in a game of seven card stud with a pair of aces showing, it takes a very good poker player to raise the ante. Sangeron wasn't that good. He leaned forward in his chair and peered intently at my co-pilot.

'Very well, Mr Duncan.'

Matt puffed leisurely at the cigarette, his eyes still boring into the Indonesian. 'I don't want you to make a fool of yourself Mr Sangeron. At the moment, this is just between you and us. Once you book us in down town, it becomes official. You would not only lose control of the situation; you would preclude any further possibility of us working together. Not to mention the embarrassment you would cause.'

I could not believe what I was hearing – and seeing. Matt sat there with all the assurance of the chairman of the board, completely in control. He must have been a very good policeman indeed, and I suddenly got an inkling of what was happening. Matt was using his police experience to out-manoeuvre another policeman, and the psychology was working very well. Sangeron looked off-balance for a moment, then seemed to regain some of his composure. He glanced in my direction and I did my best to match Matt's enigmatic expression.

Sangeron said slowly, 'You had better be a little more explicit Mr Duncan, and I warn you, do not waste my time. Also, do not try my patience with lies. The passengers from the hijacked Garuda flight are back in Djakarta, and they have been interrogated. I *know* you were both involved in that hijacking. Whatever you say, you will not avoid facing charges under the Terrorism Act.'

'Then you will face the same charges, Mr Sangeron.' Matt was smiling thinly. The Indonesian's eyes widened and mine must have done the same; I didn't know what the hell Matt was talking about either. He ground his cigarette into the ashtray with exaggerated slowness, then gazed innocuously at Sangeron. 'We both work for the same man.' Sangeron's eyes flashed disbelief. Matt said, matter-of-factly, 'Captain Adams won't mind if you use his telephone – the number is 55–8850, but I'm sure you carry those figures in your head too. However, I must ask you to be discreet, particularly if you are going to disturb the Minister at this time of night. And don't mention names – the phrase *burong utara* will identify me.'

'Son-of-a-bitch.' The Americanism had become an unconscious conscious part of my vocabulary. There were times when it was exactly the right combination of words. Matt smiled at me gently.

'Sorry, Pappy. Just one of those things.'

I stared at him. *Burong utara* –

northern bird – it suited him. It also explained how he had acquired that elusive Indonesian pilot licence on his limited experience. It explained a lot of other things too – like Matt's willingness to tag along on this whole adventure when a lesser man might have cried off long before.

Sangeron was on his feet and had crossed to the phone. The instrument was in his left hand, the fingers of his right hand hovering over the dial, hesitating. He suddenly returned the handset to its cradle and turned abruptly. 'I do not need to disturb the Minister. If you were not telling the truth, you could not possibly know so much. I accept what you say on face value.' He threw in that last sentence with the air of a man doing a big favour, trying to retain some dignity and authority. But I could see Sangeron was badly shaken.

'Very well.' The friendly, bantering tone was gone from Matt's voice. He sounded crisp, businesslike. 'Then perhaps you would answer some questions for us. As you might realize, we were in on the actual hijacking, but our knowledge stops there. We escaped from the kidnappers' hideout knowing its whereabouts and the identity of the victims, but we do not know what ransom has been demanded, or where it is to be paid. I would like that information.'

A deprecating smile crossed Sangeron's face. 'So would I, Mr Duncan. It is one of the first things I was going to ask you.'

'But there must be something by now; it's more than twenty-four hours since the kidnapping. In any case, I understand Orinassus has agreed to settle.'

'I understand the same thing, but no one knows the details. The Greek has refused to discuss the matter with anyone – police or press. All he will say is that he is co-operating and that the safe return of his daughter and the prince comes before any other consideration. He will not even disclose where the demand came from, or from whom, and he absolutely refuses to discuss anything about the ransom, except that it will be paid. According to the brief press reports, the old man is very frightened.'

Matt turned to me and said scornfully, 'Lotus Blossom could have told us, couldn't she?'

'Lotus Blossom?' Sangeron was looking from me to Matt.

'One of the hijackers – a woman. I was careless and she escaped,' I lied.

'Where? Here, in Djakarta?'

I nodded.

Sangeron indulged a satisfied smile. 'Then I will find her.' He glanced from one to the other. 'I presume she is Chinese. Do you happen to know her real name?' Matt shook his head; I did the same. Sangeron continued, 'You were leaving. May I ask where you were going?'

'No.' Matt's voice sounded harsh. 'But if you can arrest the Chinese woman, do so. Use whatever interrogation methods you need, but get the information from her. I will be in touch. Do you have a private number?'

Sangeron tore a page from his notebook, wrote a number and handed it to Matt. 'This will only be answered by myself.' The Indonesian looked earnestly at my co-pilot. 'The army is preparing to mount a search; they know General Sartono is dead. Would you like them to be dissuaded?'

Matt hesitated for a moment, then shook his head. 'No. Let them beat around the jungle and make a noise; it will keep them occupied. Besides, after our escape, the kidnappers will be expecting some sort of activity. If they've got a man in Palembang he can tell them what's going on. It will make them feel safer if they think the army has to search for the location.'

That didn't make sense to me. The fat man was no fool; he would know that Matt and I could find the place again, which meant we could just as easily pinpoint the location for the army. But Matt had the ball. Whatever he was up to eluded me for the moment, but at least he had neatly disposed of Sangeron as a threat. I wondered briefly whether he was substituting the frying pan for the fire, but I dismissed the thought. I could handle Matt.

Sangeron had moved to the door, his hand on the knob. He said suddenly

'That other young lady, the one who accompanied us to Singapore, Miss Manifold. Can I now assume she is still working with you?'

'Yes.' I felt my guts turn over as I blurted it out. Liz was back in Australia. What did Sangeron have to do with her?

I unconsciously knew the answer even before Sangeron said, 'Very well, I will send her to you.' He caught my foolish stare and said lightly, 'I dispatched a signal from my embassy in Singapore. She was arrested boarding a Qantas jet for Sydney last night.' He stared briefly at Matt. 'I will be hearing from you then, Mr Duncan.' Sangeron opened the door and stepped into the night.

'Alright, Sunshine. Give.' I had closed the door behind Sangeron and was standing with my back to it. Matt had shed his air of authority; he looked self-conscious.

'Cigarette, Frank?' He offered the packet.

'I don't need a dummy to suck, sport. What I want is some straight talking. You bastard; you fooled me with that "holier than thou" routine upstairs and all the time you're a spy for the Indonesians.'

'Only a palace spy, Frank. Don't take it to heart.'

'What do you mean, a palace spy? What are you talking about.'

Matt had risen to his feet before Sangeron left. He now returned to the chair and dropped into it, a resigned expression on his face. He crossed his legs and puffed hastily at his cigarette.

'Let me start at the beginning, Frank. I've already mentioned the confrontasi business, and how that kept me busy for a number of years. Well, after Sukarno died, there was a complete about-face. Singapore broke away from Malaysia and because the Malay race has always mistrusted the commercial expertise of the Chinese, the Malays and Indonesians – a common people with an almost common language – decided that co-operation was the order of the day. With the Chinese bastion of Singapore stuck right in their midst so to speak, the two countries decided there was strength in unity. So they began peeing in each other's pockets, at all levels.' Matt cleared his throat. ‘I came to Djakarta in ’68 as part of a government delegation hell-bent on showing the Indonesians how keen we were to co-operate. The man I had most to do with was Tuan Hamid Pahan, Minister of the Interior.’ Matt’s eyes peered darkly from his blue face. ‘Tuan Hamid and I hit it off pretty well. I spent a long weekend at his hill cottage near Bandung, and met his family.’ He shifted uncomfortably in his chair. ‘To cut a long story short, Pappy, I married his daughter.’

‘Christ!’ I took a step forward, involuntarily. ‘I didn’t know you were married.’

‘I’m not. Eisah died of cerebral malaria four years ago, at Ipoh. There were no kids, thank God, and after a while I managed to pick up the pieces. Not long after that I got the golden handshake from Special Branch and learned to fly.’ Matt smiled thinly. ‘As you know Pappy, flying jobs don’t grow on trees, especially for a new chum at my age. I bummed around for a while trying to grab hours, but it was a rat race. I knew there was flying work in

Indonesia, but getting a licence here is like trying to crack Fort Knox. I put it off as long as I could, but finally I swallowed my pride and wrote to Tuan Hamid. I got a letter back almost immediately. Of course he would help. If I came to Djakarta he would fix things up. He was true to his word – but there were strings attached.' Matt forced another smile. 'It seems that the flying profession in this country attracts all kinds of unsavoury types – CIA men, ASIO, et cetera. Tuan Hamid asked me to keep my eyes and ears open and to pass on little snippets to him. Nothing official of course – as my father-in-law he was only too glad to help me further my career. But if I could return the favour from time to time . . . You've got the picture Frank. That's what I mean when I said I was a palace spy. *Burong utara* was a sort of joke – Eisah used to call me her little bird from the north. The old man latched on to it, that's all.'

'Son-of-a-bitch.' Matt wasn't the only one who suffered from a limited vocabulary at times. I reached for a cigarette and heard the sound of a car pulling up outside. I crossed quickly to the door and opened it onto the street. Standing in the pool of light from the open doorway was Liz.

Chapter Eighteen

SHE looked pale and drawn. One half of me wanted to throw my arms around her, but the bitter half prevailed. I couldn't forget that she had used me, and had held out an emotional promise as bait. A promise she never intended to keep.

'Hello, Frank.' Her voice was soft, but her eyes couldn't quite meet mine.

'Hello, Liz. Come in.'

She glanced around the room, taking in the packed suitcase and the two automatics lying on the coffee table alongside my hastily assembled mementoes. Matt eyed her coldly and I saw the greeting freeze on her lips. She turned back in my direction.

'What's been happening, Frank?

Sangeron arrived back from Singapore this morning and has given me no peace. Then suddenly, he puts me in a car and sends me to you.'

'Don't worry about it, Liz. The kidnapping went off OK. I'm sure that's all you really care about.'

A grim smile played around the corners of her mouth. 'My, but we've grown cynical. And Matt looks as though his pet rabbit has died.' She turned on him abruptly. 'What was it Matt, myxomatosis?'

'Disappointment, I'd say. Wouldn't you, Pappy?'

'Indubitably.' I was caught halfway between Liz's attempt to ease the tension and Matt's firm admonishment. Liz had been through the mill; there was no doubt about that. She still managed to look beautiful, but the gauntness and the dark shadows under the eyes evoked a sympathy I couldn't really spare. She turned her big brown eyes on me.

'Have you got a cigarette, Frank?' I lit one for her and she sat on the edge of the settee.

'Don't get too comfortable. We're

leaving in a minute. You can come or stay – suit yourself.'

'What is it, Frank? Do you think I planned this operation?'

'You went along with it.'

'Of course I did; that's my job.' She was looking at me oddly. 'But there were some things that were all my own idea.' Her brown eyes were working overtime. 'How did you find out . . .?' Her forehead creased suddenly in concern. 'And what are you and Matt doing here? It can't be over yet.'

'It isn't. As far as we know it's only just begun, but that's got nothing to do with us. Not anymore it hasn't. As for how we found out – you should have instructed your Chinese playmates not to leave the ASIO call-sign lying around where people could see it.'

Liz was looking at me strangely. She said, finally, 'Alright, Frank, so the old firm's in this up to its neck. Wouldn't you like to know why?'

'What for? So you can con me again? I think I'd rather leave things as they are if you don't mind.' I was very interested to know, but Liz would tell me anyway –

on my terms though, not hers.

'Nobody conned you, Frank. It was a straightforward business proposition.'

'Straightforward? Christ! If this is how ASIO does things in a straightforward way I'd hate them to get devious.'

I was conscious of Matt watching us, an amused expression on his face. Liz followed my gaze and said suddenly, 'Do you think I could talk to you alone for a couple of minutes, Frank?'

I was about to protest but Matt said laconically, 'Go ahead, Pappy. I've got to pack anyway.' He stood up. 'Besides, it's better if I don't hear things which I might feel obliged to pass on if friend Sangeron applies the pressure.'

I looked at Matt sharply and he said. 'I give him another couple of hours at the most, then he'll be on the phone to Tuan Hamid no matter what time it is. Sangeron's the worrying type, but so is the Minister. He won't back me at the expense of his own position.' Matt grinned wickedly. 'It's time I left this country anyway; I have what I came for – experience. Besides, there's no future in a place where you can't trust your own father-in-law.' He stepped through the front door and turned left towards his own apartment further along the block. Liz was staring at me, uncomprehending.

I said, 'He's done a little freelance work for the Indonesians.'

'I see. Is that why Sangeron let me go?'

'Yes.'

'And does he know . . . things?'

'Some. But not enough to satisfy him. The army is busy searching for the hideout. If they find it, I think they'll go in boots and all, and to hell with the hostages.'

'Damn.' Liz stood up and paced the floor. 'We can't let things fall apart now – not when they are so near completion.'

I said sarcastically, 'I wouldn't say it was that close. A lot can happen in three weeks.'

She stopped and turned abruptly. The hard lines of her face came as something of a shock. 'Just how much *do* you know, Frank? Perhaps you can tell me how the army found out General Sartono is dead.'

'Sangeron told them, I suppose. I'm afraid it was me who told Sangeron.'

Liz helped herself to a cigarette from the packet lying on the coffee table. I extended my lighter and she drew in deeply. There was a trace of bitterness in her voice. 'We've played this badly, haven't we?' I said nothing. She continued, 'You should have been put in the picture before this. You might not have helped, but I don't think you would have deliberately gotten in our way either. Now it's probably too late.'

The troubled expression on Liz's face bothered me. I knew she had used me – would do it again given half a chance, yet the feelings this woman had awakened could not be ignored. I said softly, almost sociably, 'If you're worried about the army, I wouldn't. A ground search would be useless and they'd need the resources of the United States Air Force to find the place from the air in the time available. Unless someone flew right overhead they would miss it completely.' I realized why Matt was against withdrawing the army from the search. If he was expecting trouble from

Sangeron, it could have made the Indonesian smell a rat a little sooner. Matt reckoned we had a couple of hours; it was little enough time. Hopefully, Sangeron's attention would be elsewhere for the moment – looking for Lotus Blossom.

The expression in Liz's eyes changed abruptly. She said, suddenly, 'Could *you* find the place again, Frank?' She was looking at me intently.

'I could – but I'm not going to. I told you, leave me out of it.'

A hand strayed unconsciously to her brown hair and she sat hesitantly on the edge of the settee. She patted the brightly-coloured upholstery. 'Sit down please, Frank.' Her eyes were pleading. I hesitated for a moment, then crossed to the chair Matt had recently vacated. Liz looked at me gratefully. 'Thank you. There are things I want to tell you. But I promise not to ask you any favours. If you decide to go back to the oil camp, it will be your own decision – no coercion – except that you will be on the same rates of pay.' She smiled. 'Is that being fair?'

'Go on.'

She settled herself more comfortably on the settee. 'Firstly, ASIO did not initiate this operation, but by a fortunate coincidence we have been able to take control, and thereby guarantee that it will fail.'

'What are you talking about?' I had been prepared for a patriotic appeal to my better nature. Liz's matter-of-fact statement that it was just another ASIO double-cross shouldn't have surprised me, but it did. I hadn't figured things that way at all.

'I'm talking about something which would not be in anyone's interests if it succeeded – except maybe a handful of Chinese anarchists. The Chinese have had the best of these countries out here for well over a hundred years. They grew fat on the native population and dislike having to take a back seat.'

'Save the lecture, Liz. I know the scene. You were talking about anarchists. That's a strange word to apply to Chinese these days – I thought they died out with Sun Yat Sen.'

'Now who's lecturing?' Liz smiled

thinly. 'Alright, we'll call them colonists, then, for want of a better word. The point is, a group of these people who are disenchanted with the regime in independent New Guinea are planning to seize a small island off Papua and go into business for themselves – a kind of miniature Singapore.'

I helped myself to a cigarette and took my time lighting it. I said through the smoke, 'Then why is ASIO getting its balls in a knot? The poor buggers have to go somewhere. From what I've heard, Taiwan isn't much better than Red China – just different. Some of the islands off Papua are uninhabited, so where's the harm? I think it's a bloody good idea, in fact.'

'So you're a philosopher as well as a scholar?' Liz was looking at me with an amused expression on her face. 'It's not quite that simple. To begin with, the territory belongs to New Guinea, but leaving rightful ownership aside, it so happens that the island they have chosen is mineral rich – including uranium . . .'

'Ah. That explains *our* interest then. Can't let anyone jeopardize our uranium markets can we? Especially if we have to compete with *Chinese* businessmen instead of a few naïve fuzzy wuzzies.' I drew angrily on my cigarette and said scornfully, 'It's a bloody good job you *didn't* put me in the picture earlier. I'd have been tempted to warn the fat man you were trying to stuff him up.'

Liz raised her eyebrows. 'Now who's being naïve? If they get away with this, they have three hundred million blood brothers to the north ready to back them up – or do you think the yellow peril is a myth?'

'I think it's exaggerated to hell. Anyway, finish your story.'

Liz tried not to look exasperated, but she didn't quite succeed. 'Then let's stop arguing the rights and wrongs. The dissidents have the backing of a group of Melbourne Chinese who, no doubt with huge profits in mind, agreed to finance the operation. Being businessmen first they decided to hire professionals. An emissary went to Surabaja to negotiate with the League of the Lotus . . .'

'Woo Tang Sim . . .'

Liz smiled softly. 'Yes, Tang Sim

who, in addition to being the Tong chief executive in Indonesia, is also an ASIO sleeper.' Judging by the satisfied look on Liz's face, she expected a reaction. I disappointed her; I wasn't that surprised. ASIO had a network of people scattered throughout the Far East, and the Chinese were a good bet in countries like Indonesia. Their second-class citizen status made them already feel betrayed, so it was usually an easy recruitment, particularly for Australia which could offer immigration privileges as a final reward. No doubt Woo Tang Sim had this thought in mind when he informed ASIO of the plot. To many disestablished Chinese, Australia offered the kind of new start which had attracted so many European immigrants to the United States at the turn of the century. But immigration to Down Under was difficult these days for anybody, and for a Chinese, almost impossible. I could appreciate Woo Tang Sim's reasoning.

I said derisively, 'So you let the operation go ahead with a built-in doublecross. Why not just arrest the Melbourne Chinese?' I used a Matt-type gesture and stroked my jaw. 'No, that wouldn't do, would it? Cut the cancer out at its source is the ASIO way.' I looked at her speculatively. 'Are you *sure* Fleming isn't running this binge?'

'As far as you're concerned Frank, I'm running it. Even Hughes in Singapore doesn't know what's going on.' My eyebrows raised involuntarily. That little snippet *did* surprise me. Liz noticed the expression. 'Arthur Hughes has to appear clean. The prince was under ASIO protection and Arthur will no doubt be running around in circles at the moment, which is what we want. He is not a good enough actor to be in on the operation. In the meantime, his best efforts will be convincing and there's no harm in him pulling the other way. He won't find out anything.'

My expression had gone hard. 'That's not the only reason, is it?' As Liz gazed at me innocuously, I spat, 'Now I know why Matt and I were led into this by the nose. Just a couple of bum pilots out for a quick buck – nothing to tie us in with the old firm. Meanwhile, ASIO is co-operating madly with everyone in sight to rescue the poor prince and princess. And if anything goes wrong, me and Matt go for the high jump and ASIO comes out smelling like a rose. They never heard of Frank Adams and Matt Duncan. It's fucking marvellous.'

Liz's eyes had clouded over. Her expression was almost wistful and her voice had become very soft. 'You're not the only one in the firing line, Frank, except that I came into it with my eyes open. I knew the risks before I volunteered.'

'You? What are you handing me? The company will back you to the hilt . . . No! It won't be like that will it? It was never like that . . .' I was thinking now – thinking good. If ASIO were taking these kind of precautions, they wouldn't be using a known agent. And if Liz had been resident in Surabaja for the past two years, she would be on someone's file in Indonesia – Sangeron's most likely. Yet I was sure he didn't know her identity, and that made no sense either.

I said, suddenly more kindly, 'What did you tell Arthur Hughes, Liz? Let me guess – on no account to contact

Sangeron, and if the Indonesian contacted him, to deny any knowledge of the three of us. No wonder the bastard was waiting to arrest us back here, and why he had you pulled off that Qantas plane.' I was smiling grimly. I remembered something. 'But you gave Sangeron a phone number – I thought at the time it was for the office.'

'That's what you were supposed to think,' she said, self-consciously. 'Having Sangeron along could have proved embarrassing, then I realized I could turn it to advantage. I knew you would tell him certain things. That couldn't be helped. But I also knew you would never mention the ASIO connection, although you possibly expected me to do so at some time. So I gave him the first number that came into my head – a girlfriend's flat in Melbourne.'

I laughed involuntarily. 'You're good, Liz. Bloody good. You convinced me at the same time that Singapore was where the action was. What else did you tell Hughes? To get me and Matt onto that Garuda flight come hell or high water?'

'Yes. And also to kill an hour talking

to Matt. That way, Arthur couldn't spend too much time with you. Hughes is no fool. He might have picked something up from you.'

I gazed at her with frank admiration. Despite being the meat in the sandwhich, I couldn't help admiring the way she had done her job. I said lightly, 'Your two years in Surabaja – how long was it really?'

'Not quite two weeks. The flat belongs to Tang Sim – so does the travel agency.'

This time I laughed out loud. But it was a bitter laugh. 'Boy! Did you take me in.'

Liz turned her brown eyes on me. 'It wasn't all a line, Frank.'

I looked up sharply. 'What's this. More of that "there'll be other nights" routine. Cut it out, Liz. I've been that trip and the cure isn't easy.'

'There is no cure, Frank.'

I turned away. What was the damned woman trying to do, turn my insides to butter? It would have been the easiest thing in the world to respond to her. But for what? Another journey through the meat grinder? Liz was a professional, and would go to any lengths.

Her voice came from a long way off. 'I've levelled with you this time. I haven't held anything back.'

I turned to face her. 'No . . . You've even told me how you are in as much danger as me and Matt. Well, in that case you can do the same as we're doing and get the hell out of here. I'm not going back to that oil camp – not for you *or* your big brown eyes.'

I heard the sound of a car pulling up at the front door. Liz and I exchanged worried glances and I had one of the two automatics in my hand as the door opened and Matt stood there.

'I got us a taxi, Pappy. I recommend we don't waste any time.'

I let out a slow breath and tucked the gun inside my shirt. Matt picked up the other weapon from the coffee table and hid it in his waistband.

I turned to Liz. 'Coming?' She nodded slowly and stood up. I grabbed my suitcase in one hand and my expensive radio in the other. Matt grabbed up my curios and we went outside to the car.

The taxi bumped and swayed along the badly lighted streets, Liz sandwiched between Matt and me in the back seat.

'Where are we going?' Her voice sounded unconcerned, disinterested almost.

'To see a certain Chinaman who owes us some money. I hope he also has some answers.

'Chong Bee?'

My head snapped in her direction, but in the unlighted car I couldn't see her face. I said deliberately, 'What do you know about Chong Bee, Liz? I don't think I ever spoke his name. Did you, Matt?'

'No, Pappy. Not at any time.' There was an edge to Matt's voice.

Liz said quietly, 'Why do you think Arthur Hughes spent so much time talking to you about Chinese habits and customs, Matt? It would hardly be the topic uppermost in his mind with everything else that was happening.'

I said, incredulously, '*You* put him up to it?'

'Yes. But not for the reason you're probably thinking. I was trying to warn you in an oblique way. It also provided an excuse for Hughes to keep Matt talking.' A note of resignation crept into her voice. 'I couldn't say anything outright; it would have led to too many unanswerable questions at the time. Now it doesn't matter. I wanted to put you on your guard with Chong Bee. He is a high-ranking member of the League of the Lotus.'

I sat stunned for several seconds, conscious of Matt's heavy breathing too. I had been expecting something after the parting conversation with Hughes, but not that. I found my voice. 'Are you sure?'

'Absolutely. I wanted to warn you, but you'll realize why I couldn't. Tang Sim must have become suspicious; I'm sure that was why we had our unwelcome visitor on the *Sea Cat*. He was for real. The previous tail was a put-up job for your benefit.'

'So that was why you wanted me to collect your gear from the flat. You were afraid Woo Tang wasn't playing any more. Why? Did you think he'd pulled a double-cross?'

'No. Just looking after Tong interests I'd say. The afternoon I went to pick up the boat – while you were away rescuing your Chinaman and his family – I found Woo Tang in a highly nervous state. I asked him whether something had gone wrong with the operation. He said no, that it was Tong business. A large amount of League funds were missing. The name "Chong Bee" was mentioned, in passing, as the Tong treasurer and I put two and two together.'

'Son-of-a-bitch!' I scrambled through my pockets for a cigarette. 'But Woo Tang never mentioned Chong Bee during our interview. Yet he must have known I had disappeared with Chong Bee during the night. He could have met the plane at Juanda when we landed.'

Liz said quietly, 'I don't think Tang Sim suspected Chong Bee at all. It was Chong Bee who reported the robbery, and you're forgetting something. As fellow Tong members, it was the job of both of them to deceive you. Chong Bee could have justified most of his actions in that way.'

Matt butted in. 'You're going to have

to explain a lot of this to me, Pappy. You lost me ten minutes ago.' A match flared as he lit a cigarette.

I could sympathize with him; I wasn't feeling over-informed myself. I said slowly, 'Woo Tang only talked to me about double-crossing the fat man, Matt – not about Chong Bee. Seems our frightened friend is one hell of a good actor as well as a thief. I think he's conned us from the word go – maybe even dating back to before Ling Ma was killed.' I suppressed the anger that had risen within me and went on, 'I'll explain it when I understand it myself, Matt. Right now I'm thinking about a certain winding road near Ambon – a road just made for ambush.'

During the last ten of the forty-five minutes it took to drive to the airport, Liz had skilfully steered the conversation back to the kidnapping. She hadn't asked in so many words, but I knew she was hoping Matt and I would go back and finish the job. *After* we had talked to Chong Bee. I don't think she was under any illusions about which came first on my list of priorities.

The final touches of the ASIO plan were as simple and well thought-out as the rest had been. The ransom demanded of Avis Orinassus was a ship and a small supply of arms. The vessel would embark two hundred Chinese at Port Moresby and transport them to their island. When they were safely ashore, Melbourne would signal to the oil camp. Matt and myself were then supposed to fly the hostages and kidnappers direct to the island where the hostages would be put on board the ship and sent on their merry way. That was the original plan; the ASIO version was slightly different.

The ship would be intercepted at sea and the Greek crew replaced by ASIO personnel who would also take possession of the arms. The Chinese would be allowed to embark and once at sea, the original Greek crew would be returned to the ship. After that, it would be anybody's guess which country would accept the Chinese passengers as immigrants; they would not be allowed to return to Port Moresby. The New Guinea Government, with considerable

Australian help, would be rid of the troublemakers once and for all. The 'safely ashore' signal would be sent from Melbourne, but the reception awaiting the kidnappers on the island would not be quite what they expected. It was neat and tidy, and I could see Liz's point. Without someone to fly everybody out of the oil camp when the time came, the victims' lives could be in very real danger. I hadn't said as much to Liz, but I was prepared to reconsider my decision about going back. My attitude had softened towards her; I was more than grateful for the information she had supplied about Chong Bee. And *he* was one little bastard I wanted to see in a hurry. I looked forward to the meeting with sweet anticipation. I caught myself unconsciously patting the gun at my waist as I savoured our collision course.

The taxi pulled into the airport car park and we piled out. When the car pulled away, leaving us standing there on the broken gravel surrounded by our bags, there was still a good hour to spare before we could take off. I picked up my suitcase, took Liz by the arm and headed for the southern end of the large building, towards the domestic terminal.

The place was in semi-darkness. The porters had all gone home and apart from the odd security guard plodding his 3 am vigil, the terminal was virtually deserted. A dim light shone from the small office at one end of the customs warehouse, but I noted with relief that Santi's office was in darkness. It was not unknown for Santi to spend the night at the airport, playing cards with his clove-scented cronies. I also wouldn't have put it past the greasy little bastard to hang around for the sake of it, keeping an eye on Charlie Delta, the pride of Hudy's fleet.

Charlie Delta glistened dully at the southern end of the tarmac. The nightly rain had stopped now, but one or two drops still clung to the old Dakota, and the windscreen was heavy with dew. I glanced up. The dark windows of the tower peered sightlessly at the apron below. There was no controller on duty, which was just as well; we weren't putting in a flight plan anyway. A hurried departure before the aerodrome opened for business was the order of the day. I opened the door of Charlie Delta and helped Liz and Matt climb aboard. I passed in the luggage and jumped up after them. Through the rain-splattered windows I could see the army Dakota parked a few yards away. There was no one guarding it, so the cat was not yet out of the bag. That was a relief.

There was enough faint, reflected light inside the aircraft to discern outlines if not details. I unhitched a row of canvas seats, lowered them into place and we all sat. I took out the cigarettes, passed them around and was in the act of lighting Matt's when the cockpit door opened and a strong torch pierced the gloom.

'Stay very still.' I let the lighter go out and sat rigid with the unlighted cigarette sticking to my bottom lip as I recognized the lisp. A slim hand moved slightly ahead of the torch so that we could all see the gun Lotus Blossom was holding. She moved slowly down the fuselage.

'Your gun, Captain. Put it on the floor please – yours too Mr Duncan.' The torch beam flashed briefly on Liz. 'And you. Are you armed?'

'No.' Liz's voice was strained.

'We will see,' said the lisp. 'Hurry please, Captain. Your gun.'

I flicked the dead cigarette from my lip and slowly reached for the automatic. There was no temptation to start a shooting match – it would have been suicide. I lowered the automatic to the plywood floor and heard rather than saw Matt do the same.

'Kick the guns this way please.'

I used my right leg and sent each weapon sliding a few feet along the sloping floor. Lotus Blossom made no attempt to pick them up; with the gun and torch she had her hands full. I saw a dainty foot come out and kick at the two automatics. She kept the movement going until both weapons slid through the open doorway and clattered onto the tarmac.

'Good. That was most sensible. Now please close the door and then precede me to the flight deck.'

With both Liz and Lotus Blossom standing between the two pilot seats, the cockpit was crowded. Matt and I went through the pre-start drill in silence except for the occasional checklist call which required an answer. On Charlie Delta most of our movements were automatic – a Dak is no Concorde. I gave Matt the nod and he punched the starboard starter switch and followed quickly with the port; the engines burst into life, revelling in the cool night air. From now on, Lotus Blossom didn't need the gun in her hand to make me act quickly. The noise as Charlie Delta shattered the early morning stillness would attract unwelcome attention. The sooner we were out of here the better – even if we were heading north towards the oil camp instead of south-east. I released the brakes and taxied at a fast speed towards the waiting threshold of the north runway.

The runway was in darkness but I knew its magnetic direction so what came next was easy. I zeroed my gyro and stuck to it like glue, opening the throttles wide as we roared into the night. This kind of caper could become habit-forming.

I kept the climb going to eight thousand feet and levelled out. Lotus Blossom once again told Matt to vacate his seat and as she climbed into it I heard her tell the others to go back to the cabin. She put on Matt's headset and sat with the gun in her lap, in easy reach.

'You know the direction by now, Captain. In case you've forgotten the details, I will remind you when the time comes. In the meantime, set course for Palembang.'

'Where the hell do you think I'm going?'

'There's no need to be rude, Captain Adams. And if you are going to Palembang I suggest you adjust your heading – you've picked up some drift again.'

Damn the woman! Who did she think she was – a bloody check captain? I liked to fly my own way and if it wasn't quite airline standard – well, I didn't work for a bloody airline, did I? I grudgingly eased the wheel a little to port and set up an intercept on the ADF.

I reached for a cigarette. 'I have to give you an "A" for perseverance. How long were you waiting back there?'

'Long enough, Captain. I had to contact friends and make some inquiries, but otherwise, it was not difficult. I should be grateful that you are, what is the word, predictable. Who is the woman?'

'That is nothing to do with you – or this job,' I said sharply.

She chuckled. 'Very well. Then I will see she comes to no harm – unless you make it necessary, which I feel sure you won't.'

I reached to the lower pedestal and switched in the auto-pilot. There was a slight jolt as the servo-mechanism took charge of the aircraft, then we settled down. Like everything else on Charlie Delta, 'George' was getting a little long in the tooth. I stretched my arms high above my head and yawned into the intercom.

'I've nearly forgotten what it's like to sleep in a bed at night.'

'Then you should have stayed at the camp, Captain. We tried to make you comfortable.'

'Yes . . .' I nodded sleepily, keeping the

stretch going until I felt the fingers of my left hand make contact with the little zip in the headlining. I surreptitiously slid the zip open a few inches, and lowered my hands. Two minutes later when I once again found it necessary to interrupt our casual conversation by easing my tired muscles, I let my left hand penetrate deep into the opening. It came out holding the thirty-eight.

Her eyes widened briefly as she looked into the short barrel, and a hand moved instinctively for the gun in her lap.

'You'll never make it,' I said tightly.

Slowly the tenseness went out of her body; I saw her shoulders sag. 'I keep underestimating you, Captain Adams. Can I try another appeal to your mercenary instincts?'

'No. But you can pass me that gun in your lap. By the barrel please.'

I motioned her out of the seat and followed as she went through the door into the cabin. The dome light was on so no explanations were necessary. Matt eyed the thirty-eight.

'I wondered what you'd done with that, Pappy.'

I tossed him the small automatic I had taken from the girl. 'Keep Lotus Blossom out of my hair, Matt – and don't lose your concentration. I haven't any more of these for a rainy day.' I waved the thirty-eight. 'Do you want to come up front for a while, Liz?' She looked surprised, then nodded, pleased.

We had climbed three hundred feet in my absence from the cockpit with all the weight aft of the centre of gravity it was to be expected. I slid into my seat, disconnected the auto-pilot and put Charlie Delta into a climbing turn to starboard. We would need eleven thousand feet to clear the mountains to the south. The old C47 took her own sweet time getting there, but finally I was able to put 'George' back on the job and relax. I had thought about asking Liz to watch Lotus Blossom, but at the last second reason told me not to. The two women might be on opposing sides, but for the moment they had a common interest. If and when I went back to the oil camp, it would be because *I* had decided to go. I hadn't made my mind up.

I invited Liz to put on Matt's headset. The intercom produced a tinny, metallic sound, but it was better than shouting above the roar of a pair of Pratt and Whitney 1830s. I forced a grin. 'Alone at last.'

I saw her lips purse tightly. 'Don't make fun of me Frank. I'm not made of wood.'

'What are you made of then, Liz? Some exotic mixture of sugar and spice and all things nice – or is it slugs and snails and puppy dogs' tails – or something in-between perhaps? You tell me, because I'm damned if I know what makes you tick.'

'I didn't realize I'd hurt you so badly, Frank.'

'Oh you didn't hurt me, Liz. Shattered a dream or two maybe, but I wouldn't go so far as to say you hurt me. That would be overdoing it.' I groped in my pocket for a cigarette and stuffed it hastily in my mouth.

Liz said quietly, 'If it makes you feel any better, I think I'm falling in love with you.' I looked up and saw her eyes were glistening. Suddenly she threw her head back and let out a strained laugh. 'So the joke's on me you see. That must make you feel better.'

'Stop it. You don't know what you're saying.'

'I'm hysterical. Is that what you think? Well, maybe I am.' There was no mistaking the bitterness that had crept into her voice. 'I never wanted this damned job in the first place – and you're right, I did leave Melbourne with instructions to "charm the arse off you" as it was put. But somehow, my chemistry got mixed up in all the bull.' She ran a hand characteristically through her hair. 'So I guess I asked for it.'

'Are you being completely straight, Liz. This has nothing to do with going back to Sumatra, or anything like that?'

She turned to look at me, squarely. 'I don't care if you go to hell, Frank – so long as you take me with you. I want to see this job finished only because I want to see the last of it. It's almost become an obsession, but not for the company or anything like that. As far as I'm concerned, those Chinese can have their rotten bloody island.'

I stretched a hand across the cockpit. 'OK, Liz. Let's play fresh starts.' She hesitated for a moment then took my proferred hand.

Her smile was shy at first, then it seemed to light up the cockpit.

Chapter Nineteen

SUNRISE revealed small patches of white mist clinging to valley floors on the southern slopes of the mountain range. The coastline, still thirty miles away, was obscured in morning haze as I sent Liz to fetch Lotus Blossom. I still considered it safer not to leave the two girls alone together in the cabin, so I was going to have to use the Chinese girl again as co-pilot. If Liz felt hurt at my lack of absolute trust, she didn't show it, maybe because I had hinted at a possible return to the oil camp if things worked out. And I think she could understand my obsession to confront Chong Bee.

Lotus Blossom settled into Matt's seat

and put on the headset. She glanced at the retarded power levers and the unwinding altimeter.

'Are we landing, Captain?' Her eyes scanned the horizon. 'Where is this – southern Java? That must mean Semadang. You are being foolish – or should I say foolhardy.' Her American accent was very strong.

The auto-pilot was doing the flying. I turned to look at her. 'Why? What is so special about Semadang?'

Her eyes were bright. 'It is where General Sartono was taken before he disappeared. According to my friends in Djakarta, the army knows the general is dead and have sent people to Semadang. If you land there it will mean big trouble, for all of us.'

I looked at her stupidly. Her opening remark about my being foolhardy had given me the clue. It was the reason why I had asked her that particular question. But I was still unprepared for the answer. It seemed possible that she didn't know of our part in the general's disappearance. Yet she obviously did not know – and she had not known about the involvement of the League of the Lotus. After Liz had confirmed the League's activities, I thought Lotus Blossom had deceived me. I now realized that she was genuinely in the dark – about a lot of things. I wondered why or how.

I stared at her thoughtfully. 'When did you leave the States?'

Her almond eyes widened. 'I've never been in the States.' She smiled suddenly. 'Oh! My accent. That is a product of the Philippines. My mother took me there when I was three years old. My brother and I were brought up there – we went to an American mission school near Cavite.' Her face darkened. 'But people of my race do not fare well in the Philippines either. It seems no one wants us any more, unless we go back to China and allow ourselves to be re-educated.' She laughed bitterly. 'That's a funny one; *go back* to China. I've never been there, and what's more, I have no desire to go. Theirs is a philosophy I neither understand nor approve of, and as for Taiwan ...' Lotus Blossom's voice trailed off and her face clouded over. I knew what she was thinking. To many expatriate Chinese, Taiwan was a bad joke. I didn't necessarily agree with her, but I could appreciate her feelings.

I said, quietly, 'Where were you born?'

She looked up quickly. A thin smile crossed her lips. 'What is this, Captain – a quiz show? OK. If it's my life story you want, you can have it, but it's not much to write home about. I was born in Lae at the end of World War Two, a child of the new "peace" which would embrace the world forever after. Only for my family, there was to be no peace. It was a time of witch-hunting and revenge. One year after the end of the war, when I was about the same age, and my older brother nearly three, my father went on trial as a Japanese collaborator. His defence was that he had survived, had done the best for his wife and family in difficult times. But he was foolish enough to tell the truth – that he believed in the Greater East Asia Co-Prosperity Sphere – an Asia for the Asiatics. In those enlightened days, that was tantamount to confessing treason. He was sentenced to death – later commuted to life imprisonment.'

Hard lines of bitterness set around her mouth and she unconsciously pushed a strand of long dark hair from her face. 'You can imagine what it was like for my mother after that. She lost any civil rights she might have had. We were forced to move out of our home and live like coolies and my mother had to sell her body to put food in our mouths.

'After two years, she could stand no more. She put my brother and I on a cargo boat and took us to the Philippines.' Lotus Blossom smiled grimly. 'I was only three years old, Captain, yet I can remember that voyage. My mother crying and holding us close on the pitching deck, trying to protect us from the rain and lightning. When we arrived at Manila, the only difference was that my mother did not have to face the looks of scorn and derision when she walked down a street – not the derisive glances reserved for a traitor's wife that is. She still collected her share of the other kind – the ones reserved for prostitutes, because despite all her dreams of a new life in a new land, that was all there was. She kept us alive for five years in that way and I watched her grow old before her time. Then the exhaustion, gonorrhoea and shame combined to bring everything to a merciful end. She just lay down one morning after a night's "work" and never got up again. Paul and I were sent to the mission orphanage at Cavite where we received our share of the extra "discipline" deserving of the offspring of a street woman.' Lotus Blossom tossed her head, a gesture of stolen pride. 'So there you are, Captain – a pretty story to tell your grandchildren.'

'I'm sorry.' I said it feelingly.

There were plenty of minor tragedies being reported straight after the war, but the passage of time had lost them in obscurity. Yet Lotus Blossom's tragedy was still going on, would be with her the rest of her life.

'What about your father? Is he alive?'

'Oh yes, he's alive. He's even out of prison.' The bitterness in her voice was very strong now. 'That's the beauty of western "justice". A life-sentenced murderer in Britain can be released after fifteen years. The merciful judges in my father's case decided that twenty-five years was enough for him, so they eventually let him out. Except that during those twenty-five years, they didn't treat him very well. He had the usual diseases – malaria, beri beri, denghu fever, but he survived. Yet when he was released from prison and started eating proper food again, he discovered that the bugs which had ravaged his body for all those years had all but destroyed his thyroid gland. So he is condemned to another kind of discomfort.'

'The fat man!'

She smiled thinly. 'Yes, Captain – the fat man. Prison destroyed his body but not his mind. His dream kept him alive and when he finally sent for me and Paul to say the dream was ready, I cried with joy. We had spent long years preparing for the day. Paul should have been the pilot but his eyesight is weak so he learnt about radio and morse code instead.'

'And you learned to fly?'

'Yes, I learned to fly. It was always

intended that I should play my part, then my father told me there was money to hire professionals and it would be better that way.' Her eyes focussed on the middle distance. 'Tragically, he was wrong.'

Charlie Delta had droned her way down to four thousand feet and was crossing the coast. Ten miles away to the east I caught a glimpse of Semadang as the sun glinted off tin roofs. I peered intently ahead. Just discernible through the sea-haze was the long, flat shape of our island.

The *Sea Cat* was moored half-way along the beach and I could make out the waving figures of Chong Bee and his brood as I turned onto final approach to the west, the sun at my back. Lotus Blossom repeated her proficiency with the gear and flap levers and I peered ahead to where I intended to touch down. But my mind wasn't on the landing. I was thinking about what Lotus Blossom had told me, and I knew she hadn't done it to evoke sympathy. Yet sympathy was what I felt – for her and her cause. I was suffering from the great Australian weakness – compassion for the underdog. I wished she could get away with it. The beach rushed under the nose and I felt Charlie Delta thump unceremoniously onto the sand in a most un-Adams-like landing.

'You'd better stay on board. I have business here which could turn out to be unpleasant. Also, I think it would be better if you are not seen.'

Lotus Blossom looked at me strangely and smiled quietly. 'Alright, Captain.'

I avoided her eyes as I climbed out of my seat and headed aft, wild thoughts running through my head. They were not all concerned with Chong Bee.

Matt had already opened the rear door and jumped to the beach. Liz stood in the doorway waiting for me. I leaped to the sand and helped her down.

'Come on. I think you'll be interested in this.'

Liz glanced towards the cockpit. 'What about her?'

'She's better staying on board. I want to surprise our Chinese friend. If he sees Lotus Blossom it might give him time to concoct something. He's a formidable liar.'

Doubt flashed briefly in Liz's eyes as she dropped to the beach beside me. Matt was already heading along the sand towards the oncoming Chong Bee. I grabbed Liz by the hand and pulled her into a short run as we caught up with my co-pilot.

'What's your hurry, Sunshine?'

He slowed down and turned to look at me. His face was flushed. He said breathlessly, 'Just thought we should put on a show for Chong Bee. It's what he would expect.'

I glanced along the beach to where the Chinaman was hurrying towards us, then back at Matt. There was something wrong with his eyes. They seemed to be having trouble looking straight at me. I heard Chong Bee shout. I glanced back in his direction and saw him wave. Even from fifty yards away I could see the broad smile on his face.

'Captain.' He reached us, breathless, and began pumping my hand like it would give milk. He gulped air. 'You were quick. We did not expect you for another day, or perhaps . . .'

'Perhaps not at all, eh Chong Bee. You should have more faith; if not in us, then certainly in all that gold.'

His happy expression stayed right where it was. 'The gold is safe, Captain. I have divided it into shares. Yours is waiting for you; you will see.' He looked speculatively at Liz. There was curiosity on his face, but no alarm.

I said casually, 'This is my fiancée, Miss Manifold. Liz, this is the gentleman I was telling you about – Mr Chong Bee Ng. Mr Chong is a thief and an accomplished liar. He may also be a murderer. All talents he could have acquired in his former position as a senior lieutenant in the League of the Lotus. We shall find out.'

Chong Bee had gone white. I kept a sweet smile on my face but my eyes matched his – hard and unyielding. Even the flabbiness of his cheeks could not disguise the ruthless set of his mouth. I was meeting the real Chong Bee for the first time. I wouldn't describe it as a pleasant experience, but there was a great deal of satisfaction seeing him naked, robbed of his guise of genial coward.

Our eyes remained locked as I said sociably to the others, 'Chong Bee has divided our gold into shares, only he can't count. I'm sure when we see what he's done we'll discover he's miscalculated by two thousand ounces. Hardly an oversight.'

He said viciously, 'You are clever, Captain. Perhaps too clever for your own good.'

'Don't threaten me, Old China, or I might leave you to rot here on this beach. You deserve it, but your kids don't, so I'm willing to be co-operative. But don't push your luck.'

The change of expression in his eyes was involuntary. I'm sure he would have preferred his poker face right then but I had given him an opening and he was ready to grab it. It was only a split second before his other features caught up with his eyes, then his business expression was completely in place. His hands gestured for good measure as he said, more reasonably, 'Very well, Captain. Then we can still do business.'

I smiled derisively. 'No, Chong Bee, we can't do business. What we can do is bargain, and it's not the same thing. As a businessman you have nothing to offer. I know where the rest of the gold is and there's nothing to prevent us from just taking it. So right at this minute, all the gold belongs to us. However, I am prepared to pay you two thousand ounces – *the* two thousand ounces, for information.' As he looked at me, disbelieving, I continued, 'I want the truth, Chong Bee – the whole truth. If you leave out so much as a semi-colon you won't get a bloody cent. *That* I promise.'

His face blanched. I saw a flash of anger which he brought under control, but it was a battle. Chong Bee did not like playing second fiddle. Whilst he was putting on an act, fooling people, he could adopt *any* attitude in the secret knowledge that he was still in control. But this was different. There were no disguises left, no bushes in which to hide. He was in the open, vulnerable, and he no longer held the best hand. For a man accustomed to the almost limitless life-

or-death power of a Tong boss, it must have been a very unpalatable position. I watched the changing lines of conflict on his face as he gradually came to terms with it. Finally he nodded. 'Alright, Captain . . .'

I prodded him in the chest. 'Then sit down, Chong Bee. I'm sure you would rather talk to us here than in front of your wife.'

Mrs Chong and the kids were waiting near the launch a hundred yards away. They might be growing impatient, but they would not interrupt a business conference. We sat in a semi-circle on the beach facing Chong Bee, and invited him to start talking. In the absence of a microphone, I indulged a peacock-like display of the gun in my belt. He got the message. It was his stage. The best way to lie convincingly is merely to embellish the truth; change emphases here and there and keep outright prevarication to a bare minimum. And Chong Bee had done exactly that – for some of the time. There had been a sprinkling of lies, a great deal of fact-twisting, and *total* deception. But it had been handled like the expert Chong Bee was. Some of his near-truths were so near to the bloody truth it was no wonder he had been convincing.

For Chong Bee, it had started the day General Sartono had walked into his office and demanded fifty-one per cent of the business. That much was true. Except that it had happened six months earlier, not six years as Chong Bee had first led us to believe. The general had quickly gone through the company books and had then requested Chong Bee to open the safe, an action Chong Bee had attempted to resist with every excuse he could think of. But General Sartono would not be put off and the Chinaman was forced to reveal his secret.

As Tong treasurer, Chong Bee had been buying Tong gold with Tong money for several years, making a substantial purchase of the precious metal every six months or so. The Tong hoard, now amounting to two thousand ounces, was concealed in its secret hiding place behind a removable panel in the false wall. But Chong Bee had not only purchased Tong gold, he had gradually acquired his own nest-egg which he had foolishly deposited in the old Chubb safe. General Sartono had been more than pleased when he discovered this extra prosperity of his new business partnership. Naturally, and inevitably, he insisted on taking possession of one of the safe keys.

When instructions came through from Woo Tang to kidnap the general, Chong Bee's blood had run cold. Had the Tong discovered something? Did they know about Chong Bee's secret hoard which, by Tong ethics he was not allowed to own, and could never justify? In fact, it would have earned him a Tong death sentence.

Chong Bee had discovered by accident his bugged telephone which had obviously been planted by the general. The Chinaman had learned to remove and replace the bug so that his private calls remained private. But now it set him thinking. Had the Tong made the plant because they suspected him? There had followed a bad week during which Chong Bee allowed his mind to explore every unpleasant possibility – and work out a plan of escape at the same time. He could not ignore the Tong instruction to have General Sartono kidnapped and taken to Semadang. He was still pondering the mechanics when Ling Ma had been killed – accidentally in a gunfight, just as Chong Bee had first told us. His eyes clouded over as he remembered. Ling Ma's death had genuinely grieved him. It had also solved his problem.

Matt's blue face remained impassive as Chong Bee unfolded his story. Liz was listening with unfeigned interest. When Chong Bee spoke of Ling Ma, Liz had turned her big brown eyes on me and smiled softly in sympathy. It took a big effort to return the smile but I managed it. The alternative would have been to shrug and I wasn't feeling that enigmatic. I turned to Chong Bee and said bitingly, 'So it was you who tortured the general – to find out where he had hidden his key.'

'Not me personally, Captain. But the key was mine – I was entitled to it.'

'Then why didn't you use it before we

left Ambon the first time? Or was the two thousand ounces you had stolen from the League going to be enough?' My voice was bitter. This flabby Chinese bastard had conned me all down the line and it was really starting to hurt. I had thought at first that only the bodies had been changed. I now realized the coffins had been switched. When the General had been put on board, he was lying on top of a fortune in Tong gold.

Chong Bee said simply, 'There wasn't time. The General was – stubborn. The key only came into my possession minutes before you arrived.'

I glowered at him. 'You've been bloody clever, sport – at every turn. But you must have had to trust a lot of people to do your dirty work. Doesn't that worry you?'

Chong Bee glanced at Matt and said something in Chinese. I snapped around, annoyed, but Matt pre-empted the outburst I had ready.

'It's an old Chinese custom, Pappy. Use blood-cousins for the tricky jobs. That way you start off with ninety per cent loyalty, and as long as you pay well for the other ten per cent, the system is guaranteed.'

'And were the two jokers who faked that ambush in the banana plantation your cousins too, Chong Bee?' My fists were clenched tight. 'You shit! I crippled one of those poor bastards.'

The Chinaman stared at me impassively. I was fighting to control my anger. He had played it close to the chest all the way; no wonder Woo Tang had not questioned me about him. As far as the elegant Chinaman was concerned, Chong Bee was playing me for a sucker.

Woo Tang had interviewed me in my hotel room just to ensure that I was still going ahead with the job – had no intention of backing out. He had thrown red herrings at me as justification for the meeting, and his expressed interest in the fat man's demise was just a ruse to keep my interest. This meant Liz must have mentioned *my* particular interest in the fat man. I gave her an old-fashioned look and stood up.

'Let's go Matt – time to get our feet wet.'

He slowly clambered to his feet and

smiled laconically. 'Yeah. I guess the General won't mind if we disturb him. He can't take it with him, as they say.'

Chong Bee was looking at us oddly. A slow smile started on his face. 'So! You bluffed me, Captain Adams. I would congratulate you, only it seems you also bluffed yourself.' He was grinning hugely now; the self-satisfied look on his face made me want to smash it in. But instead I just stared at him incredulously. I didn't know what the hell he was so pleased about.

He said quietly, 'The gold is not in the coffin. That would have been foolish would it not?' His eyes had grown larger, his expression confident. For a few seconds he was back in control and he was savouring the experience. He said finally, 'The gold is where I put it after we left Ambon. Under the floorboards of your aircraft.'

I stared at him foolishly, hearing a distant 'Christ!' from Matt. No wonder Chong Bee had waited for us. I had thought it was because he couldn't face a long voyage in command of the *Sea Cat*. I should have known better.

'Come *on*, Pappy.' Matt was tugging at my arm and I suddenly snapped out of it. He started to run towards Charlie Delta; my mind dropped back in gear as I followed. We were too late! Even as we took those first frantic steps, the sound of a Pratt and Whitney shattered the early morning. I heard the other engine start up and watched helplessly as Charlie Delta lumbered into a turn at the far end of the beach and moved towards us in a take-off run.

I reached Matt's side, breathless. 'For Christ's sake . . .'

I caught a glimpse of a determined Lotus Blossom in the left hand seat as Charlie Delta roared past, tail off the ground. My eyes were following the speeding aircraft when my expression suddenly turned to horror.

Chong Bee was standing in Charlie Delta's path, waving his arms furiously, shouting frantically. I saw the aircraft lurch sideways as the port propeller struck Chong Bee before my screamed warning could have any effect. There was a sickening, dreadful thud. The Chinaman soared through the air in a grotesque arc and disappeared into the sea thirty feet away. He was dead before he hit the water.

'My God!' Liz's scream reached me and I turned to look at her, my mind numb. Her face was buried in her hands. Further along the beach the Chong Bee family was running towards us. I was suddenly conscious of Matt at my elbow.

'Jesus, Pappy. What was the stupid bastard trying to do?'

I turned towards him. The expression on his face frightened me; if *I* looked like that too, then it was time to pull myself together.

Charlie Delta was climbing gently away to the north west as I came up to Liz and put an arm round her shoulder.

'Come on, honey. Those kids are going to need us.'

The twin-Mercs burbled gently as I helped Mrs Chong and the children onto the Semadang beach. The kids were crying; their mother wore an expression of deep shock. There were no words that would help. I pushed the *Sea Cat*'s bow off the beach and jumped aboard. As Matt gunned the motors I turned and waved, but I could have spared myself the effort. The three of them were staring sightlessly back towards the island.

I scrambled into the well-deck and returned Liz's blank gaze. There was nothing more we could have done – we had ourselves to worry about now. Our first stop would be for fuel – but not at Semadang. I had baulked at taking the surviving Chong Bees there; I glanced at the town from about a mile away as we roared in a westerly direction along the coast. There was a village about twenty miles away where we could purchase gasoline and oil. Half the enormous roll of rupiah notes Madame Chong had in her handbag now nestled in my pocket. By stacking forty four-gallon drums in the well-deck, we could carry enough fuel to make Australia, and thanks to Madame Chong's contribution, we could afford to pay for it. She had the best of the bargain. Chong Bee's two-thirds share of the eleven hundred ounces had gone ashore with her and the kids. Mine and Matt's amounted to a conservative fifty thousand bucks. It was not enough to retire on, but it would get us started again. I passed around the cigarettes. Liz's expression told me she had things to say – but they would have to wait. First things first; the *Sea Cat*'s tanks were close to empty after the long haul from Surabaja. I stood on the bridge, next to Matt, peering anxiously ahead for the thatched roofs of the village. Thirty minutes later when Matt edged the *Sea Cat* into the ramshackle jetty, I was already on the bow deck, ready to jump ashore. I wanted to get the business over with and be away from Indonesian territory as quickly as possible.

It took less than an hour. While I arranged the fuel, Matt and Liz went shopping for provisions, including fresh water. And with Matt to keep her company there was no risk that Liz would forget the beer and cigarettes. She didn't. When we pulled away from the jetty I glanced at the fuel drums stacked on deck, then at the pile of goods in the cabin and realized we had all but cleaned out the village. But we had paid top price and the merchants had been eager to serve us, so if they ran short, that was their business.

Liz made a lunch of tinned meat and bananas and when we sat down to eat at noon, we were well out to sea. Matt had lashed the wheel to keep us roughly on course during the mealtime and we sat around the table in the cabin, sipping warm beer and filling our bellies. It was the opportunity Liz had been waiting for. The expression in her eyes was coolly appraising.

'I want to thank you, Frank.' As I lowered the beer bottle from my lips and looked at her quizzically, she said, 'You deliberately created the opportunity for Lotus Blossom to steal the aeroplane, didn't you?' She ignored my blank expression and continued, 'I've been thinking about it. It was the best way – providing she can handle the flying, and you'd know best about that.' She ran a hand through her bouncy hair. 'The operation can now get back on schedule and we can stop worrying.' Liz smiled gently. 'If I can pull any weight when we get back home I'll recommend that you get paid anyway. I think you and Matt have earned it.'

I set the bottle down slowly and gazed at her for several seconds. I said, finally, 'I'm not admitting to anything, Liz. As far as I'm concerned, Lotus Blossom pulled a swifty – that's the way it was and that's the way I want you to tell it.' Liz's smile had taken on a benevolent quality; she was willing to humour me. I ignored her patronizing expression and said firmly, 'And I don't want you to mention the gold either. Because as far as I'm concerned, we *haven't* seen the last of it. If you tell it the way I want you to, then me and Matt can arrange to be on that island when Charlie Delta arrives. The aircraft belongs to Hudy, our employer. Even ASIO can't object if we feel an obligation to get it back to him.'

'Frank! You can't . . .' Liz had lost her benign expression. 'That gold doesn't belong to you – you can't just help yourself.'

'Can't I? You just bloody watch me. It used to belong to the Tong but they've lost it. As far as I'm concerned it belongs to anyone who can find it.' I winked at Matt. 'Right, sport?'

'Wrong, Frank.' The expression in his eyes startled me. It was like the odd one he had been wearing on the island – almost guilty. I stared at him.

'What's the matter? Your policeman's conscience worrying you or something? Don't be bloody stupid—' I stopped in mid-stream. Something was really bothering Matt, but I hadn't identified it. He looked thoroughly self-conscious, glancing from me to Liz and licking his lips as if about to confess it was him and not Beau Geste who had stolen the Blue Diamond.

He said hesitantly, 'Lotus Blossom won't be flying to the island. I told her it was a trap.'

'You *told* her?' Liz sounded half-hysterical. A hand flew to her mouth. 'Oh my God . . .'

I grabbed hastily at the beer bottle and took a hefty swig. Some of it went down the wrong way and I nearly choked. By the time I stopped spluttering, Matt's words had sunk in and I stared at him incredulously.

‘Matt, do you know what you’ve done?’

He smiled sheepishly. ‘I’m sorry, Liz; I just couldn’t let it happen. It’s not only Lotus Blossom; I’ve lived with the Chinese a long time. I speak their language and I understand them, but even more, I like and respect them and I think they’ve had a rough deal all round in this part of the world.’

‘But what about the hostages?’ Liz said hopelessly.

‘They will be fine. They’ll be on their way home in a couple of days, then Lotus Blossom is going to take her father away and try to make his last years a bit easier.’

‘Where? The Philippines?’ I was groping desperately for a cigarette.

Matt’s dark eyes took on a spark of life; for a fraction of a second he was his old self again. Then he said blankly, not looking at me, ‘She didn’t say.’

I tried glowering at him but I couldn’t make it; I was beginning to see the funny side. I reached for a fresh beer, laughter bubbling up inside me. It might have been gallows humour, but it takes all kinds. I put the bottle on the table and said incredulously, 'So it was all for nothing.' A bitter laugh escaped in spite of myself and I picked up the beer. Matt looked at me, then at Liz.

He said significantly, 'Nothing, Pappy? I don't think it was for nothing.'

His meaning hit home and I reached for Liz's hand, squeezing it. She turned slowly and I smiled at her. Her face was in shock. Her spare hand reached unconsciously to her hair and she smiled bravely. It was going to take a long time but she would get over it. All that planning down the drain! One day she might come to feel pleased about the way things had worked out, but not yet. The operation had turned sour and the bad taste would stay with her for a long time. Gradually, it would go away and then there would be room for me. Meanwhile, in the several days it was going to take us to reach Darwin, the moonlight might work wonders. It would be something to tell our kids about one day. I let go her hand, leaving her to her thoughts. My eyes bored into my co-pilot.

'Matthew Duncan, I was right about you the first time. You really are a son-of-a-bitch.'

As he sat there, grinning, quietly getting his confidence back, the small cabin was suddenly full of the sound of twin-Mercury outboards.

There was still a long way to go, but somehow the uncomplaining engines seemed to know we were heading in the right direction.

Chapter Twenty

ON a cold morning in Melbourne three months later, I jumped out of bed at the sound of the postman's whistle, and hurriedly put on my dressing gown. Liz moaned in half-sleep and rolled over. I tucked the bedclothes high under her chin, kissed her lightly on the forehead and quietly left the room. Six weeks earlier she had left ASIO and we had embarked on life's greatest adventure – marriage.

Liz's apartment was not quite big enough for the two of us, but as she had pointedly remarked, there was no advantage in looking for a bigger place just yet. I would have to start job-hunting soon and that could take us anywhere; in the meantime, we should not waste money on a fancy apartment. I was beginning to discover what it was like being married to a practical woman – but I also had my own ideas. Liz wouldn't approve, but for the moment, what she didn't know wouldn't hurt her.

The letter I had been sweating on for days was in the mailbox. I felt a surge of excitement as I recognized the distinctive stationery of my solicitors, and I hurried indoors, sat in front of the oil heater and ripped open the envelope.

I read the covering letter first.

Dear Captain Adams,

We have received a reply (enclosed) regarding our inquiry on your behalf to Chartair-Indonesia. Should you wish us to act further in this matter, we are at your service.

Yours faithfully,
A. Fitch
Dawborn, Dawborn, Grantham & Stark
Solicitors at Law

I opened Hudy's letter with trembling fingers. It was addressed to my solicitors.

Dear Sirs,

Further to your offer to purchase our type C47 aircraft, registration PK4CD, my board of directors was interested to learn of the historical value of this aircraft, and of your client's desire to acquire PK4CD for an aeronautical museum.

The aircraft is presently located at a small airstrip on southern Luzon, Philippine Islands, where it was taken illegally ten weeks ago. Negotiations for its return are under way and should be completed shortly. If your client is willing to purchase PK4CD where it stands, and as is, then the transaction can be completed at your convenience. The price of

US$48,000.00 will include the aircraft log book but no spares. For your further information, the Indonesian Certificate of Airworthiness has approximately six months to run.

Yours faithfully,
Jugee Hudynoto
Managing Director
Chartair-Indonesia Sdn. Bhd.

I put the letter down slowly and reached for a cigarette. Good old Hudy – he would never change, the wheeler-dealing bastard. Forty-eight thousand bucks for Charlie Delta was just about twice what the old gooney bird was worth. No doubt Hudy had taken 'historic value' into account. He could be beaten down; I had spent too many hours haggling with my ex-boss not to know what a sucker he was for bargaining, but in this case it would only waste time.

I stood up, crossed to the phone and dialled a number. 'Koala Serviced Apartments,' a female voice said sweetly. 'Can I help you?'

'Mr Duncan, please.'

'Just one moment, sir. Putting you

through.'

Matt's sleepy voice came on the line. 'Hello . . .'

I spoke quietly, not wanting to wake Liz, but Matt didn't miss the excitement in my voice. I heard his sharp intake of breath as I said, 'That Guatemalan airfreight crowd we've been talking about. Get your passport out of mothballs and go see them; we're ready to deal.'

'Hudy went for it?' Excitement was running strongly through Matt's voice now.

'In spades, Sunshine. He wants forty-eight thousand, but we can afford it. Charlie Delta is still in the Philippines; we'll have to go fetch her, but first things first. Get yourself across to South America and give me a ring when you get back. I've got to go now.'

'Liz . . .?'

'. . . Doesn't know about it yet. Leave her to me.'

I hung up, stared at the telephone for several seconds, then walked into the kitchen.

Five minutes later I was on my way

back to the bedroom with two steaming cups of coffee. I would get around to telling Liz in my own sweet time; she would learn to live with it. In the meantime, there were far more interesting things she and I could get up to on a cold winter's morning. I entered the bedroom and kicked the door closed behind me.

JAMES HADLEY CHASE TITLES IN LARGE PRINT

An Ace Up My Sleeve

A Joker in the Pack

Believe This . . . You'll Believe Anything

There's a Hippie on the Highway

My Laugh Comes Last

Just Another Sucker

JON CLEARY TITLES IN LARGE PRINT

A Sound of Lightning

Mask of the Andes

Peter's Pence

The Climate of Courage

A Safe House

High Road to China

The High Commissioner

SAINT TITLES IN LARGE PRINT

The Saint and the Hapsburg Necklace

The Saint and the People Importers

The Saint and Scotland Yard

Catch the Saint

The Saint in New York

The Saint and Mr. Teal

MAIGRET TITLES IN LARGE PRINT

Maigret & The Black Sheep
Maigret & The Loner
Maigret & The Spinster
Maigret & The Millionaires
Maigret & The Hotel Majestic
Maigret & The Man on the Boulevard
Maigret & The Dosser